W6615t

Poetry
In His Country
Skin of Grace
Nineteen Masks for the Naked Poet
A New Herball
Carpenter of the Sun
A Visit to William Blake's Inn: Poems for Innocent and
  Experienced Travelers
Household Tales of Moon and Water

Short Story Collections
The Lively Anatomy of God
Childhood of the Magician

Short Stories and Essays
Angel in the Parlor

Critical Essays
Testimony of the Invisible Man

Children's Books
The Well-Mannered Balloon
Strangers' Bread
Simple Pictures Are Best
The Highest Hit
Papa's Panda
The Marzipan Moon
The Nightgown of the Sullen Moon

Fantasy Trilogy for Children
Sailing to Cythera, and Other Anatole Stories
The Island of the Grass King: Further Adventures of Anatole
Uncle Terrible: More Adventures of Anatole

Things Invisible to See

THINGS
INVISIBLE
TO SEE

Nancy Willard

Alfred A. Knopf

New York   1985

THIS IS A BORZOI BOOK
PUBLISHED BY ALFRED A. KNOPF, INC.

Library of Congress Cataloging in Publication Data

Willard, Nancy.
Things invisible to see.

I. Title.
PS3573.I444T48   1985   813'.54   84-47892
ISBN 0-394-54058-1

Grateful acknowledgment is given to Times Books for permis-
sion to reprint an excerpt from "Lay Dis Body Down" from
American Negro Folklore by J. Mason Brewster, Copyright ©
1968 by J. Mason Brewster. Reprinted by permission of Times
Books/The New York Times Book Co., Inc., a division of
Quadrangle Books.

The author is indebted to Harold F. Dixon's "Three Men on a
Raft" (*Life*, April 6, 1942) for background material to the chapter entitled "Birdlight."

Manufactured in the United States of America
Published January 14, 1985
Reprinted Once
Third Printing, March 1985

For Ilse and Howard

If thou beest borne to strange sights,
Things invisible to see . . .

John Donne, "Song"

Things Invisible to See

I

Ben and Willie

In Paradise, on the banks of the River of Time, the Lord of the Universe is playing ball with His archangels. Hundreds of spheres rest like white stones on the bottom of the river, and hundreds rise like bubbles from the water and fly to His hand that alone brings things to pass and gives them their true colors. What a show! He tosses a white ball which breaks into a yellow ball which breaks into a red ball, and in the northeast corner of the Sahara Desert the sand shifts and buries eight camels. The two herdsmen escape, and in a small town in southern Michigan Wanda Harkissian goes into labor with twins. She will name them Ben and Willie, but it's Esau and Jacob all over again.

In the damp night of the womb, when millions of chromosomes are gearing up for the game of life, the soul of Willie says to the soul of Ben, "Listen, you can be firstborn and get out of this cave first if you'll give me everything else. Brains, charm, and good looks."

"Who knows what looks good?" murmurs Ben.

"Okay, brains," says Willie. "Just give me the brains and you can have everything else."

They agree that Willie should have what the world calls brains: that is, a highly charged left hemisphere that will make him a master of languages, mathematics, and train schedules. He will be right-handed and a rich man.

To Ben go the sinister mysteries of the left hand and the dark meadows of the right hemisphere, where clocks lose their numbers and all roads lead to everywhere.

Their mother worked at the front desk of Goldberg's Cleaners & Tailors. Their father, Aaron Harkissian, used to drive the delivery truck for Clackett's Fine Foods.

They rented the bottom floor of the rundown duplex on Seventh Avenue from a man who lived in Detroit and had once owned Ann Arbor's smallest funeral home on that very site. Above them, families moved in and out; the Harkissians never introduced themselves. Behind the duplex, in a jungle of sumac, bindweed, and ailanthus, you could find half a dozen sample gravestones, nameless and without ornament, if you knew where to look. At the far end of this jungle lay the boundary of South Avenue Park.

What both boys remembered about their father, before he skidded one icy morning into the path of an oncoming car to his death, was the park after supper, that last summer with him in '31. Ben and Willie were eight. Papa would bring his glove, an old Rawlings made for a giant sloth; Ben could fit his whole face into the palm. He loved the smell of leather and sweat and that other smell he could not name which made him feel sad and powerful at the same time, the smell of games played and won by his father long before he was born, on sandlots in a town called Onaway, in northern Michigan, which furnished the rest of the world with steering wheels and said so on the sign marking the city limits.

" 'Onaway steers the world.' That's what it said," laughed Papa.

Hidden in the thumb of Papa's glove was the silver coin that had protected him all through the war, and Papa liked to tell them the story of how he'd found it. They always asked him to tell it; the jungle between South Avenue Park and Seventh Avenue was the forest in Aix, where Papa had crawled with half a dozen buddies into a trench they hadn't dug, and the grenades were zinging over their heads and the rockets were exploding on all sides of them, and there, close to his elbow, gleamed this coin. A silver coin: a man in a winged cap on one side, a skull on the other. (In the jungle it shone on Papa's outstretched hand like the wise eye of a magic animal.)

Private Harkissian tucked it into his pocket and fired at the invisible enemy beyond the trench.

Everything fell silent.

With a thin, whizzing cry, a single grenade rushed toward him, changed its mind, and veered sharply to the left, as if it had remembered a previous appointment.

Ben guessed Papa was right when he said that probably the man who lost the coin was dead. Papa said that if you could look Death in the eye (he brought the coin close to Ben's face), you could challenge him to a game of poker and maybe win a reprieve. Or gin rummy. Or dirty eights, if that was the only game you knew. (It was the only game Ben knew.) He didn't say that the coin was a powerful charm against fear, hurt, and hand grenades, but Ben grew up believing that if his father had had it in his pocket the morning his truck skidded on the ice, the coin would have saved him.

In the summer twilight that promised to go on forever, Ben and Willie and their father found seats in the half-empty bleachers in the park and watched the men work out. There were always men working out, and sometimes there were real games—Ann Arbor High against Dexter High, or Flat Rock, or Saline; or the Methodists against the Baptists, or the Broadway Rangers against the Liberty Street Badgers. It didn't matter. They'd watch anything.

Of those evenings Ben remembered that night never came till the lights began to go on at nine, and then it came all at once, and he remembered that the ball was alive, not as he and Willie and Papa were alive but dumb, inscrutable, mischievous. The players smashed it and caught it and spit on it and they still couldn't go to the places it went, high over the trees and out of sight. One minute you had it safe in your glove and the next minute you lost it.

Willie remembered the names of the teams and the statistics.

Walking home, they abandoned the jungle for the sidewalk. Under the friendly elms and the streetlights, Papa talked about the Tigers and why they should never have traded Fothergill to the White Sox. He talked about Hugh Jennings and Ty Cobb as if he knew them personally. And there was no end of stories he could tell about Ty Cobb taunting Cy Young.

"Now, let's see your fastball. I could count the stitches on the last one."

Briggs Stadium, Papa assured Ben, was a good ballpark for left-handers. And then, remembering Willie, he'd add, "Of course, it's a good ballpark for right-handers, too."

By the time Ben and Willie were fourteen, their teachers knew that Willie was destined for great things. Unlike Ben, he carried himself as if his presence on the planet were cause for the rest of humanity to rejoice. He had fine features and dark curly hair, short to keep the curl from showing, and he could make a cheap suit look expensive just by wearing it. He had small hands and flat feet. "Easy out, easy out," the kids in the infield called when he came to bat. In ninth grade he gave up baseball. He said he was giving it up forever.

People said that Ben looked like his father: the same long legs, the same loping stride and easy grace in a game. Willie, they said, took after Wanda. It was kinder than saying he looked as if he came from a different family.

In school he was always making deals. My tuna for your cream cheese. My Famous Funnies for your Ace Comics. Saturdays he packed groceries for Clackett's Fine Foods. He was ten when the banks closed in '33, and years afterward he still didn't trust the First National to keep his money. He saved it in fruit jars, lined up on a shelf in the wardrobe. And he kept his pennies separate from his nickels, and his nickels separate from his dimes, and his dimes at a safe remove from his quarters and half-dollars.

Paper dollars he took to the bank, for silver ones.

When his mother needed change for cigarettes, he loaned it to her at a penny a week interest. When Mr. Clackett gave him an Indian-head penny to buy gum (he never gave away his fine foods), Willie said, "It might be worth something," and stashed it away in a fruit jar to let it ripen. He knew that time would make treasures of his trivia. His Roosevelt-Garner campaign button. His 1907 Tigers American League pennant. He took no special pleasure in Roosevelt's victory or the Tigers' pennant beyond the hope that someday his souvenirs "might be worth something."

If Ben got a penny, he spent it on gum. Anything bigger went for comics, which he read to pieces and gave away. To his mother, he always seemed in the process of giving himself away, too, piece by piece. He'd lose his cap the first day of school, his jacket by the end of the first week. He never took a shirt off at the end of the day; he tore it off, and one by one the buttons grew weak and departed. No matter what size pants his mother bought him, they rode a couple of inches above his ankles. He was tall and awkward, with reddish blond hair that was all cowlick and no style. That was fine with Ben. All he asked of it was that it keep out of his eyes.

People said that Ben was good with his hands and that Willie couldn't change a light bulb.

But at sixteen, when Willie was working the register at Clackett's Fine Foods, Ben was no longer fixing things at Bacco's Fix-It Land. Once Ben fixed a thing, it never ran the same way again. He fixed Mrs. Bacco's faucet, and when she turned it on, no water came out, but she heard a man's voice singing "The Star-Spangled Banner" and she called the police. A policeman came and heard nothing, but he knocked the faucet several times and water gushed out. There were no charges and no explanations.

He fixed Mrs. Lieberman's Hoover and it lost all appetite for dust and paper and would pick up nothing but gold. It didn't wait for scraps to fall its way, either. Visitors complained of gold fillings vanishing from their mouths, wedding rings gliding off their fingers, and Mrs. Lieberman called a Hoover serviceman and told him to "fix it right." Unfortunately, he fixed it shortly before she lost her gold earring—an anniversary present from her husband, who owned a jewelry store—and though the cleaning woman ran the machine hither and yon through the house, it picked up dust and paper but failed to find the earring. Then Mrs. Lieberman railed against it, and the motor died, and it sulked in the cellar like an injured suitor till she gave it to the cleaning woman, who found that it ran perfectly and gave it to her dentist in exchange for a new gold molar.

By the time he was sixteen, Willie had the worst case of insomnia his mother had ever seen. Nobody knew how much money he'd saved, but thinking what he'd save for and what he'd spend it on kept Willie awake every night for hours. On the pale green Monopoly board of his future, he bought the house they lived in and the lot behind it and he raised the smallest funeral home in Ann Arbor from the dead. Everybody died, didn't they? Everybody needed a stone. It was a risk-free, steady-growth business, especially if you catered to the Negro clientele. Flu, diphtheria—everything hit harder on Catherine Street. And he'd insist on cash payments. None of this paying with a chicken here, a day's labor there.

It was during his seventeenth year that Willie shed his indifference to God and started attending St. Joseph's, which had the richest congregation in Ann Arbor. The church, a massive fortress of stone, and the parish house and the rectory faced four different streets and had the whole block between Shiawassee Avenue and Main to themselves. As the Sunday-morning custodian, Willie earned two dollars, part of which he was expected to return to the coffers of the church by way of the collection plate. He arrived an hour before the eight o'clock service, vacuumed the rector's study and the library, brewed the coffee and set the urn and cups on the long library tables. Before the ten o'clock service he washed the cups, made a fresh pot of coffee, and set everything out once more. Though he attended both services, he could take Communion only at one of them.

"The high point of Sunday morning for all of us," Father Legg told his parishioners, "should be the moment when the All Powerful joins with the weak and human."

For Willie this happened not at Communion but when Father Legg, white-haired, rosy-cheeked, and slim, looked into the kitchen and praised a properly set table or a well-scrubbed sink.

"Willie, my lad, I don't know what I'd do without you."

All this industry bred in Willie a desire to have a study as orthodox and High Church as Father Legg's, a room that spoke of authority and good taste to those invited to enter it. On the bookshelves running the length of two walls were prayer books, handbound volumes of the monthly bulletin, and curios sent to Father Legg from foreign missions. A pair of tiny shoes that once belonged to a Chinese footbinder. A grain of corn from Egypt, over a thousand years old.

On the highest shelf stood the St. Joseph's Men's Club softball trophies. Father Legg coached the team and was fond of using baseball analogies in his sermons. Wouldn't you like to pitch for God's team? Don't let temptation strike you out! Once he asked Willie, "Are you the baseball player I've been hearing so much about?"

No, answered Willie, he was not.

On the bottom shelf was a complete set of Little Blue Books, covering all forms of human knowledge, from Shakespeare to Evolution. It seemed to Willie that he could be neither as rich nor as successful as Father Legg until he owned them all.

While Willie was managing his money and plotting his success, Ben was thinking of new ways to put some real stuff on the ball he pitched for the Ann Arbor High Pioneers every Saturday during baseball season. Durkee, the coach, said you had to live the game to play it. The two years Ben had his paper route, he'd thrown fast papers, curve papers, spit papers, fadeaway papers, for a total of seven hundred and thirty throws. In the dark hours before dawn he could put a newspaper on a porch, a front step, a flowerbed, a doormat. Sunday afternoons he'd work out in South Avenue Park with whoever showed up. Tom Bacco and Tom's cousins Louis and Tony Bacco came by. And George Clackett, Jr., came, with licorice sticks in his pockets for everybody and sometimes Hershey bars if his old man was feeling generous, and Sol Lieberman came, who would have given all the gold in his father's jewelry store for Ben's left arm, and Charley LaMont, who lived in a funeral home and whose father kept corpses in the parlor, and Henry Schoonmaker, his parakeet perched on his shoulder like a sky-blue epaulet, and Stilts Moser, who galloped around the bases in such a way as to suggest that God, who winds and watches the footage of humanity, speeded up the reel when Stilts picked up a bat and swung. In him alone Durkee found no fault.

"He has the guts of a shark," said Durkee happily, tugging on his visored cap. "He's been beaned twice and look at him. Four hits in a single game, three right-handed and one left-handed. Maybe he'll go on to the Monarchs," he added. Durkee didn't follow the Negro leagues himself, but he knew talent when he saw it.

Eight games into the season of '41 Durkee got drafted, and the principal canceled baseball. Ben Harkissian and Tom Bacco and his cousins Louis and Tony, and George Clackett of the free Hersheys, and Sol Lieberman of the secret longing, and Henry Schoonmaker of the faithful parakeet and Charley LaMont and Stilts Moser met anyway, every Saturday afternoon. They kept it up all through the summer, after graduation. Kids from other neighborhoods and other schools showed up, and people who hardly knew each other filled the first fifteen rows of the bleachers and cheered. Baseball season was endless.

Five days a week that summer and into the fall, Ben sold sweatshirts and trophies at Burney's Sporting Goods and waited to be drafted. Tom and Louis and Tony also waited as they tinkered with radios and electric fans at Fix-It Land and sold bottle after bottle of Fix-All, "guaranteed to extend the life of any appliance." And George waited while he sorted the mail at the post office, and Charley waited while he drove his dad's hearse, and Stilts and the dozen other men on his construction gang waited. Sol took a defense job and dreamed of medical school. Real life would start after the war, if America entered the war.

Only Willie, born with flat feet, still had a future he could call his own. He delivered groceries for Clackett's Fine Foods and did odd jobs around the church for Father Legg and interviewed for dozens of better jobs. Prospective employers found him sharp but cold, and they'd turn him down and hire a woman. It wasn't fair, Willie knew, but who would hear his complaint? You didn't have to pay a woman what you'd pay a man for the same job.

By mid October, darkness ended the Saturday afternoon games before supper, and the faithful remnant would gather their gear and hike across the street to Mike's Grill for malts. Mike wouldn't serve Stilts, but he'd put up a drink for him all the same, and Stilts waited outside till the others came with the orders, and they'd all pile into

Tom Bacco's old green Packard, which was specially made for traveling salesmen to carry their goods and had so much room in the trunk that Charley and Henry and Tony could sit in it, with the lid bobbing over their heads.

Tom drove. He alone knew how to keep the motor from stalling. They'd drive down to the river and sit on the running board and the fenders with the empty golf course at their backs and drink from waxed paper cups the last sweetness of summer.

Night came early under the black willows, and if you stood on the golf course side you could look across the river at Island Park. You could see the fireflies. You could not see the island itself, nor the families gathered at picnic tables across the water. But you could hear them talking and laughing, you could hear their dogs barking and their kids yelling, just as if you were standing shoulder to shoulder with them, a single family in the darkness.

Henry said he'd heard that Durkee was in Manila.

"Where's Manila?" asked Ben.

Charley said he hoped America would keep out of the war.

"Look at that bird," said George, nudging Ben. "Bet you can't hit it."

"Bet I can," said Ben.

He tossed the ball to George, who backed away and pitched him a high, fast one, and Ben whammed it hard to the space where the white bird would be in three seconds, flying low and slow over the water.

The ball burst past it.

In the darkness under the willows a girl cried out. People strolling along the river on the last warm evening of autumn stopped in their tracks, chilled.

The evening star rose.

2

Clare

Clare woke up with a terrible headache in a dark room she did not know.

On the nightstand: a steel basin curved like a kidney bean, a steel pitcher, and a vase in the guise of a white cat. Pink carnations rose from its ceramic head like bright ideas.

On the facing wall: the silver body of Jesus on the cross, His head dropped to His chest. Asleep.

A window gleamed, half open, its pale curtains shifting. Under the pane, in the open eye of the window, the city skyline glimmered.

Was that her mother asleep in the easy chair, her arms resting loosely in her lap, her red hair a shadowy cap of curls?

Silence emptied the room of warmth; Clare tried to bend her knees. They were not there. She reached down and touched them. Her hand felt her knees; her knees felt nothing. She could not move her legs at all.

Before the cry rising in her throat could escape, she caught sight of the stranger.

The old woman hovered over the foot of Clare's bed, and into the room crept the fragrance of laundry drying outside and of leeks and clover and tall grass mowed early in the morning. A faded blue sunbonnet hid her face.

You see me with your spirit-eyes, daughter, said the woman. *Now run to me on your spirit-legs.*

The forget-me-nots on her skirt nodded, and in its pleated shadows flashed ferrets and mallards and owls.

She sank close to Clare and touched the girl's side. A wind swept through Clare, as if the bars of her rib cage were parting. Her own breath carried her out.

Out of her body.

Weightless and fleshless, Clare hung in the air beside the old woman and stared down at the slender body that had housed her so faithfully for seventeen years. The long brown hair fell like water down both sides of the pillow. The wide green eyes stared past her, empty. Only the bruise on her forehead was new.

I can't believe it! I can't believe time has run out!

You are not dead, my daughter, said the woman.

In the chair, Clare's mother slept on, still as a snowbank. Through the carnations on the nightstand flowed streams of light, the spawning grounds of a million tiny stars.

Molecules, said the old woman.

The steel vessels on the nightstand hummed; swarms of diamonds kept the shape of basin and pitcher.

Everything alive looks dead and everything dead looks alive, said the old woman and floated to the door, where she paused, glancing over her shoulder, and nodded for Clare to follow.

Clare hesitated.

I've known you since you were born, daughter. It was my hand guided you into your body then, same as I guided your mother into hers. She could see into the future when she was your age.

They were rolling together down the corridor like fog.

You were born here, daughter, in the women's wing. Sixth floor. So was your brother, who died before you were born.

Who are you? whispered Clare.

They passed the head nurse, asleep with her eyes open, frozen at her station.

They passed Clare's chart on the wall beside her. The chart, on which very little was written, fluttered in the rack like a flag of truce.

What's wrong with me?

Concussion by baseball. Thrower unknown—to you.

But not to you? asked Clare.

The Ancestress did not answer.

*Tomorrow morning your mother will ask you, "How do you feel?"
and you will tell her, "I can't move my legs." Doctors will give you tests
and find no damage. They will tell you they've done all they can and that
only time and rest can heal you.*

And will it? asked Clare.

That depends on the doctor you carry within you, replied the
Ancestress. *Look into this room. What do you see?*

On the bed nearest the door lay the shape of a sleeping man.

I see a house with lamps burning in two windows, answered Clare.

And in the other bed?

Clare drifted over the nightstand with its pitcher and basin
identical to hers.

Is this another house? A very dark one?

Abandoned, said the Ancestress. *So many people give up the ghost
at this hour, when pulses beat slower and hearts close down to rest.*

He's dead?

The Ancestress nodded.

And the other one—he's alive?

He has his lamp on, does he not?

And for everybody, it's the same? asked Clare.

The Ancestress nodded. *The nearly well leave many lights burning. Others leave—*

Did I leave a light burning in my house? exclaimed Clare, very
much frightened.

At the rim of her house she sank down and pushed at the warm
flesh. Cell parted from cell, rib from rib; she glided in and looked out
of her eyes at the Ancestress, who was binding the ribbon of her own
breath around Clare's head.

Then, turning toward the night, she spread pale wings that
Clare had not noticed before. The speckled bird that the Ancestress
had become darted out the window and was gone.

. . .

Until that night it was her mother, Helen Ericson Bishop, and not Clare who had the gift of second sight. On her eighth birthday Helen overheard a neighbor tell her father, "You'll never raise that girl, " and she believed she would never live long enough to grow up. The long tunnel of time leading from her past to her future closed down. Time became space, a great pathless field.

In exchange for three of her father's osteopathic treatments and two jars of honey from her father's bees, the doctor who lived across the street gave Helen an X-ray on his machine, the first one in Corunna. It found a spot hovering on her lungs like a shadowy bird.

"Let her drink a pint of cream every day and sleep outside till she's well," said the doctor.

All winter Helen slept on the back porch and woke under drifts of snow heaped high on her eiderdown, like a tombstone of cold wool. In the spring birds thumped and murmured on the roof overhead where her father scattered suet and seeds. Every morning, when the light shone milky on the wicker furniture, a raccoon stepped through the hole in the screen and stared at her for a long time before helping himself to the apples she set out for him. Once, when she threw off her blankets, a flying squirrel leapt up, sprang through the screen, and vanished into the cherry trees.

After she was well Helen discovered she could predict the sex of unborn children and the outcome of illnesses lasting more than three days. During a typhoid epidemic women came to her, begging to know whether they should order their coffins now or later. Depressed by these visits, Helen announced that the gift of prophecy had left her. Two weeks later she was declared dead of a burst appendix, during which pronouncement she left her body—she saw it lying on her bed, helpless and heavy as a fur coat in summer—and rose and passed through the walls of her room like steam.

To her surprise she did not meet the east wall of the First Congregational Church, which she knew stood next door, but found herself knee deep in snake grass on the bank of a river. The water was so clear she could see white stones resting on the bottom, like eggs, except that they were perfectly round.

On the opposite bank waited a vast silent throng that receded, as if on invisible bleachers, their faces still and strange to her, though in some she recognized her own eyes—the "Ericson eyes"—and the shape of her own face, and she knew herself to be part of that family, closest to the recently dead, the women in white, the men in black, the lovely fabric growing faint, almost threadbare among the more remote ancestors, turning, in those farthest from her, to feathers, wings, the faces of birds.

Come over, called the Ancestors.

"And I would have done it, too," Helen told Clare many years later, "if it hadn't been for the Dresden clock. Before Nell broke it, when it chimed the hour, a tiny moon came up in the window. Nobody but Mother was allowed to touch that clock, but when I was sick she carried it to my bed and put it in my hands. I died at five in the afternoon, and the clock began to chime, and I hurried back into my body to watch the moon come up."

After she was well she found she could read the minds of dogs. People brought her their dogs to train. While she housebroke the doctor's Irish setter, the family gave her room and board for a week. That winter she discovered she could hear the whistles of hunters calling their dogs, pitched beyond the range of human hearing.

Her marriage to Hal Bishop and the move to Ann Arbor changed her. She heard fewer such sounds, and the minds of animals gradually were closed to her, as if her own mind hid a sanctuary for birds and beasts to which she had lost the way. Sometimes, when she received bad news, the gift would surface, and Helen would say, "This knowing a thing before it happens is terrible. It's a power from the devil."

Hal taught chemistry at the University and did not believe in the devil. But Helen's father would say, "It's a gift from God. You're a good girl. Why shouldn't God give you a little something extra?"

3

Common Prayer

If only he'd been someplace else.

"Willie?"

Ben knew Willie was a light sleeper. The shape under the covers did not stir.

"Willie, I think I killed somebody tonight."

A hand snaked out and switched on the reading lamp hooked over the bedboard.

"What are you talking about?"

"I hit a baseball across the river at Island Park and it konked somebody."

Willie sat up.

"You know for sure it hit somebody?"

"I heard an ambulance."

"You didn't see it?"

"I ran," said Ben. "We all ran."

"Better to walk," said Willie. "When you run, you admit your guilt."

Ben shook his head.

"I should've waited. I should've waited to see how bad it was."

"What do you mean you should've waited? You want to go to jail? You want to be paying somebody's doctor bills for the next ten years?"

"I want to know who I hit."

"If it was real bad, it'll be in the paper tomorrow," Willie said reassuringly.

"Will it tell which hospital?" asked Ben.

"It always tells which hospital. For God's sake, Ben, don't hang around the hospital asking questions."

Willie turned off the light and slid back under the covers.

"It might not be serious. Don't worry about it till you know. Thank God for one thing."

"What?" asked Ben in a tight voice.

"You didn't get caught."

The light of what their mother called the hunter's moon silvered everything in the room except the balsa model Piper Cub which seemed to float just below the ceiling, out of the moon's reach. Their father had made it for Ben's fifth birthday (Willie had received a box of soldiers), and the balsa struts were so complicated and the tissue wings so delicate that neither Ben nor Willie had been allowed to touch it. Hanging on the wall just below it, their father's mitt gathered the moonlight in its sunken palm.

Lord, make it so that whoever I hit isn't hurt.

"Willie?"

Light on again.

"What is it now?"

"Can you pray that whoever I hit isn't hurt?"

"You think God listens to me and not to you?" grumbled Willie, secretly pleased, since he himself believed this was true.

"Come on, Willie. You've had more practice."

With a snort of irritation, Willie climbed out of bed, knelt at his bookcase, and pulled out *The Book of Common Prayer.*

"Can't you just pray from your bed?" asked Ben, a little awed.

"I don't address the Supreme Being of the universe lying in bed," answered Willie.

He opened the door to the wardrobe he shared with his brother.

"Guess you have to get dressed to talk to the Supreme Being of the universe, huh?" said Ben.

Willie cast him a chilly glance.

"I'm putting on a bathrobe."

Like an overgrown shepherd in a Sunday School pageant, he opened the prayer book and cleared his throat. Ben, deeply touched by all this effort on his behalf, listened attentively as Willie's voice tolled:

" 'Oh, most gracious Father, we fly unto Thee and implore Thy mercy for Thy servant lying under the visitation of Thine hand. If it be Thy will, preserve his life, that there may be place for repentance; but if Thou has otherwise appointed, let Thy mercy supply to him the want of the usual opportunity for the trimming of his lamp.' "

"How about the baseball?" asked Ben, to whom the lamp seemed a peculiar digression.

"The prayer includes all particular situations," replied Willie.

"But will God know we're talking about a baseball?" persisted Ben. "Couldn't He—I know this sounds funny, but there are so many big problems, wars and floods and ships going down and—"

"He looks into our hearts," said Willie.

"Oh. Our hearts."

Willie found his place and continued.

" 'Stir up in him such sorrow for sin and such fervent love for Thee as may in a short time do the work of many days; that among the praises which Thy saints and holy angels shall sing to the honor of Thy mercy through eternal ages, it may be to Thy unspeakable glory, that Thou hast redeemed the soul of this Thy servant from eternal death and made him partaker of the everlasting life, which is through Jesus Christ our Lord. Amen.' "

Whose prayer keeps buzzing round Your left ear? sings Gabriel.

And God answers: *That's Elena Kohn. Somebody stole her suitcase on the platform of the Nuremberg station.* The pale wings beat harder. *She had all her money and her passport in that suitcase,* He adds.

And that prayer scratching Your right shoulder?

Wei Wu, says God. *His father has been dying for forty-five days. Cancer.*

And that one passing back and forth like a film over your eyes?

Willie Harkissian in Ann Arbor, Michigan, sighs God. *Up to his old tricks.*

Willie arranged his bathrobe on a hanger and climbed back into bed. Ben closed his eyes..

If he'd walked to Mike's Grill five minutes earlier, whoever he'd hit would not have occupied that fateful space in Island Park. If Clackett had pitched to Henry instead of to Ben, the ball would have barely dribbled across the street. Henry was no hitter once darkness came on. If Sol had paid for his malt with a five-dollar bill and had to wait for Mike to make change, whoever it was would already have passed by.

To hit a ball into the darkness. That was truly a goofy thing to do.

Close your eyes. Imagine you are in outer space, standing on a distant star. Now look back at the earth. He could almost hear his father, telling him what he'd always told Ben when everything went wrong.

From a star whose single beam of light cut across the vast loneliness of inner space, Ben looked back and fell in love with the earth. It wasn't perfect, but it was there. It was better than nothing, better than empty space. On the face of the waters moved convoys, merchant ships, battleships, troop carriers. In the bowels of the deep lay destroyers, U-boats, submarines. The *Reuben James.* The *Kearney.* The galleons, rafts, longboats, and fishing craft of his ancestors, their bones and booty and baggage. The sleep of slaves, of princes, of pirates. Of men and women searching for a better life.

And over the continents, over the ragged carpet of Russia, over North America and South America kissing at the Panama Canal, over the Great Wall of China and the gigantic bean that was Australia, over the silence of Antarctica, flew swarms of fighters, their small weapons glinting in the beams of the indifferent sun.

When Ben opened his eyes, Willie was gone and everything in the room looked as if it had a hangover. The grey pallor of early morning sifted across Willie's desk, his papers stacked in two piles with their corners trued off, and across his own desk, littered with schoolwork, over which half a dozen baseball trophies stood guard. In this light, the little golden players did not look worth winning.

Why should prayers work? thought Ben. If prayers worked,

Hitler would have been stopped at the border of Poland by angels with swords of fire.

He could hear his mother moving around in the living room, which was also her bedroom. When she was tired, she slept in her clothes like a traveler, taking off nothing but her stockings and underpants. It didn't matter to Wanda what she slept in, as long as she had clean underpants when she was awake. And not torn, either. If she were in an accident, she didn't want people talking about her that way.

Since she had never, in all her life, had her own room, she did not miss having one now. If she ever made enough money to buy a house as big as the one she grew up in, she'd rent rooms, the same as her mother did. As a child Wanda would come home from school to find that her room had been rented and all her things moved into another room, vacant—but for how long? The best rooms never stayed vacant. They had brass beds and marble sinks with oval basins. Once for a whole week she slept in a brass bed and washed at a marble sink—Wanda and her mother laundered all the sheets and towels, made the beds, dusted the rooms, and after someone moved out, scrubbed the floors on their hands and knees.

Her father sent money. He never came to visit, because it turned out that he already had a wife when he married her mother, but sometimes he sent a doll to Wanda on her birthday.

To Ben as he entered the kitchen, she looked thinner, almost a stranger with short grey hair—he still could not get used to her with bobbed hair—laying the cereal dishes on the green oilcloth.

"Marsha called," she said.

"When?"

"Last night. Didn't you find my note on your bed?"

"I must have slept on it. Did she say what she wanted?"

"You think she'd tell me?"

He opened the front door and a gust of wind fluttered the newspaper at his feet. His heart racing, he picked it up and carried it to the living room and sat down on the sofa that hid his mother's bed. With studied casualness, he laid aside the comics and opened the paper and scanned the headlines.

ROOSEVELT PROPOSES OPENING MINES,
PENDING MEDIATION BOARD STUDY

"Turn on the light," said his mother. "You'll go blind."

NAVY REPORTS 11 DEAD

His eye glided past the picture of a shadowy ship sinking, and
he turned the page.

Nothing, nothing.

That meant it wasn't serious.

Like a man whose sentence has been lifted, he sped back to the
first page.

In the Navy's third report on the *Kearney*, the missing
are now listed as dead. The U.S. Destroyer *Kearney*, it
was disclosed, was torpedoed in the course of a great all-
night battle between escort warships and a Nazi U-boat
wolf pack that attacked a convoy of merchant marine men
in the bleak waters southwest of Iceland on the night of
October 16.

For the first time since the European war started, the
Navy Secretary was constrained to issue a bulletin con-
cluding with such words as "the next of kin of the missing
have been notified."

The Secretary told a press conference that the United
States, like the British, would not give out marine sinkings.
As he expressed it, German morale is depressed by having
U-boats and their crews go out and never come back,
leaving the survivors at home without word of their fate.

"You didn't read the comics first," remarked Wanda. She
handed Ben a glass of orange juice. "That's the first time I've ever seen
you pick up the paper and not head straight for *Terry and the Pirates.*"

On his way to the comics, Ben's eye caught an item on the
facing page.

A 17-year-old Washtenaw County girl suffered a concussion last night when a stray baseball struck her in the head.

Miss Clare Bishop, of 201 Orchard Drive, was taken to St. Joseph's Hospital by ambulance following the 8 P.M. accident at Island Park. She is reported in serious condition.

State police said she was walking with her parents, Mr. and Mrs. Harold Bishop, and her aunt, Mrs. Nell McGuinley, when the ball struck her.

No arrests were made.

"Call Marsha, won't you? She thinks I don't give you her messages. She's been trying to reach you for two days."

It could have been worse, he told himself. The ball could have killed her. Things could always be worse.

"I'll get out of the kitchen," said Wanda, "so you can have privacy."

When he heard the first ring, he tucked the receiver under his chin, opened the icebox, and solaced himself with the chocolate pudding Willie had passed up at dinner the night before.

"Hello," said a woman's voice. Not Marsha's.

"Can I speak to Marsha?"

"Whom shall I say is calling?" inquired the voice, in cultured tones. Couldn't be her mom. Maybe the new maid?

"Ben."

"One moment, please."

He waited a good deal longer than one moment. Marsha's house was huge. Probably it took her half an hour to walk from one end to the other. He imagined his voice, a wind-up toy of himself, padding across plush carpets from one room to the next, through shoals of what Marsha called her stepfather's Grateful Patient presents. A brass peacock, its tail set with hideous glass eyes . . . a curio cabinet full of antique spectacles. Marsha's stepfather specialized in disorders of vision.

The windup toy hadn't even reached the kitchen when Marsha came to the phone.

"Ben, the red rains have fallen. It's okay."

"What?"

"I'm not—you know."

"Well, that's wonderful," said Ben. He tried to sound relieved, but half a dozen false alarms had immunized him against taking her seriously.

"Can you get off work on Wednesday? I could cut class. We could drive into Detroit and knock around Hudson's. It's a great place for lunch on Wednesdays. They have fashion shows in the dining room."

"I can't think of anything I need to buy at Hudson's," said Ben.

"Don't you give your mom a Christmas present?"

"Yeah, but Christmas is more than a month away."

"In a month everything will be picked over," snapped Marsha. "Besides, we could ride the escalators." Taking his silence for consent, she added, "You can pick me up around ten in the morning."

Click.

She never said good-bye, and she never gave Ben a chance to say it.

Clare Bishop. Who was Clare Bishop? He knew the name of everybody in his class. Two hundred names. He didn't recognize hers. He dragged out his old yearbooks, determined to find her.

Under the junior class picture for '41, her name was listed among the missing.

She was also missing from the sophomore class picture in '40. But he found Marsha, smiling broadly, three months before her mother remarried and Marsha Kerlikoski transferred to Country Day and became Marsha Deller.

In the yearbook for '39, Clare's name appeared under the freshman class picture, and Ben searched row after row until he found her: a child with long straight hair who had closed her eyes at the wrong moment. What did she look like now, this sleeper in the middle row of two hundred ninth graders?

4

Easy as Walking on Water

Over the urgent staccato of Lowell Thomas spitting out Monday's six o'clock news, the telephone rang, and Helen Bishop, who was guiding a pillowslip through the mangle, called from the cellar, "Don't answer it, Hal. It's bad news."

"No news could be worse than what I'm hearing," said Hal. "We're practically at war."

He picked up the receiver.

"Hello?"

"Hal?" crackled a faint voice at the other end. "Hal? I can hardly hear you."

Helen's sisters sounded so exactly alike on the phone that Hal could never be sure whether he was talking to Vicky or Nell. But it sounded like long distance. It would be Vicky, calling from Grosse Pointe.

"Vicky?" he guessed.

"I hope I didn't wake anybody," said Vicky. The line snapped and roared, as if she were chewing on it.

"We're all up," said Hal.

"How's Clare?"

"Not too good," he said and felt his voice choking up.

"Call Helen to the phone. And tell her to turn off the iron. She's burning the sheets."

"What makes you think—?"

"I can smell it," said Vicky. Of her acute sense of smell Vicky would only say, "It's the aftereffects of scarlet fever" and "It runs in the family."

Almost immediately there was a distinct smell of scorched linen, and the connection opened up loud and clear, as if they'd both dropped into a lower altitude.

"Hold on," said Hal. "I'll call Helen."

He opened the door to the cellar and shouted, "Vicky's calling you from Grosse Pointe!"

Then he headed upstairs to listen on the bedroom extension. Helen clumped breathlessly into the hall and collapsed on the love seat and put the receiver to her ear.

"Here I am."

"How's Clare?" asked Vicky.

"I was with her again last night. She's having some trouble moving her legs."

"She can't walk," said Hal on the extension.

"You mean she's paralyzed?" asked Vicky.

"So far the tests don't show any nerve or muscle damage," Helen went on.

"Isn't it nice you've got Nell to help you," said Vicky.

Helen and Vicky both knew their youngest sister had never done a lick of housework all the years they were growing together. As the oldest, Helen had done it all. The ironing: her father's shirts with the little tucks in them. The dishes: her mother saved them for her, both lunch and breakfast, to do when she came home from school.

"Nell never turns her hand," said Helen. "She teaches till four, and I've got Davy to look after. He's only in first grade a half-day."

"Fred and I are bringing Grandma to your house next Wednesday," said Vicky. After Davy was born, first Nell and then Helen and Vicky had started calling their own mother and father Grandma and Grandpa. Sometimes Helen wondered if their new names had helped to hasten her parents into old age.

"We're not staying for supper," added Vicky.

"Couldn't you wait till Clare is better?" pleaded Helen.

"You owe me six months already," replied Vicky. "From the

time you had the flu. I can't stand it anymore. Grandma's getting worse."

"How worse?" inquired Hal.

"This morning she tried to pay for her breakfast. She thought I was the hostess at Christianson's."

"What about that woman you found to watch her?" asked Helen.

"She quit. Grandma hit her."

"She did?" exclaimed Hal. "She really hit her?"

"Right in the face. You can't find anybody in Grosse Pointe who wants to take care of old people. I see these ads for wonderful nursing homes in the paper—"

"No nursing home," said Helen firmly. "I won't put my mother in a nursing home. Vicky, I've got to run. The doorbell's going to ring, and I'm in my old housedress."

"Who's coming by at this hour?" asked Vicky.

"I can't tell yet. Good-bye."

The front door chimed its two tones. Before Helen could unlock the door, it opened of itself. Her youngest sister, framed in the doorway, glanced up from the depths of her purse.

"Found my key," said Nell.

Her voice triggered footsteps on the stairs. Davy, in blue sleepers, hugged his mother's legs and rubbed his cheek against her Persian lamb coat.

"Tell me 'bout the movie! Tell me 'bout the movie!" he begged.

"Vicky called," said Helen. "She's bringing Grandma here next week."

"Isn't that awful," said Nell. "Isn't that the worst you ever heard."

"We'll all have to pitch in and help," said Hal.

Nell looked hurt. "Why, of course."

"Tell me 'bout the movie!" screamed Davy.

"It starred Veronica Lake," said Nell, prying his fingers from her knees. "What I wouldn't give to have hair like hers."

She ran a grieving hand through light brown hair that curled in thin ringlets to her shoulders.

"How was your date with the piano tuner?" asked Hal. "What's his name—?"

"William Patrick Simpson," said Nell. "I found out something awful about him."

"He's married?" asked Helen.

"He's Catholic," said Nell.

"Patrick," said Helen. "Of course, with a name like that. Wouldn't you know."

She prided herself on her freedom from prejudice. Everyone in the Bishop family followed a different faith. She was Congregational, Nell was Grace Bible, and Clare was a Quaker. Nobody knew for certain what Hal believed except Hal, but Helen feared it involved reincarnation. He went to church with her only on Christmas and Easter.

"He's also married," said Nell. "His wife went to the movies with us."

"You all three went to the movies?" exclaimed Hal.

Nell nodded. "She said I'm the nicest girl Bill—she calls him Bill—has taken out since they got their separation."

"Can I have the kitty in my bed tonight?" begged Davy.

"Sweetheart, I've told you a million times," said Nell. "The kitty gives you asthma."

She hung her coat on the rack by the front door and hoisted the child to her hip, though he was getting too heavy for her to carry. At the first landing she paused for breath and groped for the switch that lit the corridor and stairs to the second landing.

Under the molding, a row of lights flashed on. Dozens of photographs of Ericsons and Bishops, frame nudging frame, seemed to open their eyes. Her parents, in their wedding picture, smiled out at her, the way they had looked before she started calling them Grandma and Grandpa. And here was Hal in his laboratory ten years ago, holding on his bare wrist the great horned owl he had tamed to sit on his desk during lectures. Time had taken the owl but hardly touched Hal. His hair was still black and wavy, parted at the side, his features still fine, though he had put on a little weight.

And there in soft focus and ivory satin, straight and simple as a Doric column, stood Nell the bride, between her sisters in their taffeta bridesmaid's dresses. Vicky and Helen might have been twins in this picture: both tall and slender—none of them had changed very much—with those green eyes that Grandpa called "the Ericson eyes," as one calls a disease or a star after the person who discovered it. Nell's eyes were brown, like the eyes of some sad, clever animal, the last of its kind on the planet.

The bridegroom was not present. The marriage had lasted six months, during which he managed not to appear in so much as a snapshot.

Nell turned off the light and the photographs fell asleep, and the light over the second landing came on.

"It's me, Grandpa," called Nell.

"I knew it was you," he called back. Grandpa Ericson was a small, pale man, nearly bald. In his white long johns, he looked like a friendly gnome. "I just wanted to light your way."

"Somebody's following us," whispered Davy.

"Those pictures can't see you," said Nell. "I've told you a hundred times they're not alive."

He's looking right at me, whispered Clare to the Ancestress. *Can he see us?*

He sees us, but he forgets what he has seen. We pass through his thoughts like water.

The two spirits floated after Nell and Davy, arrived at the rooms on the third floor, took a turn to the left, and entered the attic. It was filled with suitcases, linens, outgrown clothes, broken toys, books, framed Sunday School certificates, and half a dozen electric fans. In an overstuffed chair in the middle of the room, Grandpa was reading the Bible by the light of a floor lamp with a purple silk shade. His bed, his bookshelf, on which stood his bust of Andrew Still, founder of osteopathy, and his little bureau made a room within the larger room. Helen had installed his beehive in the window (he'd brought it all the way from Corunna) with the hope of attracting bees, though this arrangement cut off most of the natural light.

Grandpa? whispered Clare.

He did not stir, though he had good hearing for a man of his age. She followed the Ancestress out of the attic. They passed the bathroom, where the tub squatted on cracked legs over Helen's twelve sterling place settings, as if hatching them.

They passed through the closed door ahead of them into the room that Nell and Davy had shared since the divorce. "The maid's room," Helen called it, from the days when you could get a maid for nothing but her room and board. Davy was curled up in one bed, sucking his thumb hard, clutching the knotted bath towel he took with him into the uncharted waters of sleep.

On the opposite bed lay the clutter of Nell's lesson plans. Nell sat hunched over her desk, her tweed jacket thrown over her shoulders. On the lapel gleamed a golden eagle, from whose mouth dangled a heart. The heart was inscribed, in a flourishing hand, "My Heart Is with the U.S.A."

Her fourth graders liked to open the heart and say hello to Davy gazing out at them from the left side. She'd replaced Davy's father with a picture of Clark Gable till something better came along.

From where Clare hovered over the dressing table, she could look down on Nell's Madame Du Barry Beauty Box. The wooden carrying case lay open, and Madame Du Barry, silhouetted on the pale blue lid, was showing Clare her best side. Tins of rouge, eye shadow, bottles of perfume and lotion—all rose like the landscape of a toy city.

Downstairs, Helen turned off the lights.

Come, said the Ancestress. *When the human lights go out, you can see your way by the light from the stars.*

Seeing that Hal was asleep, Helen reached across him and snapped off his radio, then crawled into her own bed. His shoes, huddled together at his bedside, brought tears to her eyes. Like all his clothes, they were made to his measure and sent from England.

He'll have to buy his clothes in stores for the duration, thought Helen.

It was her last thought before she fell asleep.

The living room was dark, yet everything Clare saw wore a skin of light. The grand piano. The sofa, on which Cinnamon Monkeyshines was stretched at full length, purring, dreaming that the fire was awake in the fireplace.

In the dining room, behind the glass doors of the three china cabinets, the rims of plates and cups and saucers shone like planets.

Everything was shining in its own radiance, humming in its own dance.

You might want to try the piano, said the Ancestress.

I beg your pardon? said Clare.

Or the cat. The cat would be easy for your first time.

My first time for what? asked Clare.

On the other hand, if you try the piano, you'll know for certain. Either it plays or it does not play.

First time for what? asked Clare again.

For finding new rooms, said the Ancestress. *New houses. Watch.*

And she brushed up against the piano and disappeared, leaving a deep silence in her wake. To Clare's astonishment, the keys depressed themselves and the piano began to play.

Do you know this one? asked the piano. It spoke in the voice of the Ancestress.

Clare was silent.

The piano played a few more bars.

Now I recognize it, said Clare. *It's "O God, Our Help in Ages Past."*

Suddenly the Ancestress passed through the wood, as if the piano were no more than a shadow of itself.

Try the cat, urged the Ancestress. *Nudge right up to him, as if he were your own body.*

Clare drew close to Cinnamon Monkeyshines. Nothing happened.

It's as easy as walking on water, said the Ancestress. *Don't think about how you do it. Just do it.*

The exact moment when she entered the cat Clare did not know; it was as if a strong wind filled her and blew all her senses clean. Her ears gathered the sigh of a moth's wing outside the window and the breath of a mouse behind the wainscot, and she knew these sounds as if she'd known them always. She smelled the flesh under the mouse's fur and the sour smell of its fear. A dust ball under the radiator shifted and she spied it. An ember broke into ashes in the fireplace and she heard it. A squirrel muttered in its sleep, huddled in the eaves outside, and she was overcome with a desire to set the universe right, to sweep it clean and quiet as a bone, to rid it of all small quick moving things except herself.

Who are you? asked the Ancestress.

I am Clare, answered the cat.

Can you move the body you have entered, as I moved the keys on the piano?

Clare sent herself into every muscle and nerve. Cinnamon Monkeyshines stood up.

Not paralyzed, I see, observed the Ancestress.

The cat scampered across the room and exclaimed, *It feels wonderful!*

Time to go back, said the Ancestress.

I don't want to go back, said the cat.

Go back out of kindness to your body, Clare. Such a faithful friend your body has been to you. Think how lonely it feels now. That's a good girl.

When Clare glanced back at Cinnamon Monkeyshines, he blinked at her twice, jumped up to his spot on the sofa, and went on sleeping where he'd left off.

5

Everybody Should Learn to Swim

When Clare woke up, her legs disappointed her. A hard frost still separated them from the rest of her body. Nothing had changed.

After breakfast a large nurse with a ruddy complexion and short blond hair strode briskly into the room, pushing an empty wheelchair.

"I'm Mrs. Thatcher. This morning you're going to get some exercise, Clare."

Mrs. Thatcher cranked the bed down, helped Clare into the new pink quilted bathrobe her mother had brought, and handed Clare a comb and a mirror.

"Don't worry about the bruise on your forehead. In a week it'll turn yellow instead of blue, and in two weeks you'll hardly know it's there."

How could she not worry about the dark swelling just under her hairline? She ran her finger over it and tears sprang to her eyes. Her hair was too matted for the comb. But Mrs. Thatcher took a single lock and worked it between her fingers, and presently Clare was combing it, a few strands at a time.

"Let's braid it, Clare. That way it won't get snarled so fast."

From her pocket she drew another comb and a pair of scissors and went to work on the snarls at the back. To Clare's surprise, her touch was firm but gentle. Snip! sang the shears.

"Don't cut it," Clare pleaded.

"We don't have to cut very much," said Mrs. Thatcher. "Vase-

33

line helps." She was already braiding and banding the left side. But she did not hurry Clare, and she put the scissors back into her pocket and went on combing and chatting.

"Till you learn to use crutches, life is going to be more difficult than you've ever imagined. From now on, stairs are your enemy. Before you go anywhere, you'll ask yourself, Are the doors wide enough? Is there a bathroom on the ground floor?"

Now she was braiding the right side, gathering the strands that Clare had combed.

"When I was seventeen, I got polio. I spent four years in a chair. When my mother took me shopping for clothes, nobody wanted to wait on us. Nobody would help me try anything on. The clerks would talk about me to my mother as if I were deaf and dumb. 'Would she like this green dress? This yellow one?' But I'll tell you something. The day I took my first step was the happiest day of my life. My boyfriend stuck by me. I wanted to walk down the aisle without crutches or braces. And I did. There. Take a look at your-self."

Clare peered anxiously into the mirror. A tight, greasy braid brushed each shoulder. Mrs. Thatcher lifted Clare into the chair and pushed a pair of bedroom slippers over her bare feet. Purple silk; her mother's. At home Clare never wore slippers. Now she stared down at her feet, small, overdressed, cocked at an awkward angle on the foot rest of the wheelchair.

"Ready to meet the world," said Mrs. Thatcher and wheeled her into the hall.

The world was filled with nurses, doctors, visitors, and orderlies pushing stretchers to operating rooms, to X-ray, to the emergency room. Carts stacked high with empty breakfast trays rattled down the hall. Clare recognized the rack of charts behind the nurse's station, and here—wasn't this the room in which she had watched one man live and another man die?

Her chair turned sharply, a door opened, and she was wheeled into a large room, empty save for two sets of parallel bars and a wheelchair. Another nurse was helping a boy of about seven to walk very slowly between the bars. He was dragging his legs in their heavy braces along the floor and hanging on hard.

"You're doing *so* well!" exclaimed the nurse. "You're doing so *well*."

The boy stopped. Sweat shone in large drops on his face.

"I want the chair now," he begged.

Mrs. Thatcher and the other nurse exchanged nods.

"I'm going to buckle your legs into braces, Clare," said Mrs. Thatcher. "They feel awful, but they'll help you keep your balance. Your bars are just like his, only higher."

In this room with a crippled child and two nurses, Clare feared for the first time that she might not get well. They were not healing her. They were teaching her to take her place in that invisible nation of the handicapped.

"Hold onto the bars. Use your arms for support," said Mrs. Thatcher. "Don't worry. I have a good grip on you."

"I'm going to fall."

"No you won't. I'm right beside you. I'm holding you up. Move your legs from the hips."

That she could move them at all gave Clare a small thrill. Two dead weights. She could not feel where she was setting them down.

"My legs are too heavy," she exclaimed.

"Huh! You should've seen my first pair of braces," said Mrs. Thatcher. "They had to be forged at a blacksmith's and the straps had to be ordered from a saddlemaker. You couldn't even buy braces in the town where I grew up. People with polio were supposed to be shut away where nobody had to see them. Thank God my parents had different ideas."

By the time they returned to her room, Clare was glad to be lifted into the newly made bed.

"Somebody left you the *Reader's Digest*," observed Mrs. Thatcher.

Clare picked it up and found she was too tired to read it. She might have fallen asleep with the *Reader's Digest* clasped to her chest if a young man in a white coat and white trousers had not walked into the room.

"I'm Doctor Henderson," he said, extending his hand. Clare took it, and he pressed her fingers between his. "Did Mrs. Thatcher have you walking this morning?"

It annoyed Clare that he should ask her a question to which he almost certainly knew the answer. He glanced down at the papers on the clipboard he carried and hurried over the possibility of a reply.

"Your right leg is stronger than your left, but your left leg has more feeling in it. There's no nerve damage, no muscle damage, no fever, and no infection. Something in here"—he tapped his head— "is telling your legs they can't walk, and that's what we've got to overcome."

He gave her a broad smile.

"You won't be going back to school. But there's no need for you to shut yourself away from your friends. I had a patient who lost both arms and legs in an accident. Nicest guy in the world. Everybody loved him. He married the head nurse. Can you swim?"

"What?"

"Can you swim?"

Clare nodded her head, puzzled.

"Good. Swimming helps. There's a good pool at the YMCA."

Anger boiled up in her. She was a good swimmer, but how could she go to a public pool with her body like this?

In Paradise, the Lord of the Universe tosses a green ball which breaks into a red ball, which breaks into a gold ball, and Wanda Harkissian finds, in the lining of her winter coat, a silver coin with a skull on one side and a winged man on the other, strung on a thread of elastic.

"Ben," she says at breakfast, "isn't this the coin you lost years ago at the Y?"

She drops it into his open palm, and Ben sees himself on a hot day in July, eight years old, running along the edge of the pool. He always told people a bigger kid pushed him in at the deep end, because the truth sounded so goofy: he jumped in because he thought the water would hold him up. Water had always been friendly to him. Why should it do otherwise?

He sank swiftly into aquamarine, saw the ladder stretching still and blue, down, down under the water—how tall it stood! how far it reached!—resting its feet on the bottom like a great tree. Above him the white legs of swimmers churned the shining lid of the water into silver globes. He sank. He touched the floor of this vast, still room, felt the water push him almost to the surface; but he had fallen too far, and the shining lid was both near and far off, like land seen from the prow of a ship.

Then everything around him shattered, as the man who dived in to save Ben collided with him.

For weeks Ben would not go near the water at all. When he and Willie passed the Y, they crossed to the opposite side of the street.

Everybody should learn to swim, his father told him, and he gave Ben the coin to wear on an elastic thread around his neck while he made his peace with the water. For a month Ben paddled at the shallow end while the young man who taught swimming led the other children out into deep water. One day Ben allowed himself to be led beyond his depth. He clung to the edge of the pool and kicked and he let go and swam across the pool, steadily and with great purpose, as if he were answering a summons from the other side.

Two days later Ben could neither find nor remember having lost the talisman he was sure had helped him.

Now, after so many years, the skull and winged man flashed in the morning light. Going into hiding had not tarnished them. Wanda said it wasn't the coin but his own courage that had carried Ben across the pool. Ben guessed she was right; but couldn't the coin still have a power of its own, the accumulated courage of the unknown soldier who lost it, and of his father who'd found it long ago, and of himself, who'd both found it and lost it, and found it again?

"I could send it to her with a note," said Ben at breakfast. Willie stopped chewing his cornflakes. "Who?"

"Clare Bishop."

"Who?"

"Clare Bishop. The girl I hit. She's still in the hospital."

"You called the hospital?"

Ben nodded. "They wouldn't tell me how badly she was hurt."

"Get yourself a good lawyer," said Willie. "I'm not loaning you a cent."

"I've got to talk to her."

"You're off your trolley."

Wanda came into the kitchen, ready to leave for work—she always left a half hour before they did—and they both stood up to kiss her good-bye.

6

A Book of Gold

The attic door stood open. Grandpa Ericson sat in the overstuffed chair, his hat in his hand, his coat thrown over his shoulders like a cape, singing,

> "Thro' many dangers, toils, and snares,
> I have already come;
> 'Tis grace hath brought me safe thus far—"

"Good-bye, Grandpa," said Davy from the doorway.

Grandpa stopped singing.

"Davy, who sat under the terebinth tree?"

"The men of Shechem. And Abraham," answered Davy.

"And why did they sit under the terebinth tree?"

"Because when the leaves rustled, they were whispering the secrets of the future."

"Correct," said Grandpa. "Take a penny from the jar. I'm leaving the penny jar in your care while I'm gone. Is your aunt from Grossey Pointe here?"

It amused him to speak of his own daughters as if they were other people's relatives. And he had a way of saying "Grosse Pointe" that reminded Vicky she hadn't always had it so good.

"You forgot to pack your books," said Davy.

"They've got a public library in Grossey Pointe," said Grandpa. "And before you know it I'll be back. Let's go downstairs."

He took Davy's hand and pulled himself up. They both sang the last verse.

> "When we've been there ten thousand years,
>   Bright shining as the sun,
>   We've no less days to sing God's praise
>   Than when we first begun."

Halfway down the second flight of stairs, he asked, "Is your grandmother in the house?"

"No, Grandpa. You're safe."

Here's where I saw Clare, thought Davy. And that other lady. In my dream.

At the dining room table, Helen and Vicky and Nell sat with the book of days open on the lace tablecloth before them, a leather-bound account book in which Vicky had recorded, for the last three years, Grandpa days and Grandma days. Grandpa's were blue, Grandma's bright red. They were worked like cross stitch over the empty spaces under the names of Helen and Nell and Vicky. A simple pattern: when Helen and Nell had Grandma, Vicky had Grandpa. When Vicky had Grandma, Helen and Nell had Grandpa. Nobody needed credit for having Grandpa. He was no trouble to anyone.

Vicky kept strict account of their payments. Now she was showing Helen and Nell how many Grandma days they owed. One hundred and eighty days came to six months. No credit extended on account of illness.

"I don't know how we're going to manage when Clare comes home," said Helen. "If only Grandma doesn't try to run away."

"Keep her busy," said Vicky. "She loves to scour pots. She scoured a hole clean through my double boiler."

The aroma of roast chicken appeared in their midst like an unannounced guest, and Vicky, remembering that she never stayed for dinner, rose and announced that she never stayed for dinner while Helen, remembering that it was good manners to offer people a drink at this hour, waved toward the sideboard and said, "Have some Harvey's Bristol Cream."

It was the only alcoholic beverage she kept in the house. She'd called Vicky to ask what she should buy for her play-reading group, since you couldn't expect all your guests to drink Sparkling Catawba grape juice.

Vicky eyed it suspiciously. "Is that the same bottle you bought three years ago?"

"For my club," said Helen.

"Heavens, don't open it just for me," said Vicky.

And Nell called out from the hall, "Davy and Grandpa are here."

Grandpa walked slowly down the front walk, Davy on one side, his cane on the other. Hal followed them with the suitcase.

"That sky means snow," he said, but nobody was listening.

Vicky climbed into the driver's seat of the Olds, and Helen and Nell and Hal and Davy lined up by the rear door, which hung open like a broken wing. Grandpa settled himself into the back seat, then leaned forward and inquired of Vicky, "Where is your mother?"

"Fred's walking her around the block," replied Vicky. "He should be bringing her back any minute now. We'll drive around the corner and wait for him. I don't want Grandma to see the car."

A slamming of doors. The car hugged the curb and glided out of sight.

"Wave," said Helen.

The little group at the curbside waved.

"They can't see us anymore," said Nell.

But Helen went on waving.

"When Hal and I said good-bye to the Crombergs in Berlin, they waved their handkerchiefs till our train was out of sight," she said. "You never know when it will be the last time."

"It's a queer business," said Hal, "when a wife can't lay eyes on her husband without picking a quarrel."

From the other end of the block, Fred approached with Grandma, wrapped in her sealskin coat, bulky with the sweaters she wore even in warm weather.

Davy thought: I don't like Grandma but I like her braids. They make a little bridge across her head.

"No overcoat," said Nell. "Fred has no overcoat."

"Fred is the only man I know who puts on a three-piece suit to go outside and mail a letter," said Helen.

"Stockbrokers always wear suits," said Nell.

"He shaved his mustache," observed Hal.

Nell shrugged.

"What else could he do? A client told him he looked like Hitler."

Under the light banter, Grandma did not hear the good-byes, did not see Fred twinkle down the block to the getaway car waiting around the corner.

He made it, thought Helen. They're on the way home. Out of sight, out of mind.

Grandma looked east from where they'd come, west to where they'd gone.

"Where's Peter? Where's Peter?" she asked.

"Grandpa's in Grosse Pointe with Vicky," said Helen.

"Never here when he's needed!" Grandma cried. "I got two men coming to fix the porch. He promised he'd fetch ladders."

"Hal, take her suitcase to the guest room," said Helen.

But Hal had already gone into the house, and Helen picked up the suitcase and carried it up herself.

The guest room on the second floor was as formal as the attic was cluttered. A peach satin bolster, bedspread, and ruffled duster. A double-globed milk-glass lamp that turned into flowered moons when Helen touched the switch. Silver mirrors on the dressing table; cut-glass perfume bottles. Nobody ever used the perfume, which had aged to the deep brown of old woodwork. On the wall over the bed hovered an angel that Clare had painted. Its body followed the contours of a large crack.

In front of the open suitcase, Grandma examined, arranged, and sorted, as if appraising goods at a rummage sale. The black suit was in good condition. The blue sweater was mended on both elbows. Two nightgowns like flannel tents were wrapped around a jar of Kaopectate (the wholesale size) and five rolls of toilet paper. She had once had an attack of diarrhea in church and ever afterward kept an emergency supply of toilet paper wadded in the top of her stocking, the way some women carry money. And the pink ribbed underpants and sleeveless undershirts—it was a joke among Helen and Vicky and Nell while they were growing up that all the women in their family together hadn't enough to fill one bra.

"Let's put your things away in the drawers, shall we?" said Helen.

But Grandma wanted nothing put away. She hung all her clothes on hooks at the back of the closet door. "I want everything out where I can see it," she said.

The radiators began to pound and clang. By evening a suffocating heat filled the house.

At bedtime Grandma locked her door. Unlocked it. Called out to Helen, who was already in bed, "Did you lock the door?"

"I locked it," Helen called back.

"Good. I just wanted to be sure."

The door of the guest room closed. The dresser bumped against it. Next came the scraping and dragging of the chest of drawers. But was the front door locked? Patiently, relentlessly, she dragged the dresser away from the door, opened it, and shouted into the hall, "Did you lock the front door?"

"I locked it," replied Helen.

She was lying in the dark, her borrowed copy of *Outward Bound* open to her place, face down on her chest. When Grandma was asleep, she would turn on the light and finish the play. It wasn't the sort of play she would have chosen, but she wasn't on the committee to choose what the play-reading group would present every month. At least nobody swore in this one; she was thankful for that. She could hardly bring herself to say "damn" in front of the other women. Only Debbie Lieberman loved to swear and throw herself into the naughty speeches.

I'll have to drop out of the group now that I've got Clare and Grandma to take care of, she thought.

She would miss that group. She would especially miss the

women not connected with the University—women like those she'd grown up with—whose company she preferred to that of the other faculty wives.

She climbed out of bed, tiptoed over to Hal, reached across his chest, and snapped off the radio he used to put himself to sleep. He slept like a pharaoh laid out for the voyage to the hereafter; not a wrinkle perturbed his blankets. In college, halfway through his first night in the dorm, his roommate had waked him and then apologized: "I'm terribly sorry—I thought you were dead."

She pulled the covers close to her chin. Hal liked fresh air, and he opened the window wide, even in winter; but the window opened over her bed, not his, and she felt the full force of the breeze. He was twenty years older than Helen, and there was no use trying to change him. She never knew his age till they got the marriage license, and she'd hardly ever thought of it since, except to marvel at the difference between their ages: when I was born, he was graduating from the University. When I was starting school, he was finishing his Ph.D. at Harvard. If anybody had told him, "You're going to marry a kindergartener from Corunna . . ."

She felt at the foot of her bed for the comforter and pulled that over her, too.

Dear God, help Clare walk.

She thought she ought to say more, but she never prayed for more than one thing at a time, so as not to appear greedy. Besides, it was hard for her to hold more than one problem in her head at once. She prayed only for other people, and she never prayed for anything she felt was downright impossible.

The Lord's Prayer and a poem she'd learned in Sunday School: these were the only formal prayers she knew by heart.

Once she'd heard a man on the radio urge all his listeners to pray for peace at the same time—he gave them the time and the words of the prayer—and he assured them that he would be praying too. A thousand prayers coming in at once would flood the mailrooms of heaven. A thousand identical prayers would sound like one large prayer and be easier to understand than a clutter of small ones, and God would notice and would incline His ear.

But maybe God would like the poem best?
Oh, I always feel foolish saying words that aren't my own.
I sound like Clare now. I sound like that Mrs. Brewster who takes Clare to Friends' Meeting with her on Sundays.
Do I still remember that poem? Or have I lost it?

Abou Ben Adhem (may his tribe increase!)
Awoke one night from a deep dream of peace,
And saw, within the moonlight in his room,
Making it rich, and like a lily in bloom,
An angel writing in a book of gold:—
Exceeding peace had made Ben Adhem bold,
And to the presence in the room he said,
"What writest thou?"—The vision raised its head,
And with a look made of all sweet accord,
Answered, "The names of those who love the Lord."
"And is mine one?" said Abou. "Nay, not so,"
Replied the angel. Abou spoke more low,
But cheerily still; and said, "I pray thee then,
Write me as one that loves his fellow-men."

The angel wrote, and vanished. The next night
It came again with a great wakening light,
And showed the names whom love of God had blessed,
And lo! Ben Adhem's name led all the rest.

Good. I haven't lost it.

Close to the window, an owl whistled. All those nights when she had gotten up to nurse Clare, she had heard the owl. No, not this owl, but its great-great-great grandfather, maybe. At the foot of the pine tree, Clare, as a child, liked to gather the white bones of ferrets and mice, small as darning needles, which the owl had picked clean.

So many things dying in that tree, or being born, coming into the world, going out of it. Never forget. No. Twenty years, but never forget. He came too early. Six months. Didn't even live long enough to be named. She'd heard him cry. Through her drugged sleep, she'd heard the nurse's voice: "Shall I bathe him? He'd fit in a teacup." And the doctor: "If I were at my old hospital in Philadelphia, I could save him." And herself in the bathroom—would she ever forget?—pumping her milk into the sink. And later, her face pressed to the glass partition behind which the preemies slept, each in its own box, begging him to stay, crooning to him the song her mother sang to her, though he couldn't hear her through the glass:

> "Here comes the sandman,
> Stealing away on the tips of his toes."

She could never sing that song to Clare. Kept it locked up inside her.

> "He scatters the sand
> With his own little hand
> In the eyes of the sleeping children."

Who cares for him now? Will we meet in heaven? He would be twenty years old—going off to fight, maybe. Good to be spared that. Gone.

Gone?

Sometimes a door opens in her sleep and she sees him, three years old, in a little blue coat and leggings, standing close to her. They are on a platform, waiting, and the train stops. She gets on, the doors of the car close, the train starts up, she reaches for his hand—but where is he?

She gets off at the next stop, in tears.

"Don't you cry," says the ticketman. "Didn't you know the next train will take you back where you came from?"

"A boy in a blue coat and leggings?" murmurs a man in line behind her. "Why, he's all right. Why, he's waiting for you."

She catches the next train, and it goes in the right direction, but it does not stop at the station where a little boy in a blue coat and leggings is waiting for her.

"Don't you cry," says the ticketman. "Don't you cry. Didn't you know the next train will take you back where you came from?"

"Your little boy's waitin' for you," says the lady in front of her. "I saw him. He's not goin' anywhere. He'll be there."

But the next train goes farther and farther away from the platform where a little boy in a blue coat is waiting for her, and she can't find the train back, though now and then she meets someone who says, "A little boy in a blue coat and leggings? Yes, ma'am. I saw him. He's all right. He's waitin' for his mama on the platform. Take the next train west and get off at the seventh stop."

But there's only one train going west: an express.

If I could just find my boy, said Helen to herself. Or if he could just find me.

She turned over on her stomach.

And felt, in the same moment, a small hand drawing the comforter over her shoulders.

7

Everything Looks Good

Only Wanda knew the truth: her sons had been arguing since the day they were born, bawling at each other in the crib.

In the sandpile they'd argue: Red is better than blue. No, blue is better than red. No, dummy, red is better. Better! Biking up the street in summer, it was chocolate versus vanilla. Sledding: Snow is better than ice. No, ice is better. No, snow. They agreed on nothing and they took sides on everything.

When they started getting an allowance, they had to decide: Is Kresge's better than Woolworth's? When baseball season arrived: Is Babe Ruth better than Lou Gehrig? Goose Goslin better than Charley Gehringer? Willie chose the quiet, steady players who could be counted on in the outfield and who caused no scandals. Ben inclined toward outlandish pitchers and crazy hitters, who narrowly escaped suspension and got fined for bad conduct, their lives one long train of pranks.

Later they argued about girls in general (how did you do it with a girl?) and then about girls in particular (with whom? when?). As Ben's knowledge outstripped his brother's—Willie did not date very much; girls always expected you to pay—they argued about Marsha.

"She's beautiful," said Ben. "She's Rita Hayworth and Veronica Lake."

"Too much makeup," grumbled Willie. "And her clothes are terrible."

"She buys them in thrift shops," said Ben. "She's real saving."

"Thrift shops! Her stepfather is rolling."

"She loves bargains. She never buys the first dress she sees. She loves to shop."

Willie stopped to consider whether this was a point for his side or Ben's.

"What do women do when they shop?" he asked cautiously.

"They look at stuff. They—feel it. Marsha loves to touch things. Combs. Dresses. Magazines. She loves magazines."

Not what his mother did, Willie knew. Wanda, with her grocery list, hunting down the cheapest cut of meat. He dropped the subject of Marsha and turned to Marsha's real estate. They'd argued about this before. Which was better, the old grey duplex where Marsha lived before her mother's divorce or the new house in Barton Hills she'd moved into after her mother married Dr. Deller?

"The new one has a lotus pond and two gardens," said Willie. "You'd have to be crazy to choose the old house."

"The old one had a sand lot," said Ben.

"Marsha needs a sand lot?"

"And the new one is full of the first Mrs. Deller's stuff. Those awful figurines on every table."

"They're probably worth thousands," said Willie.

Ben parked the old Studebaker that he and Willie owned together (Wanda hated to drive) and hurried up the front walk. Usually Marsha made him wait, and Ben took it for granted that he would wait for half an hour in the library, just off the vestibule, during which time nobody would speak to him, not even the maid who let him in.

Today, however, the door opened, and Marsha slouched in the doorway. Black suit, black stockings, her huge black purse, and a white fur jacket. Her blond hair was piled high, and a diamond comb gleamed over one ear.

"How do you like me?" She grinned. "I got the jacket yesterday. It's real rabbit."

She pointed one toe and flashed a spiky heel studded with rhinestones.

"God broke the mold when he made you," said Ben.
Mold! exclaimed God. *I never repeat myself.*

The sidewalks were crowded with shoppers, mostly middle-aged women, pushing into the store or watching the mechanical figures in the windows, swagged and wreathed for Christmas, though Thanksgiving was still a week away. A family of snowmen, nodding like imbeciles. Santa in a golden sleigh, compelled to wave. Half a dozen elves whose hands pounded and stitched and sawed, and from somewhere—a cloud, perhaps—Bing Crosby singing "Silent Night" with the little catch in his voice.

"Let's share a room in the door," said Marsha. She pushed Ben ahead of her into the revolving door and squeezed in behind him. The door wedged tight. Panic froze him. A man in the section behind them tapped the glass, and Marsha started to laugh.

"Ben, move your feet!"

He moved them. The door opened. Why did she like to humiliate him? I've got to be patient, he told himself. He had made a bargain with God: If I am kind and helpful to everyone I meet from this day forward, God will forgive me for striking down Clare Bishop, even if I don't tell her I did it. Why should I tell? What good would it do? In his mind rose a jeweler's balance. The words "Clare Bishop's concussion" hovered over the right pan, and a throng of faces, known and unknown, floated in the other one, the faces of everyone he would help for the rest of his life.

They passed the perfume counter. Marsha paused at a rack of men's leather caps.

"Nobody would know if I took one," she said.

"Marsha, please."

"The stuff on the main floor is overpriced. Think of all the times I've paid too much. I could take that cap and even the score."

"Don't," said Ben. "That man is watching us."

"Which man?"

"That man next to the bathrobes. If you wore your glasses, you'd see him."

She shrugged.

"Some day when I'm alone in here, I'll take it."

"You don't need that cap," said Ben.

"It was for you," she said. "I was taking it for you."

Riding the escalator to the ninth floor, she whispered in his ear, "What I really want for Christmas is butterfly-wing eye shadow, but I don't think it's been invented yet."

The dining room was nearly full. All women, he noticed, and a few elderly men. Oriental carpets, white tablecloths, French windows with drapes of rose satin—oh, he didn't belong here. A matronly hostess showed them to a table for two by a window.

"I want a table in the middle of the room," said Marsha. "I don't want to miss anything."

She hung her purse on the chair and slipped off her jacket and sat down. She had a way of taking off her jacket that made you think she was taking off everything.

"This beats taking an exam in calculus," she said.

"Why are you taking calculus?" demanded Ben.

"Because I'm good at it," replied Marsha.

The waiter, in a red dinner jacket and green vest, brought two menus and stood discreetly aside.

"Crab," said Marsha, glancing at the menu. "Have the stuffed crab. I'm paying."

Ben knew she wanted him to pay, and he knew she did not like him to contradict her. Was she testing him? Whether he paid or not, he would fail.

The waiter stepped forward, sleek as a muskrat, pencil poised over his pad, and turned to Marsha, who turned to Ben.

"What looks good to you?" she asked him.

"Everything," said Ben. "Everything looks good."

"I'll have plain Jell-O and tea," said Marsha to the waiter. "I'm on a diet. My friend will have everything."

"I beg your pardon?" said the waiter.

"I said everything. The crab, the broiled spring chicken, the oyster croquette, the celery soufflé, the black bass baked in cream, the shrimp, the celery and pineapple salad, the raisins molded in wine jelly, the pistachio cake, the chestnut parfait. And coffee and tea."

"That's luncheons number one, two, three, four, and five," said the waiter. "I think I'd better move you to a larger table."

"I don't want to move," said Marsha. "You can bring an extra table over here."

"Marsha, the crab is fine," pleaded Ben.

But the awful feast had been set into motion. Two more waiters emerged from the kitchen bearing the extra table and three stands for the trays, which they unfolded to the left and right of Ben. The muskrat waiter brought a large bowl of shrimps on ice and set it before him.

"The shrimp," he announced. A butler announcing arrivals. "And the sauce for the shrimp."

"Fast service," remarked Marsha. "Those women behind you were here before us, and they're still waiting."

The whole dining room—right down to the curtains, thought Ben—was watching them. *Everything. Everything looks good.* His words and their consequences were as irreversible as if he'd rubbed a magic lamp—and here they came, bass and oyster and chicken and crab, bowing down to his appetite, under their steaming silver covers.

Ben lifted the first cover. The bass was dressed for the occasion in a pewter coat striped with black. Bread crumbs nestled like sleep around its upturned eyes: a small dead prince on a bed of rice.

"You're a real glutton," Marsha observed. Her Jell-O and tea had not arrived.

"A glutton for punishment," said Ben and started in on the bass.

Suddenly a woman's voice crackling through a loudspeaker commanded their attention.

"Our model number one is wearing a navy crêpe dinner dress, formalized with a lovely net yoke accented with ostrich feathers. Notice the self-buttons at the waist and wrist. The split skirt opens on a knee-length petticoat of white embossed organdy. Number one. Available on the ninth floor."

The model swept by them. Tall. Dark. Her number flashed on a white oval plaque the size of a dinner plate that dangled from her wrist. She looked straight at Ben, twirled, struck a pose, and passed on.

"Is she for sale?" asked Ben.

"You'd buy her if she were, wouldn't you?" said Marsha.

"Nope," answered Ben quickly.

"She's tall," said Marsha. "You like tall, dark women."

"I don't, Marsha."

"Like that sultry cheerleader you went out with last fall."

"She means nothing to me," said Ben. "There was nothing between us."

"Our model number two is wearing a lamé peach plaid dinner dress with corseletted bodice and a trailing sash and cap sleeves," purred the voice.

Another model, tall and red-haired, stepped up to Ben and smiled.

"Go ahead," said Marsha. "Look if you want to."

"I don't want to," he said.

"Beauty," she sighed. "I'd kill for it. The girls at Country Day are all so beautiful. I feel like a ferret among doves."

"You're beautiful," said Ben.

"My chin sticks out. My nose is too big."

"That's not true. I love you the way you are."

" 'Let me not to the marriage of true minds admit impediment,' " said Marsha. " 'Love's not love which alters when it alteration finds.' "

Love? True minds? Marsha always made Ben feel as if an exquisite wild animal had developed a taste for him; he felt honored, excited, and afraid.

"And our third model is wearing—" here little gasps of delight sprang up from those nearest the door through which she was entering—"a satin and tulle wedding dress with fitted bodice—"

Marsha began to weep. "I'm sorry, Ben. I always cry at weddings."

Ben did not see the bride, only heard her pass in a rustle of satin as Marsha leaned toward him.

"Ben, let's get married. They're not drafting married men. You wouldn't have to go."

"I'm not afraid of going," he said. "In fact, I'm thinking of enlisting."

"You're crazy!" said Marsha. "You want to go out and get shot up?"

"If we enter the war, somebody's got to go," he said.

"Look here. My stepfather could find you a job in a defense plant. He knows a lot of people. You're not being unpatriotic if you don't go."

Ben put down his knife and fork. With all the interruptions, he had scarcely touched the fish.

"Marsha, I just think we shouldn't get married till you finish high school. And till we can get through a whole month without fighting."

"Everybody fights. It's perfectly normal. You always put the blame on me. You don't trust me."

"I do trust you."

The Jell-O and tea arrived. Marsha shoved it aside.

"If we were married we wouldn't fight. That's what we fight about—getting married."

"Marsha," Ben said, folding his napkin, "there's no way I can eat all this."

"Leave it," she snapped.

"I'll ask the waiter for—"

"You don't ask for a doggy bag at Hudson's. Leave it. I'm having a chocolate sundae. I'm addicted to chocolate. I have to have it every three hours."

An elderly woman in a wheelchair caught Ben's eye. The young boy pushing her toward the door was her grandson, perhaps. Ben saw himself pushing her, forever and ever, chained to her helplessness. Freedom. Oh, God, I'm addicted to freedom.

"What are you thinking?" asked Marsha.

"I'm thinking that I'm addicted to you."

It wasn't what he'd meant to say.

"If we were married," said Marsha, "you could have me every three hours."

A spasm of terror made him shudder. He would grow old like

the ancient woman in the chair, and her grandson would grow old, and Marsha's body in time would turn on itself, turn bent and shapeless. Panic swept through him.

"I can't wait three hours," he said.

Marsha grabbed her purse and her jacket.

"Come on. I know a place we can go."

The waiter, seeing them rise, hurried over with the check. Though she usually added it and checked it to the penny, now Marsha left a fistful of bills on the table and walked quickly out of the dining room. Once in the corridor they ran for the elevator.

"Basement, please," said Marsha, to the heavyset girl in the maroon uniform, who shifted on her stool and pushed the lowest button: B.

"Here's where you find the real bargains," Marsha said, as they got off. "The same names as upstairs, but without the labels. My mom used to bring me here the week before school opened and buy all my stuff."

Ben followed her, past counters heaped with blouses, sweaters, brassières, scarves. Women were reaching for things, pinching them, rubbing them between their fingers. Marsha turned abruptly down a small corridor, passed the door marked LADIES, and stopped at the door next to it: EMPLOYEES ONLY. She opened it.

"Come *on*," she urged. "It's all right."

He followed her, his mouth dry, into a small room.

Nothing here but a chaise and a low table. For magazines. But there were no magazines. Through the thin walls he heard toilets flushing.

"Nobody ever comes in here," she said, throwing her purse and her jacket on the floor.

When he unbuttoned her blouse, his hand met something cold and smooth. The leather cap dropped at his feet.

"It's yours," she said. "I took it for you."

"Oh, Marsha."

"Nobody caught me. Nobody ever catches me."

8

Dear Doctor Well

Everybody had a cure for her.

Nell, who had once dated a Christian Scientist, sent her pamphlets which explained that she was God's perfect child and therefore the paralysis was an illusion. On one of the pamphlets was scrawled a message: "Sounds crazy—but worth a try!"

Mrs. Lieberman sent her a newspaper clipping about a polio patient who painted "The Last Supper" on velvet, holding the paintbrush between his toes.

Hal ordered her copies of "Nuts May Save the Race" and "What is the Matter with the American Stomach?" from the Battle Creek Sanitarium, where he went once a year on a private vacation to enjoy the company of vegetarians and celebrities in search of their lost youth.

"That's where I'd like to take you," he said. "They've got heated pools. Just like Warm Springs. Look what Warm Springs did for Roosevelt."

Helen brought the advertisements that still arrived in the mail for Grandpa, even though he no longer practiced osteopathy. Oh, praise the benefits of Dr. Herrick's sugar-coated vegetable pills, a blessing to the afflicted, and Dr. Herrick's Red Pepper Plasters, which restore health and vigor to the weak, and Dr. Herrick's Pain-Killing Magic Oil, which for forty years has been a merciful friend to the suffering and is not of an oily nature and is very pleasant! There were also pamphlets for people who found themselves cutting teeth in their elbows or who were born with special problems such as four-inch tails.

"A four-inch tail!" exclaimed Helen. "Clare, things could always be worse."

Mrs. Clackett, the grocer's wife, sent her half a dozen back issues of *The Herbalist's Almanac*, which her husband gave to all his customers at Christmas. Clare read the testimonials, keeping a sharp eye out for cases similar to her own. "Dear Doctor Well: I wish to sincerely thank you for your Wahoo Bark of Root. I can hardly believe it was so effective." But what was Wahoo? "Dear Doctor Well: Since I have been taking Black Haw I feel so much better. I do not have those bearing down pains and I shall continue to praise Black Haw."

Clare couldn't be sure if she had met Black Haw before, under a different name. When she found the names of herbs she knew, it was like coming across the name of an old friend in the newspaper. Grandpa had told her about the herbs and about the love affairs between sicknesses and their cures that started when the first Headache met Pennyroyal, and Sprain called for Wormwood, and Loss of Appetite demanded Sarsaparilla, and Cramps took Skullcap to bed, and Cankers rejoiced in Golden Seal, and Fevers cooled toward Slippery Elm. He introduced her to good friends, silent friends, named Boneset and Periwinkle and Life Everlasting, who traveled where she could not go, bustling through the trade centers of the brain and resting in the crepuscular chambers of the heart, rowing through secret canals in the ear, or floating between the islets of Langerhans by the dark continent of the liver. The blessings of Juniper and Ginger were upon her always. Grandpa asked her, "What did God give us for the healing of nations?" and she answered, "The leaves of the tree of life," and he said, "Correct. Take a penny from the jar. Take two. That was a hard one."

A nurse's aide named Ginny chose Clare for her special project. She wore a pale blue uniform and was planning to lose fifty pounds in the near future. She stopped by every morning to help Clare dress and every afternoon to see what new magazines Helen might have brought. She sat by Clare's bed, flipping the pages, deciding what ads she'd ask Clare to cut out for her: Merle Oberon or Claudette Colbert maybe, for Woodbury Cold Cream. *Life* always had those nice conversation ads that were so useful for amusing bored patients.

"Here's one we can do, Clare. You read the general. I'll be the general's daughter."

"Me? The general?"

"Or maybe you'd rather be the daughter."

"I'll read the general," said Clare.

Ginny drew a chair close to the bed and cleared her throat. "The General Joins the Regulars!"

GINNY: My dad, the general, is a man of few words and strong determination.

CLARE: When you get into trouble, face the enemy and fight it out.

GINNY: You and your pitched battles with constipation! Did it ever occur to you to find the *cause* of your trouble? Dad, come down to breakfast; I want to show you something.

CLARE: Now, what's the miracle?

GINNY: No miracle at all, just a crisp toasty breakfast, Kellogg's All-Bran. If your trouble is the kind that's due to lack of proper "bulk" in the diet, All-Bran will really correct the cause of it. But you should eat it every day and drink plenty of water.

CLARE: This tastes like a million. If All-Bran can make me join the regulars, I'm enlisting for the duration.

"There's a Sanforized ad we could do, if you're feeling up to it," said Ginny.

"No, thank you," said Clare. "But if you want to cut anything out, go ahead. Take the whole magazine."

To her relief, Mrs. Thatcher arrived with Clare's braces. She acknowledged Ginny with a curt nod, then knelt and buckled Clare's legs into place.

"Now, Clare, get up by yourself, the way I showed you."

Clare twisted around in her chair, shifting her weight to her braced legs.

She took one crutch and hoisted herself up on it.

She reached for the other and tucked it under her arm and adjusted her weight.

Now she was standing, facing the nurse.

"Are we ready to see the world?" asked Mrs. Thatcher, and she glided around to Clare's right side.

The tip of the crutch edged forward on the smooth floor as Clare put her weight on it. Mrs. Thatcher pushed her foot against the tip to keep it from slipping.

"Right crutch, left foot—left crutch, right foot," she sang out. Clare's braced legs clattered across the floor. "Let's walk to the playroom in the children's wing. It's at the end of the hall."

A large paper turkey eyed them from the door of the glass partition that separated this end of the corridor from the children's rooms. By the time Clare reached it, the muscles in her arms were trembling.

"We'll rest a few minutes," said Mrs. Thatcher. "I'm sure braces don't have to be so heavy. Someday, someone will find a way of making them lighter."

Leaning on the door frame, Clare watched a little boy in a blue bathrobe walking up and down the hall, pushing the big metal frame that supported his I.V. The tube from the bottle snaked up his sleeve and disappeared.

"Ready?" said Mrs. Thatcher, taking Clare's arm.

In the playroom they found Ginny, reading the magazines on the coffee table. Most had lost their covers and some of their pages as well. An empty milk bottle and a scattering of clothespins—oh, who could have left them on the table, these tokens of home?

"Clare, let me help you into one of the straight chairs," said Mrs. Thatcher. "The settee is like quicksand. I'll be back in a few minutes. You can ask Ginny if you need anything."

Ginny grunted and went on combing her short brown hair with her fingers. On a high shelf out of everyone's reach, behind a sign which said Don't Touch, the radio played continuously: two women were arguing.

"Ma Perkins." Ginny yawned. "Doesn't it play anything else?"

The boy on the I.V. sat down at the table between Ginny and Clare and cleared a little space among the magazines and began to drop the clothespins into the milk bottle, raising his hand higher each time to increase the difficulty.

"Is that fun?" asked Clare.

"It teaches patience," said the boy. "I have a hole in my heart." Seeing that Clare was impressed, he asked, "Do you know how big your heart is?"

Clare shook her head, and he held up his fist.

"Your heart is as big as your fist and it grows at the same rate," he told her.

On his pale chest, just above his half-buttoned pajama top, two gold medals gleamed.

"Did you get those medals in the gift shop?" asked Clare.

The boy shook his head. "My mom gave them to me. I don't know where she got them. This one's St. Anthony and this one's St. Joseph."

Noting that she wore none, he opened his bathrobe a little wider and showed her a paper medal pinned to his pajamas that read HERO: I HAD MY SHOT TODAY.

"Maybe," he said, "you could get one of these."

"But I haven't had my shot."

"I'll ask the nurse to give you a medal anyway," said the boy.

"She can wear mine," said a voice none of them recognized, and they all turned in surprise.

A young man in a purple and gold varsity jacket was dangling a silver coin strung on a thread of elastic. He was tall, with an open face and blue eyes and reddish blond hair that was all cowlick and no style, and Clare recognized him at once. Everyone at school recognized him. Once when Clare dropped her wallet while she was trying to open her locker, he'd leaned down and picked it up. In the jostle and din between classes, he'd picked up her wallet and handed it to her. "You dropped your wallet," he said. She was too flustered to say thank you. She managed a quick nod of her head and he disappeared down the hall. For weeks afterward, the sight of him made her tremble. She learned his schedule and looked forward to the few minutes between classes when their paths crossed. She watched him in the cafeteria and remembered what he ate and what he left untouched. She memorized his clothes and fell in love with the way he rolled up his shirt sleeves. Saturdays she watched him play, glad that he did not notice her in the stands. Once she'd stopped at Burney's to buy a sweatshirt for Davy, and to her alarm Ben came over and asked, "Can I help you?" He looked right at her; he could see she was trembling all over. *Help you?* She turned and ran out of the store. Whenever she saw him on the street, she lowered her head, afraid he could hear her heart pounding. But always his gaze passed through her. Until this moment.

The little boy on the I.V. took the coin and studied it.

"That's not a medal," he said. "Gee, what a keen skull."

Ben took the coin from the boy and handed it to Clare, who was so nervous she could scarcely hold it.

"It's an antique," he said. "Very rare."

He was talking to her just the way he'd talk to anyone. Like we were already friends, she thought. The fluttering in her stomach subsided. In this dingy lounge, it seemed as if they really were friends, and she found herself eager to talk.

"It's very unusual," she said. She handed it back.

"Don't you want to wear it?"

She was dying to wear it. But what good would it do? When he left, he would never come back, and she would look at it fifty times a day and want him to come back. She would tremble and want him all over again, this boy who had spoken to her only twice before: *You dropped your wallet. Can I help you?*

"No," she said, "it's yours. You keep it."

Disappointed, he pocketed the coin. Then he glanced around the room and saw, as if for the first time, the paper turkeys taped to the walls in the corridor.

"Well, happy Thanksgiving," he said, turning to go but not going.

"Today isn't Thanksgiving," said the boy. "What's your name?"

"Ben."

"I'm Toby. Aren't you going to stay?"

Ginny put down her torn copy of *Beauty Secrets of the Stars;* she hadn't turned a page since Ben entered the room. Now she leaned across the table and asked, "Who are you here to visit?"

"My uncle. He's seriously hurt. He's got a broken leg."

"In this place a broken leg isn't serious," said Ginny.

"How'd he break it?" asked Toby.

"Hit-and-run accident," said Ben. "He was left in the road with a broken leg. They never caught the driver."

"Just like you, honey," said Ginny, nodding to Clare.

"A car hit you?" asked Ben.

"A baseball," said Clare.

"If you ever find the guy that did it," said Ginny, "I hope you take him to court for every penny he's worth."

"I bet he's a Nazi," said Toby.

"I bet he's not," said Clare. "We don't have Nazis in America."

"He could be a Nazi spy," said Toby.

"To wreck somebody's life and get away with it," said Ginny. "It's awful."

"My life isn't wrecked," said Clare. "I'm going to study at home. I got accepted at Michigan for next year. Everybody in our family goes to Michigan."

"What are you studying to be?" asked Ben.

"An artist."

"You should get married," said Ben. "A pretty girl like you."

Ginny shot him a look: For God's sake, shut up. But Clare did not flinch.

"It takes five minutes to get married," she said. "And then what? You can't just be married."

"I could," sighed Ginny. "I—"

A clatter in the corridor drowned her out.

"Dinner's here," she said and jumped up. "I'll get the wheelchair."

Without a word Toby pushed his I.V. out of the playroom and scooted down the corridor. After Ginny had lifted Clare into the chair, she drew Ben aside.

"You want to wheel her back to room three-fifteen? I think she'd like that."

In her room Ben watched Ginny swing the arm of Clare's table over her lap and set the tray on it.

"Enjoy your dinner," she said and hurried out.

"Guess it's time to go," said Ben. He did not move.

"Don't go," said Clare. She could not bear to think of the emptiness he would leave behind him. "They always give me enough for two. Pull up that chair—that regular one."

He pulled up the only other chair in the room, and Clare lifted the silver helmet from the dinner plate and exposed a pale corpse of broccoli and a perfectly round veal patty that appeared to have been rolled in sand.

"Have some fried chicken," said Clare. She handed him the knife. "I hope you remembered to bring the watermelon."

He stared at her.

"Mother makes the best potato salad in the world," she went on, tapping the broccoli with her fork.

"I—"

"Oh, please. I can't eat all this."

She cut the patty in two and gave him the knife and fork and began to cut her half into bites with the spoon.

"We can't go swimming for at least an hour," she said.

"That's all right," said Ben. "We can sit on the beach and talk."

"Homemade ice cream for dessert."

"What flavor?"

She unveiled a watery custard with burnt edges. "Jade."

Ben laid down his fork.

"You know something? Most people in your shoes—your *situation*, I mean—would be totally depressed."

"When you leave," said Clare, "I'll be terribly depressed. I'll wonder if you're ever coming back. Are you coming back?"

"I haven't left yet, and you're talking about me coming back," said Ben with a smile. But Clare was not smiling. He would leave and she would never see him again.

"Please don't leave. I'll ask Mrs. Thatcher to bring in one of the comfortable chairs. There are comfortable chairs for the relatives who want to stay all night."

"I'm not a relative," said Ben.

"You might be. You might be my distant cousin. You look very distant, sitting over there."

Ben moved his chair around to her side of the table.

He's forgotten about visiting his uncle, thought Clare. But only something extraordinary would make him stay.

"You can meet my ghost," said Clare.

"She does look a little like a ghost," said Ben.

"You've seen her?"

"She was just here."

"*Who* was just here?"

"The nurse," said Ben.

"I don't mean the nurse," exclaimed Clare. "I mean the spirit-woman who comes at night. She's the reason I don't go nuts in this place. We travel together."

"You travel together?"

"My spirit travels. I leave my body behind."

"Jesus," whispered Ben.

"I'm talking too much, I know. Now I'll be quiet. What about you?"

"Me?"

"You haven't told me anything about you."

"There's not much to tell," said Ben. He knew he couldn't invent anything as good as her ghost.

"Start at the beginning," said Clare. "You wake up. You get dressed and eat breakfast in the dining room."

"No, in the kitchen," Ben said.

"All right, in the kitchen. You sit down at the kitchen table with your mom and dad."

"No, I sit down with my brother. Mom never sits down for breakfast."

"My mom doesn't, either. Okay, you sit down with your brother."

A nurse Clare did not know popped her head in the doorway.

"Finished with your dinner?"

"Yes, thank you. Could you help me back to bed?"

When the nurse left, she seemed to draw the last threads of twilight after her. The room was dark; the sky in the window was dark and starless as a well. On the horizon the city crouched like a strange animal, its hundreds of eyes shining. The bells next door were tolling for vespers.

"Tell me more about you," said Clare. "I may look like I'm dead, but I'll be listening."

She lay motionless, hands folded on her chest, her face so white that Ben was suddenly terrified she really might be dying.

"Do you want me to call the nurse?"

"Don't call anyone. You don't have to talk if you don't want to."

He sat down again and waited for her to open her eyes.

Was it very late? Had he fallen asleep? His legs felt stiff; one foot was asleep, and it prickled back to life as he tried to put his weight on it. He tipped his watch toward the doorway, and by the light from the corridor he saw the hands: midnight. The nurses had forgotten him and gone to roost. Everything around him had gone to its appointed place. He stood up and stretched, then bent down to look at Clare. He held his breath. He could go now. She would not miss him.

He leaned over and kissed her cheek.

9

Five for Your Happiest Day on Earth

"If you'd just let Mr. Knochen come to the house and give a demonstration," pleaded Nell, spearing an artichoke out of the salad. "There must be some dead person you'd like to communicate with."

"The Bible says, 'Thou shalt not traffic with magicians,'" said Helen. "Or ghosts or soothsayers or wizards."

"Where does it say that?" demanded Nell.

"Give me the Bible and I'll find it," said Helen. "If Grandpa were here, he could find it right away. Who told you about this man?"

"Debbie Lieberman and Marie Clackett."

"I saw some ghosts once," said Davy and was glad that nobody heard him. The two women he'd seen on the landing by the photographs—were they ghosts? One of them had looked like Clare.

Grandma stopped humming. In her sealskin coat and black straw hat, she looked like a great shaggy beast.

"Hal," said Grandma, and she reached over and patted his hand, "did anyone ever tell you that you have beautiful ears?"

Hal laughed, and Davy felt sure he was not laughing at Grandma.

"You did," he chuckled. "You're the only one."

"I'll be leaving right after lunch," she said. "I'll be taking the bus."

"There are no buses running today," said Helen. "It's Thanksgiving."

"And it's raining," added Nell. "You don't want to go in the rain."

"I never thought we'd get through the turkey without Clare to carve it," said Helen. She stole a loving glance at Hal, who was chewing his soy cutlet and who could not have carved a turkey if his life depended on it.

"Where *is* Clare?" asked Grandma, surprised.

"Oh, Grandma," groaned Nell. "She's in the hospital. Remember?"

"Is she sick?" asked Grandma.

"Paralyzed," said Hal.

"We told you," said Davy.

Grandma squinted at Davy, not certain whether she knew him or not, and not wanting them to scold her if she asked his name. She decided that she did know him and that it would not be wise to ask.

"How old are you?" she inquired.

"You asked me that this morning," said the boy.

"Hush," said Nell. "It won't hurt you to tell her again."

"I'm five," said Davy.

"Five," Grandma exclaimed. "Already five?"

"Show Grandma the turkey you drew for Clare," said Helen.

"It's wrapped up," said Davy.

"Clare painted this cup," said Nell, changing the subject. "Isn't it nice? Davy set the table, and he gave me this cup."

She held it aloft. It was plain as an eggshell on the outside, but inside danced a riot of angels.

"We have an ancestor who was painter to the Kaiser," said Grandma.

"You already said that," said Davy. He did not believe in this ancestor, since nobody except Grandma knew anything about him.

"Hush," said Nell. "You know she forgets."

He hushed, but he could not understand why she forgot so often. Aunt Helen forgot things too, but differently. Sometimes she forgot where she put her watch or her ring. To keep from forgetting, she would say severely to her ring, "I am putting you on the sill," or she would remind her watch she was putting it on the china cabinet, and sometimes she would explain to both the ring and the watch why she hated to wear anything that encumbered her hands when she washed the dishes and polished the silver.

"Do we have any coffee?" asked Nell. "I mean real coffee. Not the Battle Creek Sanitarium stuff."

"Nobody drinks coffee but you," said Helen. "I keep forgetting to buy it."

"I thought there was one can left."

"Can we get some more Ovaltine?" asked Davy.

"Someday," said Nell. "Someday we'll get another jar of Ovaltine."

Ovaltine and Cream of Wheat. Once when he had to stay in bed with asthma, Aunt Helen gave him Ovaltine and Cream of Wheat, all he wanted, and Clare saved the silver seal with the raised letters OVALTINE inside the lid of the jar and sent away for an Orphan Annie cup. It had a red plastic top, so you could shake the Ovaltine and the milk together inside, and Orphan Annie on the front was holding another cup, just like this one, and on the front of that cup was a still smaller Orphan Annie holding yet another cup, though of course you couldn't see it. He could only see the first two, but he knew they went on forever, each Orphan Annie holding the image of herself, tinier and tinier. Probably nobody could see the tiniest one, except God.

Those were good times. Clare brought the Sears catalogue and sat on the edge of his bed, and they would turn the pages of the toy section and say "Dibs on that train" or "Dibs on that sled," and whoever said it first won. Having dibs on the sled was almost as good as having the real sled if you were sick and couldn't use it. She brought *Better Homes & Gardens* and *Good Housekeeping* and *Parents' Magazine,* and they looked for coupons that said no salesman would call, and Clare put his name on all of them. And after he was well the mailman brought him samples of Gerber's cereal and a book on the wonders of the Frigidaire, showing in pictures how much better it was to keep food in an electric Frigidaire than wait for a man to bring the ice, and a Br'er Rabbit cookbook, which Clare said was like any other cookbook except that all the recipes called for molasses.

. . .

Nell opened the kitchen cupboard and gazed with a sinking heart at four cans of soy Protose and a box of Dr. Jackson's Meal, which showed Dr. Jackson in white swimming trunks, looking fit and youthful. There was a big box of seaweed snacks. There was no coffee.

What difference did it make? You couldn't really enjoy your coffee with Hal casting baleful glances at you every time you took a sip.

Suddenly, behind the Koepplinger's Health Bread she spied a tea bag. Enough for one cup, maybe two. She put the water on to boil, and soon the teakettle was hissing and jiggling the way it always did since Helen pulled out the whistle. Nell's spirits lifted.

The tea was strong and black. She drank it slowly and listened to the clatter of silverware in the next room.

There was a scraping of chairs, and Helen hurried into the kitchen. "Grandma's headed for the front door," she said. "Where's that basket of clothes?"

"On the back porch. She won't get out," Nell assured her. "I locked the door."

In the front hall they found Grandma shaking the doorknob.

"It's been lovely," she said, "but I have to leave. I got five men coming to work on the house."

"Today is Thanksgiving," said Nell. "Nobody works on Thanksgiving."

"I have to go home *now*," said Grandma darkly.

"Grandma, you promised you'd help me hang up the clothes," said Helen. "I did a big wash this morning. We have to hang up the clothes."

"In the rain?" asked Hal.

"Why not in the rain?" said Helen.

From the dining room they could keep an eye on her. The clean sheets fluttered over the spirea bushes that trailed their dead wands against the French doors. The clothesline was strung around the pole like a spider's web, and when the sheets billowed out, it seemed to Helen that Grandma was rigging a peculiar ship.

"Look at the crows," said Nell. "Three, four, five of them out in the pear tree."

"Three for a wedding, four for a birth, five for your happiest day on earth," said Helen.

Grandma turned the clothesline a little and started hanging up towels.

"She's some help to you anyhow," said Hal.

"Those are the same clothes she hung up this morning," said Helen. "I keep the basket handy. Gives me fifteen minutes of peace."

"She hangs 'em up and I take 'em down," said Nell. "Has anyone seen my shoes?"

She always missed her shoes when it was time to clear the table and had to set off in search of them.

"Davy," said Helen, "these are my best Dresden plates. Can you carry them very carefully to the kitchen? One at a time."

Davy carried his own plate out first and set it on the sink while Helen collected the gravy boat and the platter bearing the ruins of the turkey. Before she reached the kitchen, Davy came running back.

"Aunt Helen, my mom drank up all the angels! Her cup is bald!"

And he waved the cup at her that Clare had painted. It was now totally blank. For a moment she felt as if Clare herself had been erased through that casual mistake. Then she could hear Clare telling her, Don't worry, Mother. I can fix it. I'll paint even better angels next time.

"Oh, Lord," she said, "that was water paint and India ink. I never drink out of that cup. Will it hurt her, Hal?"

"Her hair will fall out and she will die of violent cramps," said Hal. "And she won't feel a thing. She's strong as a horse."

"Angels in the tummy," sang Davy.

"Don't tell her," said Helen. "She'll feel better if she doesn't know."

Helen washed the cup gently. She'd rather have lost the cup than the angels. Lost things, she felt certain, had a life of their own.

They came back to their families like stray dogs. Maybe there really was an ancestor who'd painted the Kaiser's portrait; maybe one of his paintings would find its way to America.

That's where Clare's talent comes from, she thought. From that ancestor. Not from Hal or me.

10

A Man in a Winged Cap

Everything in the room was saying good-bye to her.

"Your last night here," said the lamp.

"You won't be seeing me again," said the basin.

"Tomorrow you'll sleep in your own bed," said the pillow.

Ginny had spent half the afternoon helping her pack.

"That's five nights running he's come to see you. He's madly in love with you, Clare."

"He didn't come on Thanksgiving," said Clare. "The one day we have good food he doesn't come."

There had been cranberry jelly and dressing and two slices of white meat, and in the corner of her tray a paper turkey made by the Girl Scouts.

"You know he's not coming for the food," said Ginny. "Oh, God, I'm going to miss you, Clare. I never personally met anybody who made love for the first time in a hospital bed."

Clare could see that Ginny wanted to hear all about it, but somehow the thing seemed too private to share. And where should she start? In bed? Or before, when she told him her dream about being locked in the high school gym, which was all decorated with crepe paper for the sock hop, and her friends were standing around in little groups, waiting for the band to start up, and Clare was there, too, as hale and free as anybody, and the band struck up "The White Cliffs of Dover," and it was at that moment Clare felt herself starting to fade, to lose her substance till she was nothing but a big black-and-white snapshot, propped on a fold-out stand right in the middle of the dance floor—just like the big cardboard Santa Claus drinking Coca-Cola in the window of Clackett's Fine Foods. The boy who looked as if he were going to ask her to dance lost interest and went off to find somebody more permanent. Her math teacher, one of the chaperones, picked Clare up and carried her down to the janitor's office and left her there.

Without color, without dimension, without a body to call her own, she listened to the laughter and music overhead, the dance of life, from which she was excluded.

"I never noticed you in school," Ben had said.

"I noticed you," Clare had answered.

Though they were sisters by experience now, Clare could not tell Ginny. Not until Ginny told first. Ginny snapped Clare's overnight case shut and pushed it into the closet and sat down on her bed.

"My first time was in a woods, with a guy I didn't even like very much. I was a sophomore in high school and he was a freshman, but he looked older. I thought he was at least a junior when he called me up and asked me would I like to go for a walk. Some walk. It was a five-mile hike. We walked clean out of town. I remember the moon, huge and yellow. The harvest moon, he called it. We crossed one cow pasture and then another cow pasture, and he kept saying it was a shortcut home, and all of a sudden in the middle of nowhere he stops and turns to me and says, 'You're an older woman. You've had a lot of experience. Show me how to do it.' That's just how he put it to me. I was flabbergasted. I said he had me all wrong. I told him I was saving myself for marriage. He looked kind of hurt and mumbled something about no hard feelings and heading back into town."

She paused, puzzled by what she had just said, as if the story were new to her.

"He said he knew a shortcut. We plunged into the darkest woods I have ever seen. I mean, I couldn't see *anything*. Not even my own hands. Everything was just *gone*. And I was beginning to wonder if we were going in the right direction when suddenly we heard breathing."

"I'd have died right there," said Clare.

"*Heavy* breathing all around us, and stamping and running. My hand rammed into something huge and warm and furry, and I screamed and screamed—Lord, how I screamed! And Hubert said, 'It's cows. Stay where you are. It's nothing but a herd of cows.' So we stood quiet and they passed us. I never saw those cows. I just felt their big bodies brush up against mine, and I heard them stamping and snorting, and when the last cow was gone I was so glad that I flopped down on the ground and started to laugh. And Hubert flopped down on top of me and laughed, too. And I had no more sense of saving myself for marriage than those cows did. I was so glad not to be trampled to death, so glad to be alive."

"That's how I felt," said Clare, "so glad to be alive."

"You're real lucky," said Ginny. "If we get into the war, there won't be any men left for us except the old and the married. Even if Ben is drafted, you'll know you belong to somebody. You have somebody."

"I don't want to belong to anybody," said Clare quietly.

"Honey, don't you worry. You'll be walking as good as new one of these days. You'll be walking to the altar as good as anybody."

Ben was gone, and yet, Clare thought, he had never left the room. The chair he'd sat in praised him, the curtains he'd drawn still held the place where his hand touched them. And every fiber of Clare's body carried the message, passing it from cell to cell, like a fire that warms but does not destroy: Ben was here. Ben was here. Here.

The clock in the convent struck twelve. What are they doing over there now? thought Clare. She listened for the faint final stroke and heard a ping of glass shattered far away. The thirteenth stroke.

The Ancestress hovered at the foot of the bed. Clare had not seen her for five nights.

I'm ready, said Clare.

She never asked where they were going. How much easier it was now, to slip like fog out of her flesh and gather her shadow self together, yet not a shadow either, but a flame, a lamp invisible to the eyes of the body.

Tonight I shall follow you, said the Ancestress. *I shall protect you, but you must be your own guide. Let the way choose you, and go where you are needed.*

Almost immediately they moved into the deep darkness of a long journey, a darkness filled with the gathering of waves into crested hills and their retreat into gleaming valleys, the net of green phosphorescence under the water's skin, the cries of men going under, the bombs that sent them there, the moon that watched. Clare heard the gathering, the imperceptible tugs of the moon.

Before I left my bone-house for good, said the Ancestress, *I was surprised that I could hear the world's hum long after my other senses winked out. All languages are open to you now, Clare.*

A deep chill caught them. They passed through a stone wall and came out through a tapestry on the other side into a large, badly lit room. Under a chandelier of carved beasts whose eyes hid candles, two men were studying the tapestry. The shorter of the two wore a white suit, and from his crown of golden antlers rose a swastika of pearls. The other might have been a diplomat, impeccable and unobtrusive in his three-piece suit. Black.

Gobelin, Herr Goering? asked the gentleman in black.

Of course, Herr Death, was the reply.

Statues, tapestries, bishops' staves, silver goblets, and Persian carpets lay heaped like an offering before a desk nearly eight yards long. Pale blond, inlaid with bronze swastikas. Two large golden candlesticks glittered at either end.

Splendid desk, Herr Goering, observed the gentleman in black.

Mahogany, said Goering. *Notice my inkstand, Herr Death.*

Black marble?

Onyx, replied Goering.

And an exquisite yardstick, added the gentleman in black. *Jade?*

Green ivory. With rubies to mark the centimeters.

And what's this? A painting of the Kaiser?

It was used for packing, replied Goering.

I must say, exclaimed the gentleman in black, *I've done rather well by you.*

Reichsmarschall, whispered Goering. *That's all I want now. To be Reichsmarschall.*

And now, said the gentleman in black, *if you'll show me that coin.*

Stand under the lamp, said Goering.

In the light cast by the eyes of the beasts, Goering drew out a black leather box and opened it.

Just as you described, Herr Death. On one side, a man in a winged cap, holding a staff twisted with snakes. On the other, a skull.

The gentleman in black turned the coin over in his hand, as if his palm were a balance and he were weighing it.

This is not the lost coin, Herr Goering. This is a copy.

Herr Death, I assure you—

A copy. A poor trick, Herr Goering. You took the pattern from old tales about me. What power did you think I would give you in exchange? The power to meet your own death? He reached over and dropped the coin into the box and snapped it shut. *Don't you know that to those who serve me the power is already given?*

II

Sunrise Jams, Childhood Preserves

"Don't let them come in yet," said Clare. "I want to surprise them."

Mrs. Thatcher put her head out the door again.

"They're still at the nurse's station."

She leaned toward Clare, who put her arm around the other woman for support.

"Up we go—crutches into place," she said.

Curtain going up, act one, thought Clare, and the doorway was filled with an audience: her mother and father and Nell and Grandma and Davy, all bundled in winter coats, shy as peasants brought into the glittering rooms of the rich.

"Look, Hal!" exclaimed Helen. "She's standing! She can stand all by herself!"

They surged into the room, and Mrs. Thatcher stepped protectively toward Clare.

"Give her a hug," said Mrs. Thatcher. "You won't fall, will you, Clare?" And she gripped Clare firmly around the waist.

Helen leaned over and kissed Clare's cheek, gingerly. Does she think I'm contagious? thought Clare. Only Davy did not seem to be afraid of her. He held up a little metal box painted like a cereal carton and danced around her. "Look at the bank I got at the gift shop. Read what it says, Clare. Read what it says."

"Mouse Crusties," said Clare. "It says Mouse Crusties."

"I'm sorry I can't stay," said Grandma. "I have a meeting."

Nell rolled her eyes at Clare.

77

"Grandma, we're bringing Clare home today. You can skip your meeting."

"I *got* to go," said Grandma. "I'm the main speaker."

"She drives you nuts," whispered Nell into Clare's ear. "Absolutely nuts."

"If you'll take her suitcase"—Mrs. Thatcher handed Clare's overnight bag to Hal—"I'll bring her down in the wheelchair."

"Oh, we brought a wheelchair," said Helen proudly.

"That's all right, Mrs. Bishop. We can use one of the hospital chairs to move her."

"Here's your new coat, Clare," said Nell. "It's the first time you've had a chance to wear it."

Fake fur, the color of dry sand. Everybody in school was wearing fake fur. How new it smelled! Drawing it around her, she felt light-headed and a little frightened.

My God, her feet! thought Nell. Poor dead birds propped on the footrest.

And she turned her gaze elsewhere.

It's like the day we brought Clare home from the hospital, thought Helen. All that new equipment, the sterilizer, the bottle warmer, the Bathinette. I was afraid I'd never learn to take care of her. Terrified of giving her a bath.

Mrs. Thatcher wheeled Clare past the nurse's station, and the nurse behind the desk smiled.

"Isn't it wonderful to be going home?" she said.

At the elevator they waited respectfully for Mrs. Thatcher to push the button for down, and when the door opened and a crowd of other visitors surged out, Clare was grateful for her brisk manner.

"Out of the way, please. Wheelchair here. Please make room."

She eased the chair in backwards, so that Clare would be facing the door and could watch the numbers light up. Fifth floor, fourth floor, third floor, falling like a temperature.

"Is everyone going to the ground floor?" called a voice from the back.

The elevator stopped with a small jolt that sent Davy rising on tiptoes. Helen found herself gripping the arm of the chair.

They passed the gift shop, the outpatient waiting room; they passed through heavy glass doors into the parking lot. The thin dusting of snow, the cold sunlight, the crisp bones of the trees, left Clare speechless. The leaves—when had they gone? Her breath steamed out of her mouth and vanished. From the hospital window, with its bland sky and distant city, she had known none of this.

"Clare," said Mrs. Thatcher, "you can ride in the front seat."

She opened the front door of the Buick and drew the wheelchair close.

"Now, Mr. Bishop, if you'll just go around to her left side, and lock your arm around her waist."

Carefully, Hal slid his arm around Clare.

"You have to *lock* your arm," said Mrs. Thatcher. "Clench your biceps."

"Uff," said Hal.

"The most important job you have right now is keeping your arm there. When you're walking, watch her feet and walk right with her, stride for stride."

"Papa, your arm is quivering like jelly!"

They all laughed, except Hal.

"That's no arm," said Mrs. Thatcher. "That's an iron bar."

Clare plumped down into the front seat, and Nell and Davy and Grandma and Helen, who had been watching helplessly, snapped to life and crowded into the back seat.

"I don't think I'll ever be able to get out again," said Clare. "I'll have to live in the car."

"Oh, you can't live in the car," said Helen earnestly. "I've got your room all fixed up for you."

"I hope your room is on the ground floor, Clare," said Mrs. Thatcher.

"Second floor," said Hal.

"There's no bathroom on the first floor," said Helen. "Isn't that ridiculous? We have four bathrooms and none on the first floor."

"Clare will do fine," said Mrs. Thatcher. "She's got grit and then some, Mrs. Bishop. Not many of my patients meet a new boyfriend in the hospital."

"He's not my boyfriend," said Clare.

"You wait," said Mrs. Thatcher. "He'll call. I can tell when they're going to call. I can tell from the way they say good-bye."

Clare felt a pang of remorse. "I never said good-bye to Ginny."

"I'll tell her good-bye for you," said Mrs. Thatcher. "She'll be so pleased you remembered her."

As they turned out of the parking lot into traffic, Helen leaned forward from the back seat.

"Did your friend say he'd call?"

"He said he might drop by sometime."

"I can't wait to meet him," said Nell.

"How's Bill?" asked Clare, changing the subject. "Are you still seeing much of him?"

"Bill and Heidi," Nell said. "Last week we went dancing at Whitmore Lake. First he danced with Heidi. Then he danced with me. Then he danced with Heidi. Then he danced with me. Then he danced with Heidi. Then he danced with me. The next morning Heidi called to say *he* couldn't get out of bed, and she'd lost the medal she'd received at her First Communion, and she felt real bad about it because if you're wearing your First Communion medal when you die, you go straight to heaven. You skip right over the other place."

"Oh, Lord," said Helen.

They drove in silence for some time. At last Helen remarked, "Hal, this isn't the way home."

"It's the long way home. I thought Clare might like to see her old school," said Hal, as if she had renounced it forever.

"Well, slow down, Hal, so she can look," said Helen.

Clare turned, all unsuspecting, and saw that school, too, had gone on without her. Two boys were crossing the playfield, kicking a football across the patches of snow. Funny to pass the school at eleven o'clock on a weekday morning, to be outside the classroom when she should have been inside, listening to Miss Fairmont talk about irregular French verbs. Did the teachers miss her? She had always been a good student. Never came late to class, never fooled around in the halls. It wasn't fair to keep her out just because she couldn't walk up the stairs.

"You should ask some of your friends over to visit you," said Helen.

Friends, thought Hal. She doesn't have any friends. Always got her nose in a book.

It took Clare nearly a quarter of an hour to walk up the front path and even longer to go upstairs to her own room, with everyone clenching and hugging and squeezing and pushing and hanging onto her, and Helen saying over and over, "Remember, Hal, your arm is an iron bar" and "Clench your biceps," as if these phrases would protect Clare, so that when she finally arrived and was helped into her own bed, she never wanted to leave it again.

And immediately thought: I must leave this room. Must know I can leave it.

Already she could feel herself becoming a child in this undisturbed space which preserved the layers of her childhood intact, like the nine layers of Troy. But in reverse: the bottom layer was the most recent. The lowest shelves, within easy reach, were crammed with her books and her school papers and two jars that said Sunrise Strawberry Jam and held erasers. Just above the books could be found her India ink and her pens and sketch books and oils and the water paints she'd used as a child to make pictures and birthday cards for relatives.

Above the paints, on a high shelf where the air was rare enough for cobwebs to grow undisturbed, lived her Storybook Dolls, all bisque and satin and taffeta, none taller than her hand; some still stood framed in their white boxes with pink polka dots, and two still clutched the tiny folder that listed the whole series of dolls a little girl could acquire if she were rich enough. Fairy Tales. Foreign Lands. Nursery Rhymes. Nobody Clare knew was rich enough to own them all.

And above the dolls, just below the ceiling, hidden away in plain boxes were the oldest treasures: her christening dress and the silver cup and brush she'd been given when she was born and a glass baby bottle, streaked with amber from frequent sterilizing in hard water.

On the ceiling itself her father had pasted paper stars the month before she was born, hoping perhaps for a son who would be interested in astronomy. They glowed in the dark. Lying in her crib, lulled by the murmur of adult voices downstairs, she had watched the stars before she knew how to call anything by its name, had heard the clatter of dishes in the kitchen below mark mealtimes, and the deep silence of afternoons stretching across the long days before she started going to school.

The doctors had sent her home, had done all they could for her, and she was no better. Grass covered the roads she had traveled to other lives, other places. The Ancestress, the journey over the water, Death himself, were snapshots from a voyage vaguely remembered, and soon these, too, would be lost. What day was it? What time? She dropped on all fours and crawled, dragging her legs after her, pulling herself forward with her arms. Sliding downstairs on her stomach was as easy as coasting down a hill. It was so much easier to crawl than to use the crutches.

That evening when her father sat reading the newspaper in the living room after supper, she curled up at his feet on the hearth beside Cinnamon Monkeyshines, who kept watch over the fire, and Davy brought her the Sears catalogue. *Dibs on that doll. Dibs on that icebox.* Now he let her have the best things on each page, as she used to do for him.

It was to this preserve of childhood that Ben came.

12

Did Jesus Charge a Dollar
for Raising the Dead?

The east part of Ann Arbor once belonged to trees, Indians, and Englishmen. The Englishmen and the Indians went the way of all flesh, leaving nothing but their names—Iroquois Drive, Devonshire Place. The trees were luckier. Here, an orchard. There, a stand of hickory. What the realtors call "stately old homes" have taken root under their branches. *Stately:* large rooms, window seats, French doors, a third-floor room for the maid. *Old:* a bathtub on legs, and behind the electric icebox, a door for the iceman, who no longer comes. Lilacs, spirea, forsythia in season; a rusty rose arbor, tottering; a goldfish pond in the backyard. Elm. Maple. Mountain ash.

Number 201 Orchard Drive was so different from Ben's house on the north side of Main as to make him think he had crossed the frontier of a different nation. Pear trees lined both sides of the walk and roofed his passage with bent wands bearing light burdens of snow. The pears were long gone. Two months earlier a Negro man and his wife had come over from the west side and begged Helen for the windfall. Helen said yes, and the windfall was collected and canned. Row upon row of the Bishops' pears shone in the kitchen of a frame house on Catherine Street.

Ben crunched up the front walk; the snow underfoot felt clean and unused, as if it had been stored in mothballs. He rang the bell twice.

When the door opened, he was facing a woman who looked very much like Clare, only older.

"Come right in," she said. "I'm Clare's mother. I'll tell Clare you're here."

He stepped into the hallway, and Helen went to the foot of the stairs and hollered, "CLA-YER! He's HERE!"

A little boy clumped down the stairs, almost hidden behind the pungent swag of evergreen that wreathed the banister.

"Aunt Helen—"

"This is Davy, my sister's boy."

"Aunt Helen, Clare says to give her ten minutes. She wants to come down for lunch."

"You may as well come in and wait by the fire," said Helen and motioned for Ben to follow her.

The living room was as crammed as a shop. There was a grand piano in one corner and a low black jade pedestal, intricately carved with leaves and blossoms; nothing heavier than a handkerchief could have sat on it. Massive gold frames held a pair of landscapes, all shade and twilight and cows drinking at a dark river and cottages under willows that trailed their boughs like feathers of lead.

There was a large cream brocade sofa against one wall, and two overstuffed chairs of wine plush on either side of the fireplace, and a glass-topped coffee table between them, under which a tiger cat slept like an exhibit, offering its belly to the fire.

There was a black sofa with wooden dividers in the back, and a whatnot shelf supported by columns of polished spools—how many years of making and mending had used so much thread?— whose surfaces held ashtrays from China enameled with egrets and a wooden box from Persia which showed an emperor hunting a gazelle and two china heads that belonged to dolls whose bodies had long gone.

There was a small round table whose four feet ended in claws and from whose open drawer spilled photographs and bridge tallies and old Christmas cards.

The Oriental rug underfoot gave Ben the feeling that all these wonders were precariously balanced on an island of flowers. He knew it would be polite to admire something.

"Nice sofa," he said at last.

"Love seat," Helen corrected him. "It's an antique."

"Aunt Helen gets all her furniture from dead people," said Davy.

"I know it's crowded in here," said Helen, "but I hate to sell things that have been in the family. Do you want a ginger ale?"

"Me too," said Davy.

"Bring two bottles of Vernor's and two glasses from the kitchen, Davy," said Helen.

As Davy darted away, Helen took Ben's arm and led him to the mantel. A long swag of artificial holly hung down at either side of it like a rumpled snake.

"I want you to see what nice painting Clare does. She painted this pitcher when she was twelve."

On its unglazed belly, an angel rode across a navy sky on a green bird. Every feather was meticulously drawn: a bird in armor, a jeweled nightingale.

"Beautiful," he said.

"And that bowl next to the pitcher," said Helen. "She gave me that bowl for Mother's Day when she was eight."

The wooden bowl, covered with crudely painted hearts and flowers, Ben found less attractive than the pitcher.

"Pretty good for eight," he said.

"She painted angels on all my kitchen cupboards. And when we had the kitchen repainted last year, Mr. Schneider painted right over them. It broke my heart. Clare said, 'Don't worry, Mother, I'll paint you some new ones.' Nell says, 'Watch out, she'll paint on your coffin.' Come here—let me show you something."

She urged him toward the grand piano, over which hung half a dozen diplomas and certificates and one blue ribbon.

"Clare won first prize in the Scholastic Regional Art Contest, Southeastern Michigan Division, when she was fourteen."

"That's wonderful, just wonderful," said Ben. He was growing sleepy; the room was too hot.

"And she won this blue ribbon for a shadow box she entered in the Ann Arbor Garden Club Flower Show."

"Well, what do you know?"

"And here's a picture of Clare in the freshman class play. She wrote the play."

Helen pointed to the photograph of a makeshift horse wearing ballet slippers.

"Did you say Clare is in the picture?" asked Ben, puzzled.

"She's the horse. The front half."

Davy ran into the room carrying two ginger ales with Grandma right behind him, dragging her suitcase, her straw hat shoved cock-eyed on her head.

"I'm going now," she said. "It's been lovely."

"Oh, Grandma, you don't want to go now," said Nell, gliding up behind her. "We've just put lunch on the table."

"And Clare's friend Ben has come especially to meet you," said Helen. "Oh, you can't go now."

Grandma peered at Ben through her thick glasses, as if she had been asked to believe in something she could not see. Or was she listening to the muffled thumping in the hall? Did nobody else hear it except this old woman and himself, Ben wondered, and at that moment he caught sight of Clare in the mirror over the mantel. She was paddling headfirst down the stairs, pulling herself forward with her arms, dragging her legs after her as if she wanted to leave them behind; a shell she had outgrown and could not shake off.

Ben wished he had not seen her. She would not want him to see her. Not that way. He followed Helen into the dining room.

"This is Hal, Clare's father," said Helen. "He always sits down to lunch at noon, whether anyone else is here or not."

Hal, in shirt-sleeves at the head of the table, had not only sat down, he had already started to eat, spearing beets out of a bowl as steadily as a conveyer belt, forking them, eating them—*snip, snap!* He speared, spooned, snapped, chewed without mercy; he did not miss a beat.

"Glad to meet you," said Ben, though he did not feel they had met, only appraised each other, as one insect might wonder if the other is edible. He looked away and saw Clare again, this time in the mirror over the telephone table in the front hall. Nell was lifting her into the wheelchair. Was this Clare, he asked himself, this rag doll whose dress hung dark and plain, like a nun's habit? The two of them emerged from the mirror into the dining room: two time travelers entering the fourth dimension.

"Hello," said Clare.

Davy took Ben's hand.

"Here's your place," he said, "next to me."

Ben sat down at the table between Davy, who stared at him, and Grandma, who was humming under her breath. And Clare? She hardly seemed to notice he was in the room.

"Clare tells me you're a student at the University," said Helen.

"She did?" Ben's stomach sank. He had never told Clare that.

"What are you majoring in?" asked Nell.

"Geology," said Ben. The first subject that popped into his head.

"And what do you plan to do with it?" asked Hal.

Everybody was staring at Ben now, forks in midair.

"It's kind of private," he said. "I just can't talk about it."

He must be on academic probation, thought Helen, trying to imagine what could be so private about a career in geology.

"If you want an easy course, take Precious Gems!" exclaimed Nell, and Clare's stony face broke into a smile.

"Mother, tell Ben about Precious Gems."

"I can't," said Helen. "I don't even like to think about it."

"Tell it, tell it!" pleaded Davy.

"Well—" Helen wiped her mouth with her napkin and laid the napkin on the table. "Hal and I were at a faculty dinner party—we had only been married a month, and everyone was so curious about me because Hal is twenty years older than I am—we met on a blind date—and somebody started talking about pipe courses on campus, and I said, 'The biggest pipe course on campus is Precious Gems.' There was a long silence. And then the hostess said, 'The gentleman on your left is our good friend Professor Shrew, who teaches that course.' I nearly died."

"Shrew," repeated Hal, as if invoking him. "We took freshman English together."

"At Michigan," added Helen. "All our family went to Michigan. Hal, Nell, me—"

"Our other sister, her husband, my ex-husband," chimed in Nell.

"Hal," said Grandma, "did anyone ever tell you that you have beautiful ears?"

"You did," said Hal. He smiled at her.

"You tell him every day," said Davy.

"Davy, she forgets," whispered Nell.

Grandma peered at Davy. Her glasses made her eyes huge and all-knowing.

"How old are you now?" she asked.

"Five."

"Oh, that's right. I forgot."

Ben finished his salad—a Bartlett pear filled with cream cheese —and reached for the plate of hamburgers. Nell snatched it away from him.

"Give Ben a real hamburger. That's Hal's Protose."

"They look just like—" began Ben, but she cut him off.

"They're made from soybeans. Hal is a vegetarian."

"I never heard of soybean hamburgers."

"I order them from Battle Creek," said Hal, as if that explained everything. Helen had just come from the kitchen, and from the dish in her hand she forked a real hamburger onto Ben's plate.

"We've got cases and cases of Protose," said Davy.

"You've heard of the Battle Creek Sanitarium, of course," remarked Hal.

Ben shook his head no.

"I want to take Clare to the San," Hal said, as if Ben had nodded yes instead. "I want to see if Dr. Kellogg can help her."

Clare, head bowed, was eating slowly and steadily.

"Listen," exclaimed Helen. "The marching band is practicing."

Silence.

"I can't hear anything," said Ben.

"Me neither," said Nell.

"Can't you feel the vibrations?" asked Helen, turning to Ben.

Again they stopped talking and listened.

"It wouldn't be the marching band now," said Nell.

"Perhaps it's snow," said Helen.

"Pardon me?" asked Ben.

"Helen can hear the snow coming when it's still miles away," said Nell. When he did not respond, she changed the subject. "Wasn't that Ohio State game a thriller?"

"I didn't see it," said Ben.

"Goodness, I don't know how you could bear to miss it," said Helen. "We go to all the games." She almost said, "We used to go to all the games till Clare came home," but stopped herself in time. "Our seats are right on the fifty-yard line. Where are your seats?"

"My seats?"

"Where you sit," said Nell.

"I don't have any tickets."

"You never got your tickets?" exclaimed Helen. "Every student is entitled to a season ticket. You should have gotten yours in the mail the first week of classes."

"I'll call the dean of men about it on Monday," said Hal.

"That's all right," said Ben quickly. "The season's over."

"The season's over," said Hal, "and who knows if there'll be a football team next year? Did you see the headlines this morning? The Germans sank another submarine."

"If we go to war, there won't be enough men around to make up a team," said Nell.

"Do you think we *will* go to war?" asked Clare.

She had hardly spoken during the entire meal, and now her voice was as startling as a stranger's.

"We're arming ships," said Hal. "We're sending men. We can hardly be called neutral."

"I expect you'll be drafted one of these days," said Nell, beaming at Ben.

"Wait till you're drafted," said Hal. "No point in going any sooner. You can serve your country better with a good education."

In the front hall, the telephone was ringing urgently.

"Now who would call during lunch?" asked Helen and rose to

answer it. Again silence fell over the meal. Helen knew they were all listening to her, trying to piece the conversation together from her brief responses. "Here? . . . Tonight? . . . But not for supper, I hope."

She banged the receiver down without saying good-bye.

"What nerve!"

"Who was it?" asked Nell.

"Marie Clackett. Mr. Knochen will be arriving here at eight."

"I thought he wasn't coming till the seventh. That's Sunday."

"He says he has important business on Sunday."

Helen began to clear the plates.

"I think that any man who goes around saying he can call back the dead will go straight to hell. And to charge a dollar for it, too!"

"Every dollar goes to the Red Cross," Nell reminded her.

"Did Jesus charge people a dollar when he raised Lazarus?" demanded Helen.

13

Islanders

The telephone in Drake's Sandwich Shop stood in a booth at the back, behind the restrooms. Ben managed to park Hal's vast Buick in front of the shop. But should he leave Clare in the car or carry her in? Or should he go through the long hassle of getting her on crutches? During the drive after lunch she had begun to liven up, and he saw traces of the spirited girl he'd met in the hospital.

It's the heat in that house, he thought. It's enough to put anyone to sleep.

The subject of Mr. Knochen had revived her. He was an itinerant spiritualist, she explained, who arranged seances in private houses. He did not claim to be a medium, only a believer who cleared the air of doubt so the dead could make themselves heard. The dead could speak through anybody they chose—and not only a person, either. They could speak through any object, and they could send you presents from far places. Why, a man in Philadelphia had received, over several years, a two-thousand-year-old coin from India, one English farthing, ten artificial gems, a child's sleigh bell, a small seashell, and two fresh poppies out of season. He had also been robbed by spirits of a package of Turkish cigarettes. And a dead priest had sent his congregation in New York a ceramic ashtray marked Chicago Hilton. It sprang from the air and plummeted to the altar while the choir was singing "Nearer My God to Thee." The dead could even gather vibrations and spiritual vapors in the room and put on the appearance of flesh.

"Isn't there somebody you'd like to talk with in the other world?" asked Clare.

The quickness of his own reply surprised him, as if someone had spoken for him. "My dad."

Ben was glad to find Drake's nearly deserted as he shut himself into the telephone booth and dialed home. Glad not to be burdened, at this moment, with Clare. The telephone rang twice. Willie answered it.

"It's me," said Ben. "Listen, I have a big favor to ask you."

"Not a cent," said Willie.

"It's not about money. It's about Marsha."

"What about Marsha?" asked Willie, in quite a different voice.

"Can you take her to the dance tonight?"

"Why aren't you taking her?"

"I—things have gotten a little complicated here," said Ben. "Sort of involved."

"In what way involved?" persisted Willie.

"Don't ask," said Ben.

"Did you tell anyone that you were the—"

"No. Clare doesn't know I'm the one who messed up her life. It doesn't seem very important right now. Listen, the dance is at the Barton Hills Boat Club."

"Gas is twelve cents a gallon," murmured Willie.

"I'll pay for the gas."

Still Willie hesitated. "Lots of debutantes, I suppose."

Money entered silently, like an eavesdropping operator.

"Oh, lots of them. You'll have to buy Marsha a corsage. Her dress is black. Buy gardenias. She likes to wear gardenias on her wrist."

"A corsage on her wrist?"

"You have to ask for it. I'll pay," said Ben. He didn't say that Marsha often bought her own corsage, in case she didn't like the one Ben bought her.

"What shall I say when she asks why you can't take her?"

"Anything but the truth. You'll think of something."

Climbing into the car beside Clare, Ben felt sad and exhilarated: a traveler leaving home forever bound for the New World.

"Where shall we go now?" she asked.

"How about Island Park?" Again, the quickness of his own reply surprised him, as if someone had spoken for him. "Oh, Clare, I'm sorry."

"That's all right. I've always loved Island Park."

"Clare—why did you tell your folks I went to the University?"

"So they'd like you. Why did you tell them you're majoring in geology?"

"God knows," said Ben.

Indeed, said God.

In any quiet town you can find a street, a field, a stand of trees, which breaks into the dreams of its citizens years after the dreamers have left home for good. For generations of dreamers in Ann Arbor the Island has beckoned, flickered, faded, and risen again. Yet Island Park is surely not different from other parks in other cities lucky enough to be divided by one of those lazy brown rivers that join shanties and brickyards to golf courses and boat houses. In summer the water is too shallow for a rowboat, but canoes from the livery on Barton Pond thread their way past black willow and wild cherry and crab apple, among islands large enough to offer standing room only to one adult human and five muskrats, or four otters and half a dozen mallards. There are picnic tables on the right bank, where the new road runs, and tall grass along the left bank, where the old road sleeps, and a bridge between them, big enough for one car to pass over. Once, whole families of Negroes who lived by the tracks that followed the river could be seen on that bridge, fishing for carp or crayfish.

A footbridge joins the right bank to the only island that could support a population larger than one adult human and five muskrats or four otters and half a dozen mallards. On the Island—for so it is called, as if no other island were worthy of the name—stands a modest Greek temple with a roof like the lid of a fancy tureen and a colonnade running all around. Is it a circular temple proper to the worship of Hermes in winged cap and winged sandals, sacred to crossroads, the messenger of the dead? Is it sacred to the genius of this place?

No. The temple is sacred to two toilets, hidden at opposite ends behind appropriately marked doors. From far off, the graffiti on the doors do not show and the rough plaster walls might pass for Carrara marble. On a spring morning, when the black willow is leafing and the wild cherry beginning to bloom, if you are taking the Wolverine to Detroit or Battle Creek, you might look out of the train window and think you are passing the temple of love on the sacred island of Cythera, as Watteau painted it. And long after you've forgotten where you are going and why you are going there, the temple will appear to you in dreams, and you will wonder if your soul lived here before it put on its burden of flesh.

On this cloudy day the temple hung over the river like a ghostly sepulcher. Snow added its cubits to the stature of the roof, the trees, the picnic tables spread as if with that hidden fabric called "the silence cloth" by housewives who keep it under the finer damask one, to absorb the clatter of dishes and silver. Snow softened the bare limbs of the bushes.

Under its roof of ice, the river sent up bubbles: the telegraphed laments of the fish.

A single twig was now a thing of great beauty: a wand, a power, a glory. A sign.

Ben turned down Catherine Street and passed the open arcade where tomorrow morning at eight the manager of the Farmer's Market would walk up and down ringing a bell, to signify that the stalls were now open for business. During the winter only a few farmers huddled over small stoves behind their counters. Tomorrow the smell of kerosene would hang over the kale, dug out of snow fresh that morning, and over the cartons of eggs which had to be kept in the back of the trucks to prevent them from freezing.

Beyond the market rose a block of storefronts that belonged indisputably to the Negroes. There was a barbershop, a hardware store, a harness shop—in fine weather the bridles were hung around the doorway for show—and a secondhand store, which as long as anyone on the block could remember had displayed in its window a huddle of green glazed jars and liniment bottles filled with colored water. Sometimes they appeared in a row on the sidewalk. Nobody ever took them. They gave you the feeling they might cry out and the owner would hear them.

Behind the shops—and no white person had ever seen what lay behind the shops—was a graveyard for those who did not or could not get themselves properly buried in the Ebenezer Baptist cemetery. The graves looked like beds for penitents: a long slab of concrete studded with buttons, shells, beads, or nails. An iron pole joined headstone to footstone; in warm weather it held pots of geraniums and marigolds, night shade and devil's claw. There were names but no inscriptions. In the headstone of Pharoah Dawson was embedded the headlight of the Cadillac that carried him to a fiery death. From the stone of Sister Harriet Doyle rose an open hand, in whose palm gleamed a mirror, like a tiny frozen pond.

Nothing was broken, kicked over, or disturbed. Perhaps the faces on the little clay pots that grinned on the graves protected them. From deep sockets their eyes, made of mirrors or balls of white clay, seemed to glow, and though their teeth were no more than kernels of corn, a guilty visitor might see his own death grinning there. The Barbershop Cemetery, people said, was a mighty powerful place, and people went there for reasons that had nothing to do with honoring the dead.

The paved road gave way to brick and dipped sharply to the left, toward the river and the stone fortress that was the train station, a granite vision of Byzantium: towers, arches, porches, windows curved like giant keyholes, iced and glittering. Today, behind stained glass hidden by snow, the stationmaster knelt at the hearth and laid a fire. A handful of passengers stood waiting hopefully, listening for trains, postponing the moment when they must rush out to the cold platform where baggage carts waited like large, sad animals, their wheels frozen and clogged with snow.

Ben drove past the station and over the bridge. It was icier than it looked. He crept down the road to the picnic area and parked opposite the Island. Snow was falling now, weaving itself into a single fabric. He could barely make out the temple. Every familiar thing was taking itself away.

"We'd better go back," said Ben. If the car got stuck, he would have to walk a mile for help and leave Clare to freeze in the front seat. But Clare stared out the window as if she saw through the snow to next summer and the picnic tables crowded with families.

"We were walking over there. Grandpa had just asked me why the devil is called Lucifer. And I told him it meant Light-Bringer, and I was just saying the verse, 'How thou art fallen from heaven, O Lucifer, son of the morning, how art thou cut to the ground.' Then it happened. We didn't know anybody was playing baseball across the river. We never heard their voices."

"Did it hurt?" asked Ben. A dumb question, he knew. But he hungered for details. He needed to know what happened on her side of the river when he hit that ball into the dark.

"Not right away. I didn't know what hit me. I woke up in the hospital. Then it hurt a lot."

The snow hissed softly against the windshield.

"Maybe someday you'll meet the fellow that did it." Thin ice here.

"Maybe. But I don't think so."

"Of course you were ready to kill him. Whoever it was."

"I was angry at first, yes."

"But you aren't now?"

"It was an accident. It's like being angry at the river because it drowns people."

Ben shivered. The water, the earth, the very air, would take them all someday. It would take Clare and her father and mother, it would take her grandmother and her aunts and Davy and Wanda and Willie and Marsha and himself, would take all of them, would stop at nothing.

I could have killed her.

He kissed her, and without warning a piercing joy in the year's first snow filled him. Good sledding. Good packing. No school today. Time opened at his feet and unrolled its white carpet into eternity.

Clare was watching him, bright-eyed as a squirrel.

"If we take off our clothes, we'll freeze." She laughed. "How do the Eskimos do it?"

"Like this," he answered and lifted his body over hers to shield her from whatever could snatch her from him, out of this life.

14

There Is No Resisting You

Wanda sat in the kitchen, rubbing Crisco into her heels, listening for the click of the receiver.

"Was that Ben on the phone?"

"Um," said Willie.

"Is something wrong? Was he in an accident?"

"Car trouble," said Willie. He began flipping through the Yellow Pages with great purpose.

"He didn't take the car," Wanda remarked.

"He took somebody else's car. I didn't follow the whole story."

"He hit somebody in somebody else's car?" exclaimed Wanda.

"Mother, don't worry. He called to say he'll be coming home late."

"He's taking Marsha to the dance tonight, isn't he?"

Willie shook his head. "I'm taking her."

Now she felt certain Willie was shielding her from some terrible calamity.

"If Ben is in trouble, you'd tell me, wouldn't you? I've always trusted you, Willie. Of course," she added, "I've always trusted Ben, too."

"I would, Mother. You know that."

"Sit down. I'll get my slippers on and make you a cup of coffee." He looks as if he needs one, she thought.

He sat down opposite her at the kitchen table, still lost in the Yellow Pages, then jumped up.

"The florist closes at five on Friday. I've got to fly."

He arrived at Pearson's as a skinny girl with short blond curls was locking the door. She opened it a crack, just enough for her words to squeak through.

"I'm sorry, we're closed."

"You aren't closed yet," said Willie. "You just opened the door."

"I opened it to tell you we're closed."

"But you opened it," he reminded her, and, stepping back, he threw himself against the door. It flew open with a bang. The girl backed off, terrified. Willie hadn't meant to scare her. In the green smock and white collar all Pearson employees were required to wear, she looked as pious as a choirboy.

"I need a corsage!" he exclaimed. The girl stepped behind the counter. "Did you order one?" she asked in a trembling voice.

"No. Don't you have them already made up?"

"We have the individual orchids," she answered.

"How much are the orchids?"

"All we have left are the three-dollar fancies."

Willie winced. "Haven't you got anything cheaper?"

"Our miniature orchid corsages are all sold." His disappointment filled the room, and the girl felt vaguely responsible. "You might find something in the glass case. What color is her dress?"

"Whose?"

"The girl you're getting the flowers for."

What color *was* her dress? Had Ben told him? He could not remember.

"Oh, lots of colors," he said. "No one color in particular."

He pressed his nose to the glass and gazed at the enchanted sleepers: irises, daisies, carnations, roses out of season.

"Which flowers are the least expensive?" he asked.

"Daisies are the cheapest," she replied.

He ordered a corsage of three daisies but did not remember to say that it would be worn on the wrist till after the girl had written out the sales slip, and when she told him the extra ribbon would cost a nickel, he asked for a pin instead, which was free. Three daisies on the strap of her formal—if it had straps—would also look nice.

"Does the price include delivery?" asked Willie.

"No delivery," said the girl. "Our driver has already gone home."

Afterward, he remembered he should have asked for a gardenia.

He had reached home again before it occurred to him that he would need a tux. Ben's tux would hang on him. His heart sank at the thought of wearing his black suit.

His mother was putting supper on the table. Maybe she could find him a tux at the drycleaner's.

"Mr. Goldberg doesn't rent tuxes," said Wanda.

"But there must be one my size on the racks."

"You mean one of the customers'?" she asked, incredulous.

"A tux is a tux, Mother. I'll be very careful."

"I know you'll be careful," said Wanda, uncertain why borrowing a customer's tux for the evening made her feel as if she were stealing it.

"I never spill," he added. "Never."

"I know you never spill. Even when you were a baby you never spilled. Ben threw his food all over the kitchen. But you always ate very carefully."

Of course, the front desk would be closed, she told him. Willie said he did not believe in closed doors.

"Bring a bag," he said.

The janitor saw them through the window and unlocked the front door, regarding them both with a questioning expression.

"I forgot my sweater, Joe," said Wanda. "I think I left it on one of the racks."

"Well, have a look around."

Queer to have the place so dark and quiet, she thought. The stillness and the feeble light—Joe was sweeping by the light of a single bulb—made the place feel strange to her. In long paper bags, the finished garments hung on the racks, aisle after aisle of ghosts.

"We're getting warm," said Wanda. "Here's the bridals."

Neither the tuxedos nor the bridal gowns were hidden under wraps. The tuxedos in particular kept a human shape, as if inhabited by the souls of their owners. Tall, fat, thin; butlers of the night. And the brides: a cotillion of headless angels.

Willie yanked one tuxedo out of line. "How about this one?"

"Whose is it?" asked Wanda. She lit a match and peered at the tag. "B. Nesbitt. He owns that restaurant way out on Washtenaw —the fancy one with the organ. He brings his shirts in every Friday. Won't let his wife iron a thing." She sighed. "Just imagine that. He won't let her."

"It looks about my size."

"Yes, he's short like you." In the dark she did not see him wince. Hearing the janitor shuffle toward them, Willie stuffed the tuxedo into his bag.

"Did you find your sweater, Mrs. Harkissian?"

"Thanks, Joe, I did. We can let ourselves out the back door."

At home Willie appraised himself in the full-length mirror on the back of the bedroom door. To his surprise, he looked older and taller—distinguished, even. A pity he couldn't appear in a tux more often. What did tall, old, distinguished men say to rich, attractive girls? What did rich, attractive girls say to tall, old, distinguished men? He'd never taken a girl to any of the dances at school. He did not enjoy dancing, and girls always expected you to buy them a meal afterward.

From his bookshelf he pulled the *Little Blue Book of Useful Phrases* and turned to the chapter titled "Exclamations and Comments (Complimentary)."

A most extraordinary idea!
How delightful!
I like the plan very much.
It is glorious to contemplate.
You have never looked better.
He has a jolly handshake.
She possesses the highest ideals.
Such noble ideals!
It is superb!
I never flatter, on my honor.

There is no resisting you.
A most unexpected pleasure!
An excellent performance.

He turned to the section on apt quotations for all occasions, and the first example spoke directly to him:

> When as in silks my Julia goes
>   Then, then (me thinks) how sweetly flows
> That liquefaction of her clothes.

That described Marsha to a T. How could somebody who had never seen Marsha describe her so well? Oh, he never could remember so many phrases; he should have started learning them weeks ago. He flipped back to section one: "Introductory Remarks." These, at least, were shorter.

> Assuredly, but
> To be quite frank, I
> If you'll excuse my being abrupt, I
> Further than that, I might add
> Of course, but you see
> If I may speak freely, I
> Frankly, I don't see
> I strongly suspect that

A knock at the bedroom door.

"Willie—did you call Marsha and tell her that Ben isn't coming?"

"I forgot."

As he dialed, Willie hoped he wouldn't have to speak to Marsha. Not now, not when she couldn't see him, tall and distinguished, in B. Nesbitt's tuxedo.

A woman's voice answered. Not Marsha's. He realized he was holding his breath, and now he exhaled deeply.

"Is Marsha there?"

"Marsha's in the shower. Can I take a message?"

"This is Willie Harkissian. Could you tell her that I'll come by in half an hour to pick her up for the dance? Ben can't make it."

Silence.

"I'll tell her," said the woman. "Will you hold the line, please?"

She was gone a very long time, and when she returned, she sounded out of breath.

"I'm awfully sorry, but Marsha isn't feeling well."

"You mean she doesn't want to go?"

"She has a headache. Is there any place she can reach Ben?"

"I expect there is, but he didn't leave me the number."

"I'll give her that message," said the woman and hung up.

"Hell!" said Willie, slamming down the receiver. He opened the refrigerator and threw the box, with its three daisies in green tissue, into the garbage pail. "A dollar down the drain for this corsage. I can't take it back."

His mother retrieved the box.

"I haven't had a corsage in twenty-five years. I'll buy it from you," she said and went to fetch her purse.

15

Borrowed Mouths

Helen and Nell dragged the bridge table from under the piano, and something crashed and tinkled in response.

"There goes the movie projector," said Helen. "We'll get it later."

"Can I help?" Ben asked, eager to make himself useful.

Though she knew perfectly well how to set up the table, Helen turned to him and said, "Can you figure out how to unfold these legs?"

The two sisters watched approvingly as one by one the legs snapped to attention. Clare, her chair drawn up to the fireplace, exchanged smiles with Ben.

"Mother, are Aunt Vicky and Uncle Fred coming? You've brought out the Harvey's Bristol Cream."

"It's for Debbie Lieberman," said Helen.

"Debbie doesn't like sherry," Nell reminded her.

"I know," said Helen. "But she always looks to see if it's there."

"I used to work for Mrs. Lieberman," said Ben.

"What kind of work?" inquired Helen.

"I fixed her vacuum cleaner."

"Marie Clackett is coming with her," Helen went on. "Do you know the Clacketts?"

"I know Mrs. Clackett. And my brother works in Mr. Clackett's store."

"Debbie will be bringing Marie and Mr. Knochen," said Nell. "They say Mr. Knochen knows everybody. They say he can even recognize people he's never met."

Then Davy, who wanted everyone gathered together in one place, ran into the room carrying Cinnamon Monkeyshines. He set the cat down in front of the fire but could not persuade it to stay.

"Where's Uncle Hal?" he asked.

"He's napping," answered Helen.

"I'll go and wake him," said Davy.

"No, don't," said Helen. "You know he hates for people to wake him up. *This* is the way to call him."

She seated herself at the piano, opened her tattered copy of *Michigan's Favorite College Songs,* and launched into "Hail to the Victors."

"You'll wake Grandma," said Nell.

"No, I won't," answered Helen. "She's real tired. I got her up early so we could have some peace tonight."

She turned the page and began to sing:

> "I'll never forget my college days,
> I'll ne'er forget my Michigan."

Suddenly she broke off. "Do you hear voices at the door?" she asked.

"I don't hear anybody," said Ben.

"The guests will arrive in five minutes," she announced. "Davy, bring me the decanter from the sideboard. We'll put the Harvey's Bristol Cream in it. A decanter," she added, noticing his bewilderment, "is a very fancy bottle."

When the doorbell rang at last, Helen hurried to answer it, and everyone followed her.

The porch light cut through the snow, which unrolled like bandages from heaven. It wrapped the identical fur coats of Mrs. Lieberman and Mrs. Clackett. It whitened their eyebrows and dusted the veils on their hats. Between them stood Mr. Knochen, his black overcoat free of snow and disorder. Why, he might have blown in from another planet, thought Helen. Pale, thin face and white hair combed straight back, his grey fedora in one hand, as if asking for alms.

He peeled off his gloves, black leather, like the skin of an expensive fruit, exposing the pale meat below. Across Clare's mind flashed a drowning she had seen years ago at Island Park. The coroner's black-gloved hands held a mirror to the mouth of the dead boy, then drew from his pocket two silver coins and closed his eyes. *What power did you think I would give you? The power to meet your own death?*

Now she recognized him. It was Herr Death, he whom the Ancestress had taken her to see, he who had rebuked Goering for his greed. *Don't you know that to those who serve me the power is already given?* When she visited him—how long ago the Ancestress had traveled beside her, over the water!—he had seemed as dangerous and remote as an iceberg viewed through binoculars. Now the space between them was gone. He had sought her out. Had he come for her?

Too terrified to speak, she felt her body draw back from him of its own will, as if his very breath could kill her.

"Delighted to meet you, Mrs. Bishop," he was saying, "and your sister. And Davy, and Clare. And—"

"Ben Harkissian."

"Of course."

"He recognized us," whispered Nell to Helen. "What did I tell you?"

That was evidence of intuition but not of great powers, thought Helen. She took Mr. Knochen's black umbrella, which he had not opened, and his coat and his fedora, soft and flexible as a cat, and hung them on the coat rack beside Hal's hat, while he stood first on one foot, then on the other, and pulled off his thin overshoes.

He's done well for himself, thought Helen, appraising his three-piece suit. Black serge. Aloud she said, "Your overshoes are just like Hal's. I've never met anyone who had overshoes like Hal's, Mr. Knochen."

"They're Brazilian rubbers," observed Mr. Knochen. "Hard to come by, with the shortages."

Davy admired his shoes, so highly polished they shone like silver.

The fire crackling in the hearth drew the three guests, who held their hands out to warm them. Cinnamon Monkeyshines stretched himself out to his full length, and Mr. Knochen leaned down and stroked his ears.

Why, he's nearly bald, thought Nell. The way he combs those white strands over the bald spot. Making the most of what he has.

"You have nice shoes," said Davy, and knelt and patted them.

"Now you've seen him," said Nell, taking Davy's hand. "And now it's your bedtime. Say good-night to the company."

"I'm not sleepy," said Davy.

"Da-*vy*," warned Nell.

"G'night, company," said Davy and allowed himself to be bundled off to bed.

Mr. Knochen surveyed the room as if he intended to buy it.

"I see you have a table all ready, Mrs. Bishop. Splendid table. Leather?"

"I don't know," said Helen. "It was a wedding present."

"And an exquisite decanter. Crystal?"

Helen shrugged. "It's been in the family for years. I don't even remember where it came from." She recollected its purpose and added, "May I give you some Harvey's Bristol Cream?"

An amused smile crossed Mr. Knochen's face.

"No, thank you. Perhaps the ladies—"

"None for me, thanks," said Mrs. Lieberman.

"None for me, either," said Mrs. Clackett.

Hal came into the room.

"Mr. Bishop, delighted to meet you," said Mr. Knochen. He shook Hal's hand warmly, as if they were old friends.

Everyone sat down.

"I'm very interested in what happens tonight," said Hal. "I've never had any experiences along this line myself, but my sister had several of them."

"You never told me that," said Helen.

"You never asked," said Hal.

"Would you care to tell us about your sister's experiences?" asked Mr. Knochen.

"When our father died, my sister saw him in a sort of—vision. He was a thousand miles away from her when he died, and yet he appeared to her at the exact moment of his death."

"Did she know he was dead?" asked Mrs. Clackett.

"Not at the time. She was working in her garden. She stood up to brush the dirt off her hands and saw him walking backwards down the path, away from her, waving. Ten minutes later she got the call saying he was dead."

"Dead," mused Mr. Knochen. "I'm told they do not like to be called so. It's we who are dead to them. We cut ourselves off from them."

Why, *why*, thought Clare, has he come?

"I wish we could find a good doctor in the next world," said Helen. "The doctors in this one haven't done much for Clare."

Hal turned to Mr. Knochen and inquired, "Have you heard of Benjamin Rush?"

Silence.

"I thought perhaps you might know the name. The Rush Medical College in Chicago is named for Benjamin Rush."

"And did he find a good doctor in the next world?" inquired Mrs. Lieberman, smoothing her dark hair, which was drawn into a bun.

Hal smiled.

"Dr. Rush died in 1813. Through a medium in New York, he offered his services to patients pronounced incurable by the doctors living on *this* side of life." He raised his right hand, as if taking an oath. "A woman dying of stomach cancer accepted his offer, through the medium. Dr. Rush told the patient to go to bed and pray for her recovery. While she slept, he would examine her, for of course he could not diagnose or prescribe without an examination."

"And did he examine her?" exclaimed several voices, astonished.

"From the *other* side"—and here Hal raised his left hand—"he did indeed examine her, and through the medium he told her that he would handle her case. He prescribed a regimen of rest and prayer, and said that while she slept, he would perform the operation. She remained in a coma for one night and when she awoke, she knew herself to be healed. A spot of blood on the bedclothes was the only trace of the operation. And when her regular doctor examined her, he found she was completely cured."

Mr. Knochen turned to Helen. "Mrs. Bishop, have you ever spoken with anyone in the other world?"

"No. Why?"

"You have an aura around your head."

Helen touched her hair. "You see something around my head?"

He nodded. "It is a good sign. I do not see auras around the heads of those who have not yet learned to trust me."

I shall never trust you, thought Clare, and longed to wrap her arms around her mother. Around all of them.

Behind his back, Nell slipped into the room.

"Ah, your sister has rejoined us. We can begin."

From his pocket he brought a small paper dial rimmed with the letters of the alphabet.

"A one-handed clock," he said and smiled, to let them know he had made a joke. "Some spirits choose to speak through mediums. Others spell their messages, sending vibrations through our fingers, tapping them out on the table through us. We must provide for both preferences. If you will all draw your chairs around the table, please—"

There was a scuffling and scraping of chairs. Ben, who did not like Mr. Knochen's unctuous manner, wheeled Clare as far from him as he could and found places for them between Helen and Hal. Mrs. Lieberman sat on Mr. Knochen's right hand and Mrs. Clackett sat on his left. Nell squeezed her chair between Mrs. Clackett and Hal.

Mr. Knochen stood up.

"I always like to sit by the young people," he said, and with one swift movement of his chair, he parted Ben and Clare, felt in his pocket, and then glanced at the floor.

"What have you lost?" asked Helen.

"It's odd," said Mr. Knochen, "but I seem to have lost one of my good-luck charms. Has anyone seen it? Here's the mate."

And he drew forth a silver coin. They all bent forward to examine it.

"Is it Greek?" asked Mrs. Lieberman. "Isn't this Hermes in the winged cap?"

"If it were lost in this house, I'd see it right off," said Helen. "A thing like that."

"Perhaps you didn't lose it here," suggested Mrs. Clackett. "You could advertise in the papers."

"You could offer a reward," said Nell.

"I could offer a reward," agreed Mr. Knochen. "But whoever finds it must give it to me of his own free will. Stolen charms never serve the thief, do they?" He nodded at Ben.

In the jungles of Ben's childhood, the lost coin had shone on his father's palm like the wise eye of a magic animal. Ben wore it now, on an elastic string around his neck. His eyes met Clare's, and her terror paralyzed him. He could not utter a word.

"If you happen to find it—" said Mr. Knochen.

"We'll let you know right away," said Helen. "I understand how awful it is to lose something that's been in the family."

"Could we have the lights turned down, please?" Mr. Knochen said. "The firelight will be ample."

From lamp to lamp Nell walked, pulling their chains, sending them into darkness. A low, restless light from the fire flickered over their faces.

"Now, if you will take your places again—thank you. I want you all to rest your fingertips on the table, as I am doing. The little finger of each hand should be touching the corresponding finger of those on either side of you. We want a closed circle."

A movement of hands answered him, barely perceptible, like the blinking of birds. Clare's finger brushed his. It was cold and dry, and the touch sickened her.

"My dear friends," said Mr. Knochen in a low voice, "I ask that each of you come to this table as innocent as a child. Let yourselves be led by whatever happens here. Believe me, there is nothing to fear."

Helen, who had lowered her head, stole a glance at him. His eyes were closed, his whole body still as marble.

"Perhaps you are wondering why the dead must talk through borrowed mouths. Is their need so very different from ours when we use a telephone? Our voices are too small for the great distances."

Everything grew still. Even the lively fire danced behind a curfew of silence.

I don't hear the clock, thought Mrs. Clackett nervously.

"Perhaps some of you have said, 'If visions are real, why haven't I had visions? If those I lost are alive, why haven't I heard their voices?' My dear children, how easy it is to see and not see, to hear and not hear. Let us never forget St. Paul: 'There is a natural body, and there is a spiritual body.' What was mortal has put on immortality."

A rising excitement gathered them together, like pulses in an unbroken current. It seemed to Hal that the air had become too pure for breathing; every familiar sound and smell was being swabbed away.

Who left the door open? Such a terrible draft, thought Nell, but she could not rise to close it.

To all of them Mr. Knochen's voice sounded thin, an echo thrown from the top of a mountain.

"I believe the invisible will not always be hidden from us. Tonight, let there abide among us faith, hope, and charity. And the greatest of these is hope."

Not charity? thought Helen. She prided herself on knowing the Bible.

He stopped talking. He rested his hands on the table as lightly as on a keyboard seconds before a long and difficult performance.

A clean wind blew across Ben's face and brought him close to tears with the old sensations it stirred in him: that first fresh fragrance things gave him when he and the world were new together.

Then the first mingling of fragrances became a strong smell of Sen-Sen and the sweaty leather of his father's Rawlings glove, and that other smell of games played and lost by his father long before he was born.

"Dad?" he whispered.

Nothing answered him. Even the tapping ceased. The rejection stung him, embarrassed him.

"Call again," urged Mr. Knochen.

"Dad? It's me, Ben."

The comforting presence in the room began to withdraw.

"Don't go," said Ben, louder this time. "Please don't go."

Suddenly a crash made them all jump. Something struck Nell on her foot and rolled away, and she scrambled under the table after it.

"The Harvey's Bristol Cream!" she shrieked and held up the decanter. It was cracked straight down the middle. For half a second it appeared to relax. Then it split into neat halves, as if a diamond had cut it. With trembling hands, Nell placed the two halves in the middle of the table.

"Empty!" exclaimed Nell.

"Fortunately there wasn't much in it," said Helen.

"What do you mean?" demanded Mrs. Lieberman. "It was a full bottle."

"The spirits are welcome to it, I'm sure," said Helen.

"Children," said Mr. Knochen, "take hands."

Again they rested their fingertips on the table. Ben found that every part of him was shaking except his hands, which felt as if they were in another corner of the universe, dabbling and dipping themselves in the streams of no-time.

"I once had a very pious cook who told me she could smell bread baking in heaven," observed Mr. Knochen.

Is he laughing at us? Clare wondered. She was no longer afraid of him. In the firelight, his smile flickered back and forth between kindly and terrible. The smell of new-mown grass—did no one else notice it? No one. Clare glanced around for the Ancestress. No, she would not show herself here. Not now. A great desire to be comforted came over her, and she turned toward the fire. It crackled, it hissed. As a child she could sit for hours watching the dancers in the little theatre of the hearth, shifting from beast to human, from human to beast. But the figures she saw now were clearly human, a pageant played in the fire rather than the fire itself. She saw the image of Death wrestling with a woman. She saw the white scarf wrapped around the woman's head; she saw the bodice of her dress covered with medals, winking and glittering, so closely set they seemed a single fabric. The woman was taller than Death by about a foot.

Hal's voice broke the silence and the two players vanished.

"O spirits who have honored us by your coming, who among the living or the dead can heal Clare Bishop?"

Clare started at her own name. It lingered in the still air like smoke.

Tap, tap. Very slowly, the pointer moved; something behind it was groping for speech. Mr. Knochen named the letters.

"C-O-L-D."

Tap, tap.

"F-R-I-D-A-Y D-O-N-E."

"Cold Friday Done," said Mr. Knochen.

"D-I-E-D. Done died," repeated Mr. Knochen.

Tap, tap, tap.

"F-I-V-E." Pause. "T-I-M-E-S. Five times."

Nobody breathed. No further messages came forth. The pointer stretched lifeless on the little dial.

"Well, there you have it," said Mr. Knochen.

It's all a game, thought Helen. A hoax, after all.

But Hal would not give up. "Is the one we seek among the living or the dead?" he asked.

The pointer jiggled along eagerly, and Mr. Knochen spelled and muttered under his breath, and when the pointer stopped moving, he repeated the whole message.

"Cold Friday on Catherine Street."

"Catherine Street!" exclaimed Mrs. Clackett. "Why, that's a block away from the Farmer's Market."

"Is this Friday in the future or the past?" asked Hal. "Can you tell us more?"

But the pointer grew listless and would not move at all.

Mr. Knochen looked around the table. "You can't force them to speak," he said. "Is there anyone else you would like to ask for?"

Nobody spoke.

At last Helen broke the silence. "Mr. Knochen, do the people in the next world grow old?"

"I do not think they grow old," said Mr. Knochen.

"But who takes care of the babies?" asked Helen and realized that she was not addressing him at all but the darkness behind him.

And he, understanding this, did not answer.

Clare's head sank to her chest. Ben looked at her anxiously. She had fallen asleep—at such a time! Helen cupped her hand to her ear, and though they heard nothing yet, Nell and Hal cupped their hands and listened also.

"Here comes the sandman
Stealing away on the tips of his toes."

Now they all heard it, the voice of a child singing.

"He scatters the sand
With his own little hand
In the eyes of the sleeping children."

Davy? Nell said to herself and knew it was not Davy.

"Go to sleep, my baby.
Close your pretty eyes.
The mother moon will watch you
From out the darkening skies."

Peace folded its great wings over Helen.

So you did hear me! So you do remember! She saw herself holding her firstborn, his life seeping away, herself crying, "Come back! Come back!"

"The little stars are peeping
to see if you are sleeping.
Go to sleep, my baby—"

"Clare!" cried Ben.

"Go to sleep. Good-night."

Clare slept on. The voice of the child was coming from her open mouth.

Mrs. Lieberman, Mrs. Clackett, and Mr. Knochen left the house in silence, as after a funeral. Improper to ask questions, unseemly to burst out weeping. Nell hurried to her room without saying good-night, and Helen and Hal went to bed like estranged lovers, each sealed in silence from the other. Clare was crying as Ben carried her upstairs. She had caused this silence, had gone out of herself and brought it back like a sickness. And of her going forth she remembered nothing.

They sat on the edge of her bed, under her father's stars, holding hands.

"You don't remember anything?" asked Ben.

She shook her head.

"You sang about the sandman. Your voice sounded so strange."

"I don't remember."

Silence.

"Mr. Knochen is Death," said Clare suddenly. "That's who he is. Death."

"How do you know?"

"Because I've met him before. With my Ancestress. I saw him with Goering."

"You dreamed you saw him with Goering." Ben corrected her.

"No," said Clare. "I saw Goering's marble desk and his tapestry —we came in through the tapestry. Death was looking for his silver coin, and Goering offered him a counterfeit—"

She broke off with a cry. The coin, on its elastic thread, was shining on Ben's open palm.

"He knew I had it," muttered Ben. "Whoever he is, he knew I had it. He'll be hounding me for it. What good will it do me now?"

"I heard him tell Goering it gives you the power to meet your own death."

"Clare, do you really think Death is a man who walks the earth in a black suit?"

"I think that's how Death appeared to me," she said slowly. "And to all of us this evening."

Already this evening felt as if it had happened a long time ago.

"I don't want to think about Death," said Ben. "I don't want to lose you."

"Stay with me, then."

He lay down beside her, held her in the dark till her breathing, slow and steady, told him she was asleep. Then he crept downstairs to the bed Helen had made up for him on the sofa.

One by one the embers winked out. On the warm hearth, Cinnamon Monkeyshines stretched. Under its glass dome, the blue china clock struck five and for the first time in years the moon rose in the little window on its face.

16

As Quietly as a Thief

In the dark living room, the numbers of Wanda's alarm clock glowed pale green.

Two o'clock.

Wanda got up from the sofa, peered through the venetian blinds, and pattered barefoot to Willie's room and knocked on the door, gently at first, then more urgently.

"What is it?" growled Willie.

"She's still out there."

"Well, what do you want me to do about it? She's not a child."

"Bring her in the house," said Wanda. "She'll freeze."

"Christ," muttered Willie. He swung his feet out of bed and suffered as they hit the cold floor.

"Mother, I've made three trips out there already. She won't even talk to me."

"So make one more. I'll heat the coffee."

He shaved and dressed himself as meticulously as if he were meeting Marsha for a date. Then he marched to the living-room window.

In her black strapless evening gown and her white fur jacket, Marsha was pacing up and down in front of the house.

Wanda handed him his overcoat. "Bundle up. I sewed that top button."

Sleepy and angry, he buttoned his coat.

He pulled on his galoshes.

He swaddled his neck in his navy scarf.

He clamped his navy earmuffs into place.

He put on his hat and opened the front door. The moment he appeared, Marsha stopped pacing.

"Has Ben called yet?"

"No," said Willie. "I wish you'd come in. Not that I personally give a damn about you, but you're worrying my mother, and she's got to go to work tomorrow morning."

Marsha cocked her head and weighed this new information. "I *will* come in." She sounded shy and grateful. "I'm awfully cold."

Willie did not trust this change in her, but he was glad that she followed him into the house.

"The coffee's in the kitchen," he announced.

"Sit right here," Wanda said, smoothing the green oilcloth on the kitchen table. "There's plenty of cake for all of us."

"Coffee cake!" exclaimed Willie. "I didn't know you had any in the house."

"I got it for breakfast tomorrow. But it's already tomorrow."

She had set the table with her best things: the teacups and the little china pitcher and the sugar bowl painted with roses. Marsha pulled up a chair and sat down. Her blond hair, piled high on her head, was beginning to send down a strand here, a curl there. The diamond comb that held everything in place would soon fall out, Willie thought, and she'd lose it. Lose several hundred dollars worth of stones just like that. If they were real.

Marsha picked up her cup and sipped. She ate her piece of cake and then, absentmindedly, she ate Wanda's.

Such heavy makeup, thought Wanda. Regular war paint. She ought to wash her face. Or has she been bruised?

Weeping had streaked Marsha's mascara. Her hand lingered around her empty cup, warming itself. Rings shone on the fourth finger of both hands: silver and turquoise on the left, a circle of pearls set in gold on the right.

Fakes? wondered Willie.

Perfect fingernails, noted Wanda. Perfectly lovely fingernails. Fakes?

The girl reached for the third piece of cake, and Wanda signaled Willie with her eyes: *let her.*

Christ! raged Willie to himself. It isn't fair.

Suddenly Marsha put her head on her arms and started to sob. Willie felt a pang of guilt about the size of a splinter and knelt down beside her, and put his arm around her shoulders. Her white fur, very cold and soft, brushed his wrist.

"I'm sorry," he said. "I wish I could help."

To his surprise, she stopped crying and leaned her head against his shoulder, but her sly glance chilled him, as if she were reading some secret in his face. She drew her face away from him and wiped her eyes with the back of her hand.

"Could I use your bathroom? I must look like a real mess."

"Of course," said Wanda. "It's down the hall. First door to the right."

How clean is it? she thought. Never scrubbed the toilet today.

"Willie, when she comes out, you drive her home."

"She drove herself here, remember?" said Willie.

"Hush."

"She can't hear us. She's running the water."

Covering the sound of—?

They sat without speaking for some time, listening to the water.

"Maybe you should go after her," said Wanda nervously.

"We could both go," said Willie.

"No," said Wanda. "You go."

The bathroom was empty. Willie turned off the faucet. The door to the bedroom he shared with Ben stood half closed. Willie pushed it open and stepped cautiously inside. A rush of cold air made him shiver.

Through a cloud of feathers he spied the open window. He snapped on the light. His half of the room was untouched. Ben's side lay in ruins. His pillow was not merely ripped; it had been methodically slashed. His baseball had been slit open and the stuffing pulled out. Their father's mitt she had surgically dismembered, had cut it into small pieces and these pieces into smaller pieces. And the baseball trophies on Ben's desk were a rubble of golden arms and legs and bodies and empty pedestals. Willie picked up an arm and examined it. Under the gold paint, cheap metal showed through. A woman's hand could break it.

Overhead, the Piper Cub sagged like a dead insect, the balsa struts snapped, the colored tissue shredded.

17

Strangers All

When Hal opened the letter telling him he was being sent to California, Helen was calling everyone for lunch, and he tucked the letter into his pocket and said nothing about it, only handed Davy the rest of the mail.

"Anything from Ben?" asked Clare.

They were all in high spirits. The ice was thawing. Under thin, crystalline platforms that clung to the curbs, water trickled and sparkled. And with only ten days left in January, Hal had already ordered the seeds for his victory garden.

After lunch he opened his suitcase on his bed and started to pack. Helen sat on the edge of her bed and watched him.

"They didn't give you much notice," she observed.

"They gave me all they had."

"The letter doesn't say how long you'll be gone." She wondered if he knew and was simply not telling her.

"With things the way they are in the world, who knows how long?"

"I don't know why they couldn't have sent you to Willow Run. California, for heaven's sake! There are closer places you could do defense work. Nell took the car into Detroit this morning. We'll have to call a cab to take you to the station."

"Why Detroit?"

"Her dentist. She lost a filling."

"With the gas shortage she goes to Detroit for a filling? She'll have to find somebody here."

Helen watched him arrange a layer of BVDs at the bottom of the suitcase.

"At least you're too old for the fighting," she said.

Over the BVDs he made a second layer of white shirts.

"I don't know why you didn't take that commission they offered you. What's one night a week, wearing a uniform?"

"I loathe uniforms," said Hal.

"That's the most unpatriotic thing I've ever heard."

"I'm doing my share. I'm just not doing it in uniform."

As he arranged his ties in one corner of the suitcase, Helen realized that she had no idea what he would be doing. It was all top secret, of course, but even the classes he taught at the University had always been as remote to her as if they were conducted in code. She simply didn't understand a thing about his work.

He was packing his socks very carefully. He'd packed so often, and he always liked to do it himself with no help from her. Here was his shaving brush, and here was his gold razor in its purple velvet case. And his suits, made to order by a tailor. Hal picked the material from a book of swatches. Here were his shoes, made for him in England. He loves shoes, thought Helen. Yet she knew he never insisted on luxuries or noticed them in other people's houses, though he had been brought up in a household that took certain luxuries for granted.

He strapped his suits into place.

He's looking forward to this trip, thought Helen. He enjoys these long train rides away from us, when he goes to conventions and gives lectures. He enjoys the service in the dining car, and the country rushing past his window, and putting his shoes outside his berth for the porter to shine. And the night somebody went through the sleeping car and stole all the shoes, and a shoe salesman from Memphis was called to the station—that's the only pair of store-bought shoes he owns.

"Where will you be staying?"

"I can't tell you."

"But I'm your wife!"

"Helen, if I knew more, I'd tell you."

"How can I reach you if there's an emergency?"

"Call the chemistry department. Ask for Dr. Turner."

"What if I die?"

Hal chuckled. "You're too tough to die," he said, and they both burst out laughing.

It was late afternoon by the time he'd finished packing. Clare was waiting for him. He sat on her bed, under the stars he had put up so long ago. He felt immensely tired.

"Don't forget my soap," she said, certain this would make him smile. When she was little, he had brought back miniature bars of hotel soap for her dolls.

He did not smile now. "I hope you'll be walking when I see you again," he said. "I have a hunch you will be."

"Not even the nice lady in the public library could help us find out about Cold Friday," said Clare.

He frowned, but not at her. "I think the cure has got to come from you, Clare. Not from the outside."

"You don't believe we can get help from the spirits?"

"I don't know what to believe anymore. That evening with Mr. Knochen—your mother still frets over it."

"I'll be all right, Papa."

"Good."

I should ask her about Ben, he thought, but he did not know what to ask or how to ask. Tell her it doesn't matter that Ben isn't really a geology major, that he isn't even a student? Tell her that he's done the right thing to enlist the day after Pearl Harbor, not waiting to be drafted?

"The taxi's here," called Helen.

The driver came into the front hall to fetch the luggage.

"Another trip, professor? Must be a long one. You've got your big suitcase."

"I'm going to the station with him," said Helen, "but I'll want a cab as soon as the train comes. I don't like to leave Clare and Davy and Grandma alone."

"Clare can keep an eye on Davy, and Davy can keep an eye on Grandma," said the driver.

Hal and Helen settled themselves into the back seat, and the driver flipped on the meter.

"Going far?" he asked.

"West," said Hal.

"Oh, those western trains are real nice."

Click, murmured the meter.

"I hear they've dug out the old gaslight cars to move the troops. The Japs really caught us by surprise."

"They sure did," said Helen.

Hal was gazing sadly out of the window.

"All those battleships burning," the driver said. "I saw it in the newsreel."

"Awful," said Helen.

She did not want to talk about troop trains and battleships. She wanted to tell Hal she loved him. But the driver had included himself in their conversation, and she rambled on about trivial details.

"I'll take care of the garden this year," she said. "I hope you don't miss the tomatoes."

Click.

"Don't forget to put a mousetrap under the melons," said Hal.

"We have mice in the melons?" asked Helen, surprised.

"Thieves, thieves," said Hal.

The waiting room of the station was thronged with travelers. Hal checked his luggage and listened with satisfaction to the baggage cart rumbling down the platform. Far off the train whistled, and everyone shuffled toward the door.

"Do you have enough money?" Hal asked, taking out his wallet.

"You gave me money before we left, remember?"

But he pressed a twenty-dollar bill into her hand anyway.

They hurried outside, and Helen lunged toward him and caught him in a hug.

"Uff," he gasped.

"Well, I was afraid you weren't going to kiss me good-bye."

He kissed her, and the steam swirled around him.

He was gone.

As the train pulled out, Helen searched the windows of the cars for his face. Behind weeping glass, only the faces of soldiers met hers. Strangers all.

The house at twilight had never felt so empty.

"I suppose we should go ahead and eat dinner," said Helen.

"Of course we should eat dinner," said Nell. "I'm starved."

But when Helen opened the refrigerator and saw the custards and the nut loaf she had prepared yesterday for Hal, tears ran down her face.

"Maybe we don't have to have nut loaf anymore," said Davy. Helen was bringing Hal's favorite dishes to the table, without bothering to heat them. "Maybe now we can have hamburgers."

"Davy!" exclaimed Nell, who was hoping the same thing.

"I hate to eat and run," said Grandma, "but I've got to get home before dark."

"Vicky is coming to see you tomorrow," said Nell. "She'll be awfully disappointed if you're not here."

They took their places at the table. Helen ate mechanically, wiping away tears.

"Let's turn on the light," said Nell. "We'll all feel more cheerful."

"I know you've been through this kind of thing already," said Helen. She blew her nose on the paper napkin.

"It wasn't the same," said Nell. "Bob *drank*. I was glad to be rid of him. Of course it was a shock when I realized he was never coming back. And there was that awful business of listening for the key at night. Every noise—I'd think, that's Bob coming home now." She helped herself to the extra custard. "I'll bet he's dead now."

"Is Hal dead?" asked Grandma.

"Dead? Of course he's not dead," said Helen. "He's on his way to California."

After dinner they sat in the living room and listened to "Amos and Andy," out of respect for Hal, who hated to miss it and would not be able to hear it on the train. They worked on their squares for the afghan the play-reading group was making to send the boys overseas. Only Helen had hers nearly done: a cigarette floating in a blue sky. On the sky were great puffs of smoke.

"I hope Debbie doesn't mind that we're all doing cigarettes," said Helen. "The other patterns were so hard. I couldn't knit a boat or a flag if my life depended on it."

They listened to Grandma moving the furniture in her room; they listened to Kate Smith singing "God Bless America" and they all got goose bumps and felt weepy. The campus carillon struck eleven. The blue china clock on the mantel struck two; it kept its own time.

And now they could not postpone the night any longer. Helen poured water on the fire, locked the front door, locked the back door, and hid the key under the china rabbit on the sewing machine which she kept closed and used as a table; she had not sewed since Clare was a little girl.

Clare wheeled herself into the hall and glanced at the hat rack.

"Look, Papa forgot his hat."

"No he didn't," said Helen. "That's his old hat. I'm going to keep it there so burglars peeking in the window will think there's a man in the house. Are you ready to go upstairs?"

At the door of Helen's bedroom, all three women stopped. From his gold frame on the wall over Helen's bed, Hal was smiling at them.

"Do you want me or Clare to stay with you?" asked Nell. "One of us can sleep in Hal's bed."

"No thanks. I've got to get used to being alone."

"It's not so bad," said Nell. "I don't know about Hal—it's none of my business—but let me tell you one thing: I never had a good night's sleep with Bob."

"I suppose it's awful when husbands snore," said Clare.

"He didn't snore. He was always after me. I'd crawl into bed dead tired—I was working, and he hadn't held a job for six months —and he'd be lying in wait for me, all his juices worked up. And then he'd start pinching me. Pinch, pinch."

"He *pinched* you?" exclaimed Helen.

"It didn't hurt. But I knew he'd keep it up all night till I gave in. Just like a gnat, pinch, pinch, pinch, to make sure I didn't fall asleep. The only way I could get to sleep was to give in. And then he'd say, 'Let's make love all night, I could go on forever.' Well, lying around the house drinking all day, of course he could go on forever. He didn't have to be out of the house at the crack of dawn."

Silence.

"Of course, all men aren't like that," she added hastily.

"Of course," said Clare. "When you first loved each other, it was different."

When she was alone, Helen put on her nightgown and tucked the money Hal had given her behind his picture.

"Good-night, Hal," she said to the picture.

She opened the window a crack and pulled up the covers.

Silently, she began to weep.

18

V-Mail

Ben Harkissian to Clare Bishop

Fort Hood, Texas
February 3, 1942

Dear Clare,

Today we faced real bullets. A couple of machine guns are stuck at the top of the hill and they're pointed to send crossfire about a yard above the ground. Sergeant Klinehart took twenty of us a hundred yards off and told us to go after those guns. The course is full of trenches with parapets. The shellholes are mined, the barbed-wire entanglements are awful, there are dynamite charges to hurry the slowpokes, and everybody has heard stories of people whose heads got blown off—the line of fire is about eighteen inches over your head.

When I got the signal, I tore through fifteen yards of bush and headed for the first trench, and the machine gun started hammering away, and I'm pushing myself along the dirt, and something explodes to my left, I'm less than twenty yards from the trench and I come to the barbed wire. I start picking my way through but the leg of my pants gets caught and I can't work it loose and the bullets are flying and finally I just rip through. My pants are in rags from top to bottom. On to the next trench, fast. Dynamite behind, bullets overhead. I finally made it to the safety trench and was waiting for the last guy to make it through and I thought, I could get killed in this war.

You know, I thought I understood why I joined the army: to

serve my country, to start a different life. Now I wish the army hadn't taken me. I wish I had flat feet like Willie. I wish I were in the medical and could save something, or put something together. What made me think I belonged with a unit of tank destroyers?

Any more visits from the mystery man Knochen? I don't understand him. I'll never understand him. I haven't got time to worry about him, what with all the stuff I've had thrown at me these last few days. Everything I do, the thought of you is with me. Eating, drinking, sleeping. I wonder if you've pulled one of your out-of-the-body fast ones and maybe you really are with me.

Tell your Ancestress if it's not too much trouble to keep an eye out for me. I don't want to get killed and I don't want to kill anybody. I could use some help.

Love,
Ben

WRITE!

Stilts Moser to His Mother, Ernestina

February 8, 1942

Dear Mom,

First, I just want you to know that I'm fine. I haven't gone off the base into town. I don't want any trouble from the Alabamans, who are not going to welcome me with open arms, that's for sure. I read the *Birmingham News,* the *Chicago Defender,* and a few local papers. The folks here seem to worry more about Negroes than about winning the war.

The riots in Detroit really upset me. Why doesn't Roosevelt step in? The army took me to fight for my country. I'd rather stay home and fight for our own selves. What I'm living through now seems like a nightmare that we'll have to put up with till we win this war. I haven't changed much except I feel a lot older.

Send me a picture of Red, if you can get him to sit still. That dog is nicer than a lot of people I've met here. But don't worry. I've learned to obey orders and keep out of trouble.

I hope your leg is better. Please go to a doctor. You don't have to tell Cold Friday you went. Or you can put the blame on me.

Love,
Stilts

Sol Lieberman to Clare Bishop

February 8, 1942
Ann Arbor, Michigan

Dear Miss Bishop,

You don't know me, but I am a friend of your mother's. My mother is Mrs. David Lieberman (Deborah) and she knows your mother. So in a way we have already met, though not face to face.

I've heard a good deal about your accident from my mother. I hope to be a doctor someday, if the war doesn't finish us all off. My uncle is a doctor, and he told me a story that I think may interest you. A man came to my uncle and told him that he woke up one morning stone deaf. His wife had died in a car accident the month before, and he got the shakes whenever he climbed into a car. My uncle told the man he couldn't cure his deafness, but maybe he could cure his fear of cars.

The first day my uncle drove to the man's house and they sat together in the back seat. The man poured sweat and held my uncle's hand. The next day they sat in the back seat and discussed the weather. They wrote messages on a pad and passed it back and forth. The next week they sat in the front seat, half an hour a day, for a whole week. When a month passed, my uncle decided the man was ready for his first ride. He was wrong. The man threw up. I won't go into the whole story, but this happened three months ago, and now the man is driving again and he can hear better than ever. Now that gas is rationed, he said, you've taught me how to drive. Now that the news is terrible, you've taught me how to hear.

I'm telling you this story because I believe if you learn to play baseball, you might get well faster. I know you think you can't do much in a wheelchair, but this is not true. You can throw. You can catch. You can call balls and strikes. Not everybody who plays the game is perfect. Three Finger Brown was one of the best pitchers in the National League.

I'm not the best player myself, but I know the game. My uncle says you can learn something from everyone. Please call me if you want my help.

Yours truly,
Sol Lieberman

Hal Bishop to Helen Bishop

February 10, 1942

Dear Helen,

The trip here was very pleasant. I wish I could tell you something about where I live and what I'm doing in California, but I'd only give the censor extra work. So you'll have to be satisfied with a P.O. box number.

Tomorrow is the anniversary of a big event, probably the most important in my life, and the one responsible for my present happiness. I don't think anyone else could have put up with my idiosyncrasies as well as you have, and I know that I could never love anyone else as much. I don't say as much about it as I should, perhaps, but I love you very much and always shall. You have made and still make me very happy, and with our wonderful daughter I have no reason to envy anyone, and I would not change places with anyone.

I've written to Dr. Kellogg about Clare's case. I hope to take her to the San if she has not improved when I return, although I understand that Dr. Kellogg has moved to less elegant quarters (and less expensive), and the days when you could talk to Henry Ford about his colon or Johnny Weissmuller about his blood pressure are over.

Heaps of love,
Hal

Clare Bishop to Ben Harkissian

February 11, 1942

Dear Ben,

I'm enclosing a letter from Sol Lieberman, a friend of yours. Now hold your breath: he's teaching me how to play baseball. He says it will help me walk again, though God knows I can't do anything with the ball but throw it. I've had two lessons, and this morning I thought I felt a slight tingling in my right heel. Maybe I'm coming back to life.

Sol is a wonderful teacher. Before he introduced himself, he'd already decided we didn't need a big field. We could use the orchard across the street. I was awfully glad, since it takes me a year and a day to go anywhere, and I get very self-conscious about holding other people up. Sol put an old armchair in the middle of the orchard, in the snow. I watched him from the window in the upstairs hall. Then he came up to my room and we talked for a few minutes and he asked me if I was ready to start, and I said yes, and he picked me up and carried me across the street. (It's *cold* here. I wore my heavy coat and a blanket—not ideal for easy movement.)

Sol put a wastebasket full of baseballs next to me and asked if I'd played any softball before my accident. I said no, but I could swim. That made us both laugh, and from then on we trusted each other. He tied red ribbons around three trees to mark first base, second, and third, and he told me to aim for his glove. I asked him if we'd have to practice catching, and he said not till I felt ready. He knew I was afraid of the ball, and he assured me that everybody is afraid of the ball at one time or other, and that the man who beans a player feels worse than the man who gets hit. He added that he was sure the person who hit me felt awful.

"I want to show you three basic pitches," he said, just as if I were going into the Majors tomorrow. "The fastball, the curve, and the fadeaway. We'll start with the fadeaway. That's the slowest."

My slow ball was very slow indeed. I couldn't throw it more than a couple of feet. Sol came in close.

"Aim for my glove," he said.

When he saw I was getting tired, he sat down on the ground beside me and reminded me that I was now part of a great tradition. According to his uncle, baseball is older than the Torah. He also told me that Christy Mathewson was the greatest pitcher who ever lived and Babe Ruth is the greatest hitter and Ty Cobb the greatest base runner and Joe DiMaggio the greatest base stealer. He told me that Lou Gehrig would have been a bigger star if he hadn't played in the shadow of Babe Ruth. And he said I should know the statistics of the great players and loaned me his book of rules and ordered me to study it.

The next day we commenced my second lesson, and soon my arm felt as if it were no longer part of me. I don't mean only that it was tired. I mean it was free, it moved in a way the rest of me hasn't moved for months. I thought it might fly off by itself for parts unknown. People in Poughkeepsie would look up and see an arm flying among the birds. Twice Mother has invited Sol for dinner but nothing is kosher in our house, hence we have nothing he can eat, so she has given up. At night I close my eyes and see him ducking and running among the apple trees, glove raised like a giant paw.

Sunday Mrs. Brewster called to ask if I wanted a ride to Friends' Meeting. The last two times she called I said no. It just seemed such a horrendous effort, and I dreaded everyone staring at me. I remember one Sunday last year when a boy came into Meeting on crutches with his trousers folded up and pinned where his leg had been. I'd heard about the accident but didn't know he'd lost a leg. The normal waiting-for-the-spirit silence deepened to one of pain and shock. I didn't want people to feel sorry for me that way. But after the second lesson with Sol, I found it didn't matter, perhaps because I no longer feel sorry for myself. So I said yes, I'd go.

And I'm glad I went. There never were many young people in Meeting and there are even fewer now. A number of people are speaking to the question of how they remained pacifists in the last war. Mr. Brewster was a CO during the war and got sent to an army prison where he wouldn't even pick up a broom. He spent most of the war in the hospital with one thing or another, starting with typhus. Another man was a news photographer in the Navy and carried a gun all through the war but never fired it. Just before he went home, he took a couple of shots at a log to see if the gun really worked.

In the afternoon I went to a work party at the Brewsters' house. They have a Polish girl living with them, a refugee, who is still afraid to speak above a whisper. I don't know if I told you about the work parties. Half a dozen women sit in the living room among heaps of used clothing. We go over it piece by piece, we mend it, and we talk about the war. Sometimes we sing. I learned that a delegation of Friends was sent by the General Meeting to persuade Hitler that he should beat his swords into ploughshares.

Mother rolls bandages twice a week at the Red Cross and works on her square for the afghan the play-reading group is making for the soldiers. Nell is still dating Bill and they are still trying to avoid his wife, Heidi. Last week they almost succeeded. Mother had hung some blankets on the line to air, and Nell and Bill slipped between two of them and simply vanished. Heidi raved and roared and threatened. An hour later they showed up, claiming that they had been kidnapped by Martians but all particulars of the event had been erased by a mysterious ray administered to them before they were released.

I'm supposed to be keeping up with my schoolwork. The math is beyond me; it's also beyond Nell and Mother. So much for math. I read a little French but not very energetically. And novels, though all we have in the house are Poe and Dickens. I haven't been to the library in ever so long.

I do a lot of drawing. I did a good portrait of Nell, but she didn't like the little lines around her mouth and the shadows under her eyes, and last night she sneaked into my room and erased them.

Mr. Knochen hasn't been back, but I think about him a lot. Ben, be careful. I will ask my Ancestress to help you when I see her again, but when will I see her? Maybe she won't come anymore. Mother told me she lost most of her power over the invisible after she fell in love with Papa. You have to give up one for the other, she said. Most people don't have room for both.

I love you. So perhaps the Ancestress won't come, ever again.

On the other hand, she might. She comes when she's needed. But I can't ask her. She comes in her own way.

Love,
Clare

Sol Lieberman to Ben Harkissian

February 15, 1942

Dear Ben,

No doubt Clare has already written you that I'm teaching her baseball. I think if she gets to know the game, maybe she'll move a little faster down the road to a cure.

I wish the news from home were all good, but it's not. Durkee was killed in action in the Philippines. I feel just awful about it. And now that everybody on our old team has enlisted but me, I have to keep reminding myself that when the war is over, people are still going to need doctors.

Tell Clare that you're the one responsible for putting her in a wheelchair. If you get killed, God forbid, and somebody else tells her, how do you think she'll feel? It's more important to ask her forgiveness than God's. God will always be there, He can wait. But you and me and Clare and the rest of us—who knows when we'll be taken?

Take care of yourself—
Your old pal,
Sol

Ben Harkissian to Clare Bishop

Fort Hood, Texas
February 20, 1942

Dear Clare,

This is the hardest letter I'll ever have to write. And I hope I don't lose you for writing it. I couldn't bear that right now. The chance of seeing you again is what keeps me going.

I'm the one that hit you with the ball. A bunch of us were fooling around on the golf course, across from Island Park. George Clackett pitched me a ball and I hit it. I never saw where it went. But I read about you in the paper and I wanted to tell you but I kept putting it off. If I get killed, I want you to know the truth, and I want you to know it from me.

Write. Write soon. Or call. It's awfully hard for me to get a call through to the outside. Every night there are a hundred men in line for the telephone. We'll be going overseas soon. They don't tell you where you're going till you get there. I've learned to kill in a hundred different ways. I've learned how we kill and how the enemy kills. Steel darts, butterfly bombs, personnel mines, castrators (you step on one, it blows your groin out). Oh, God, I wish I could ask forgiveness for everything I'm going to have to do. I don't want to kill. I wish I could bandage the wounded or set the broken wings of birds.

Love,
Ben

P.S. You keep working out with Sol. That tingling is a good sign.

Clare Bishop to Ben Harkissian

Ann Arbor, Michigan
February 28, 1942

Dear Ben,

When I read your last letter, I nearly fell out of my chair. I won't tell you all the thoughts that raced through my head. What matters is this. If you hadn't hit that ball, we'd never have met. And I think my real life started from that moment. Oh, I ate and slept and walked around, but I was asleep. When I think about my life B.B. (before Ben), the days are all the same color, they run into each other like water. There's so much that slipped over me, so much I didn't notice or remember.

Meeting you the way I did was an awful way to wake up. But I'd rather be awake than asleep.

We hear a lot about keeping awake now. Keep awake! The enemy never sleeps! In Meeting one of the elders made my heart stop when he stood up and spoke a passage from George Fox's journal: "Now was I come up in spirit through the flaming sword, into the paradise of God. All things were new, and all the creation gave unto me another smell than before, beyond what words can utter." I believe the flaming sword is double-edged—it wakes you and it wounds you, and I thought of you and me, and if life is being taken from us, I want to be awake when it happens. I want to know what I've lost.

If you want to save things, you should be here. We're saving scrap. Paper, old tires, iron. I'd like to scrap this chair. I wish somebody would come up to me and say, "Take up your chair and walk." Are there still people around who can say that and mean it?

My baseball lessons go on. Sol is a wonderful teacher. And I love you.

Clare

Davy McGuinley to Hal Bishop
[postcard]

[picture side]

A BUSY WORKER'S CORRESPONDENCE CARD
CHECK MESSAGE DESIRED

Date . . . . .
Place . . . . .

MY DEAR	WEATHER IS	
Old Darling √	Warm	Cool √
Wifey	Wet	Dry
Hubby	Pleasant	Miserable
Folks		

I AM

  Working from . . .

    to . . .

  Buying War Bonds

  Finding Scrap √

  Thinking of You √

  Happy

  Lonesome √

FOR RECREATION I

  Swim

  Play Golf

  Play Tennis

  Go Fishing

  Bowl

  Loaf √

  Spend My Dough

  Go to Church

CAN'T COME TO VISIT YOU NOW BECAUSE

  Tires Wore Out

  Too Busy

  No Gas

  Can't Find a Horse √

GIVE MY REGARDS TO

  The Whole Family √

  The Old Gang √

  My Pals √

  The Mayor √

YOURS

  Sincerely √

  Devotedly √

  Hurriedly √

[message side]

LOVDAVY

19

A Greedy Eye

After Ben left, Willie and his mother began every morning with a discussion of Marsha.

"It's just as well he's rid of her," said Willie.

"Just as well," agreed Wanda. "Such a terrible girl."

Willie said, "Terrible," and thought of Marsha's tearstricken face and her white rabbit coat and her money and remembered how her head felt against his shoulder and the sly look she gave him, as if she were reading the future in his face.

One morning Willie observed that his mother was growing tired of this subject, and he feared that unless he mentioned Marsha first, they might not discuss her at all, and he would lose the pleasure of parading Marsha's faults, a pleasure oddly akin to prayer, for it seemed to bring him into the very presence of her to whom all this talk and energy were directed. A new morsel of information would sustain his appetite for weeks.

"Her stepfather is Dr. Deller," said Wanda. "Did you know that? Don't forget to drink your orange juice."

Willie drank it very fast.

"His specialty is eyes. He has a big wooden eye in his examining room with Arabic writing on it."

"Who told you that?"

"Mr. Nesbitt. Dr. Deller operated on him for cataracts."

"What does the writing mean?"

"I don't know," answered Wanda.

"Maybe Mr. Nesbitt could find out."

"What do you want to know for?"

"It's nice to know things like that," Willie answered.

A week later she told him what it meant: Don't have a greedy eye.

"He overcharges," she added.

In his mind Willie kept a compartment marked "Marsha, Priority," in which he filed the most casual remarks and tried to assemble them into a larger picture of their subject, while he listened for new tidbits of information floating in the stream of his mother's talk. One evening over supper his mother said, "Dr. Deller came in today."

"What for?" asked Willie.

"He brought a bunch of Marsha's dresses to be cleaned." Willie felt himself go weak. Wanda went on relentlessly. "He used to go down the street to Spotless and Cheap, but they lost a pair of his trousers, so he's switching to us. I never saw a girl with so many clothes. He told me she never gets rid of a single outfit."

When Willie stopped by Goldberg's Cleaners & Tailors at noon and offered to take her to lunch, his mother was surprised and pleased. "But I can't leave the counter till Joe comes back from his lunch break. We're awfully busy at noon."

"Is there anything I can do to make myself useful?" asked Willie.

"You can keep out of the way," she said. "I have more work than I can handle."

She brushed him aside and took an armload of shirts from a man who was drumming his fingers on the counter.

"No starch, Mr. Siegl, right? And you want 'em on hangers."

Mr. Siegl nodded. "My wife's pink dress is in that pile," he warned her. "She wants you should get the sweat out of the armpits."

Wanda filled out another slip. At the bottom she scrawled, "Sweat Under Pits."

"When will it be ready?" asked Mr. Siegl.

"Saturday, unless you want to put a rush on it."

Willie lifted the gate in the counter and closed it behind him and slipped into that vast, noisy nation of steam presses, whirling drums, women old before their time pushing bins of dirty clothes, and garments rustling on racks that stretched into infinity. He watched a girl unroll giant bags from a spool over her head and ease them down over the finished dresses that scooted down the rack toward her like obedient children waiting to be checked. A call from the far side of the room sent her running.

Mr. Siegl was gone, but another man, with an armload of table-cloths, had taken his place.

"Mother, let me bag some of the finished dresses," said Willie. "You can trust me."

He knew from the way she glanced at him over her shoulder as she wrote out a slip for the tablecloths that he was in her way.

"I could do Dr. Deller's suits. Or Marsha's dresses, if they're ready."

She shrugged, and he thought she gave him an odd look, but she said nothing, only pointed to the rack behind her.

"Marsha's dresses are at the far end. They're all marked."

The white rabbit coat told him he'd found what he wanted. He leafed through the clothes on the rack as if turning the pages of a powerful book. There was only one copy of this book in existence and only one opportunity to turn its pages. A white satin blouse. A gold lamé skirt so narrowly cut that Willie, accustomed to the sight of Wanda's stocky figure, could hardly believe that any flesh-and-blood woman could fit into it. Ah, here was an old friend: the strapless evening gown, tagged with Marsha's name and the date her mother, or Dr. Deller, or perhaps Marsha herself, would call for it. He took out his pocket notebook and tore out the page on which he had copied with great care:

> When as in silks my Marsha goes
>   Then, then (me thinks) how sweetly flows
> That liquefaction of her clothes.

He added a single line of his own: "You looked wonderful in this dress." With trembling hands he pinned it into the bodice and noticed that it was lined with stays and a stiff, heavily padded bra.

He drew a white bag over the dress and pushed it along the rack.

Only after he had bagged thirty-two dresses, all Marsha's, did he remember lunch.

He spent the next week seesawing between repentance and anticipation, both of which peaked when Wanda came home from work. In vain he waited for a cryptic confession of love on small perfumed paper, or a note saying he might call. Had he forgotten to sign his message? Had it fallen off? Had Marsha put the dress away for the duration without inspecting it? Or had she found the note ridiculous, even offensive? Angry, first at her and then at himself, he thumbed through his *Encyclopedia of Etiquette: What to Do, What to Say, What to Write, What to Wear* for a letter to copy, a rule to follow. He found a useful heading, "Accidents," but the only disasters acknowledged were accidents at the dinner table. Nevertheless, he scanned the section for useful phrases:

> Mishaps will overtake the best-regulated diner, who, however, when anything flies from the plate or the lap to the floor, should allow the servant to pick it up.
>
> If an ill-starred individual [Willie turned the page hopefully] overturns a full wine or water glass at a dinner table, profuse apologies are out of place. To give the hostess an appealing glance and say, "Pray forgive me, I am very awkward," or, "I must apologize for my stupidity, this is quite unforgiveable, I fear," is enough.

Willie read the last paragraph over twice and wrote, on stationery bearing the gold embossed crest of the Episcopal church:

> My dear Miss Deller,
>   Forgive me, I am very awkward, I must apologize for my stupidity. My pinning that poem to your dress was unforgiveable.
>   Believe me sincerely yours,
>   Willie Harkissian

Two days passed before her answer came, on a sheet that carried her name in huge block letters at the top and below it, a brief message: "Don't worry about it."

Oh, she had answered—she had accepted him! If he asked her out—but where could he take her if he asked her out? To dinner and a movie? That would be expensive, and of course she would expect him to pay. He would ask her to the movies but not to dinner.

He checked the newspaper and was delighted to see that *The Chocolate Soldier* was coming to the Michigan Theatre on Saturday. There was plenty of time to write her. He turned to the *Encyclopedia of Etiquette,* only to find that all the examples of written invitations concerned themselves with accepting or postponing dinner parties. He chose one, however, and adapted it to suit his needs.

> Dear Miss Deller,
>
> It would give me great pleasure to have you meet with me on Saturday, the sixteenth, at seven o'clock, to see Nelson Eddy in *The Chocolate Soldier,* at the Michigan. Trusting there is no previous engagement to prevent my enjoyment of your company, I am
>
> Most sincerely yours,
> Willie Harkissian

Its distance from his own life and its suggestion of good taste and the money to show it pleased him.

But what if she didn't answer? Or what if his letter got lost in the mail, or arrived too late?

That evening he telephoned her and was glad that the first voice he heard was not Marsha's.

"Whom shall I say is calling?"

"Ben Harkissian," he said and realized his error at once, but it was too late. The woman who had picked up the receiver was gone. After a long time, Marsha said "Hello?" and Willie found he had scarcely enough breath to answer.

"Hello?" she repeated.

"This is Willie Harkissian," said Willie, in faint tones.

"Willie?" she exclaimed. He could not miss the disappointment in her voice.

"It would give me great pleasure to have you meet me on Saturday the sixteenth at half past three, to see Nelson Eddy in *The Chocolate Soldier.* "

He waited for her to burst out laughing. Her quiet, grave reply surprised him.

"I'd like that very much," she said. "Thank you for asking me."

20

The March of Time
(in Five Episodes)

KLINEHART SURRENDERS!

Sergeant Klinehart inspected the two pails of potatoes: first the potatoes peeled by Private Yeager, then the potatoes peeled by Private Harkissian.

"You mean to tell me, Harkissian, that these were perfectly good potatoes when you started?"

"Yes, sir," said Ben.

"And when you peel them, they turn into faces?"

"Right before our eyes, sir," said Yeager. "Watch, sir."

Ben picked up a potato and began to peel.

"No funny business with the knife, Harkissian," said Klinehart.

"Yes, sir."

But even as Klinehart warned him, he could see that Ben was paring a potato the way anyone else would pare a potato, letting the thin peelings drop into the slop bucket. A chill gripped the sergeant as he watched the pale flesh of the potato shrivel into sunken sockets, pocked nose, smashed chin.

"There—it's happening, sir!" cried Yeager.

"Harkissian, you son of a bitch!" shouted Klinehart. "Last week I sent you to clean the latrines."

"Yes, sir, I cleaned them, sir."

"How do you explain the sulphuric geyser after every flush?"

"I don't know, sir."

"And that class on driving a tank?"

"Yes, sir," said Ben.

"You ran the tank into a tree, Harkissian."

"Yes, sir."

"And that tree was not on the field till you ran into it."

"No, sir."

Ben tossed the potato into the pail—it really looked ghastly now, like a starved child—and reached for a new one.

"Oh, sir!" exclaimed Yeager.

Behind the thin peel, Ben's knife exposed the shrunken head of General MacArthur. The Ancestress slipped quietly out of the knife, and Clare slipped quietly out of the potato.

Did you put back the tree? whispered Clare.

I put back the tree. I don't know why your army and navy call their decoding divisions MAGIC. They don't know the first thing about it.

STOP WASTE AND WIN THE WAR

"I never thought I'd look forward to an enema," said the artillery captain in the bed next to Ben's.

There were three of them in the ward: the captain, Ben, and the tall lieutenant from Nashville. The lieutenant did not talk. He marched up and down the aisle between the empty beds, his hospital gown fluttering: an archangel who had been issued the wrong robe. Up the aisle, about face, down the aisle, about face. Up the aisle.

"What are you in for?" asked the artillery captain.

"I don't know, sir," said Ben. "I've been tested for everything."

The captain farted.

"Pardon me," he said, "top secret," and discharged a new volley. "Do you notice anything?"

"What, sir?"

"About what you have just heard—do you notice anything?"

"No, sir."

"Keep your small intestine spotlessly clean," said the captain, "and you can eliminate the fumes. Listen."

One long. Two short. Two long. Two short.

"Is it code, sir?" asked Ben, astonished.

"It is," answered the artillery captain. "To be used by prisoners in separate cells, for communicating with each other."

"You mean, you can teach someone—"

"The secret is muscle tone," whispered the captain, "and holding your breath and sending air into the small intestine. Close your mouth, stop your nose, and open the back door. When you get control of those muscles, you can say anything. Listen."

Ben listened.

"Did you get the message?" asked the captain.

"It sounded like . . . "

"Like what? You can tell me."

"Like 'Remember Pearl Harbor' in Morse code."

"You hear the possibilities," said the captain. "Stripped of every weapon, the body itself is a secret agent."

"That's amazing, sir."

"My discovery can also be used for entertainment. I can do a hound—and a hare—and a machine gun—"

The arrival of Dr. Cohen and Dr. Turner cut short the performance.

"Ben," said Dr. Cohen, "we'd like to watch you peel this potato."

Dr. Turner handed Ben a potato and Dr. Cohen handed him a knife, and Ben took them up and began to pare away the skin. Dr. Cohen gathered the peelings in a paper cup, took the potato, and passed it to Dr. Turner, who passed it back.

"It's still an ordinary potato," said Dr. Turner.

In Paradise, on the banks of the River of Time, the Lord of the Universe tosses a white ball which breaks into a green ball, and Sergeant Klinehart is awarded the bed next to the artillery captain. In three days he is released, and Ben is sent on active duty to Hewitt Island, 4,200 miles from Chile, 4,300 miles from Australia, and 5,600 miles from Clare.

TRUTH AND CONSEQUENCES

Grosse Pointe
March 1, 1942

Dear Helen and Clare and Nell and Davy,

I suppose you have been reading about the riots in the *Free Press* and seen the pictures of burning crosses and the picket lines. About 700 people surrounded the Sojourner Truth homes and kept Negro defense workers from moving into the very space that our government built especially for them. All the families had paid their rent in advance, and seven of them came back to find their old apartments occupied and no place to live. The moving company charged them for storage: five dollars an hour. The Negro driver who took the first van through the picket line was hit in the head with a rock.

We are doing our part for the war effort, of course. Vicky and Fred gave a dinner party for a dozen soldiers, sight unseen. Though they marched up the front walk in strict formation, two by two, they seemed glad to be in a real home. Nice boys, from all over the country. Fred observed that most of them had bad teeth. I wonder how many will be alive at the end of the war?

Vicky's snowdrops are blooming to beat the band, just as if they hadn't heard about the shortages. I have made friends with a bumblebee, who woke too early in the season and comes to my window to be petted. He sits very still on my hand and I rub his back.

You shall see me next month, when Grandma and I change places. In the meantime, you are welcome to put my bust of Stillman in the garden. It is not metal, it is not rubber. It is marble, and no one can find such a garden decoration unpatriotic. And no one need know that Stillman is the founder of osteopathy. You can tell your friends he's a distant ancestor. If we could map the tangled roots of the tree of life, this might even turn out to be true.

Love,
Grandpa

MACHINE MAKES 10,000 STARS AN HOUR!

"They sent me a star for the window," said Wanda. "A black star."

"Be glad it isn't a gold one," said Mr. Goldberg. "A lady on our street had five sons in the Pacific. She got five stars, five gold stars, for them. How's Willie?"

People were always careful not to mention his flat feet, as if having flat feet were unpatriotic.

"Same as usual. Such a help to me. Such a steady boy."

"There ought to be a star for Willie," said Mr. Goldberg. "A steel one."

NO MORE WEATHER!

From the air Hewitt Island was a button of sand with five dead koa trees and one shanty, stitched to a sea so blue that it made you think of sapphires, butterflies, the crests of tropical birds.

"Nice little beach, sir," said Ben. The island looked no wider than two miles in any direction. "I love white sand."

"That's not sand," said the pilot. "That's guano."

"What, sir?"

"Bird shit."

Captain Cooper, the weather patrol, was sitting in a rocking chair on the front porch of the government building, knitting. He was thirty-two, prematurely grey, and he had been a meteorologist at UCLA before he was drafted and assigned to the island of Canton. At Canton he did not like being so close to Honolulu—about a thousand miles—and he asked for an assignment on Baker Island. The weather station on Baker Island was run by six men.

From them he learned that Howard Island had only four men, and he got himself transferred to Howard, which he thought would be more peaceful. On December 8 he realized his mistake, when fourteen twin-engined bombers knocked out the cabin, the weather station, and the four men. Cooper, the sole survivor, moved into a dugout. For fifty-two days he foraged for food in the rubble and played solitaire with a deck of cards that miraculously had survived intact. Not an ace was missing.

After the Navy picked him up, Cooper studied a map and asked to be transferred to Hewitt Island. His second day on Hewitt, a freak lightning storm nearly burned down the government building. Cooper pointed out the charred places to Ben as he showed him around the island.

"Everywhere I go—catastrophe," said Cooper gloomily.

The sign over the porch read:

> THE GOOD TERN
> Quiet—Dignified—Cheap
> Best Food on the Island
> One Good Tern Deserves Another

It reminded Ben of the bars around Catherine Street and Lower Main: the Paradise Bar and Grill . . . the Chosen Land . . . the Oasis. Awful things happened in such places. A man stabbed his brother in the Chosen Land. A woman was raped in the alley behind the Oasis. One good tern . . . Ben hoped he wouldn't find religious pamphlets on a table inside.

The government building—Cooper never called it a house— had a tiny kitchen, a privy, a living room with two wicker chairs, two cots, and a table. On the table stood an alarm clock. Wanda had one just like it in the kitchen at home, and Ben thought of the kitchen shelf with its musty jars of spices, their tops spattered with grease; Wanda standing at the stove in the morning, her back to him as she heated the water for coffee; Willie drumming his fingers, waiting for the toast to pop up. Gone. Yes. No—not forever.

The focus of Cooper's living room was a rubber raft packed with provisions. Anything vital to life, explained Cooper, was kept in the raft. Naturally it was a nuisance digging through the gear in the raft every time you wanted a match, but tropical storms gave no warning. You had to be prepared. Every morning he checked that items borrowed from the raft were back in place. He checked the flashlight—did the batteries still work? He checked the log book and the fountain pen—did it have enough ink? He checked the matches, the rations, the life jackets.

"Whatever you take from the raft during the day goes back into the raft at night," he explained. Then he added, as an afterthought, "The clock and the calendar do not go into the raft unless we have to evacuate the island."

In his slow, meticulous way, he explained to Ben the importance of winding the clock and marking off the days on the calendar. A busty blond knelt over the month of March and drew her hands over her exquisitely airbrushed breasts.

"The one thing you don't want to lose on this island," said Cooper, "is time."

Sometimes he dropped a stitch. Or a word.

"Catholic?" he inquired one morning.

"Me, sir?"

"You're wearing a medal."

Ben smiled. "This isn't a holy medal, sir. It's a good-luck charm. My dad brought it back from the war. The First World War."

Cooper laid aside his knitting, leaned over, and examined the coin.

"I thought it was St. Columba—the wings and all. My mother has St. Columba."

"I met a kid in the hospital who had St. Anthony, sir," said Ben, eager to keep the conversation going.

Cooper did not appear interested in the kid who had St. Anthony.

"My mother is a nun," he observed. "After Dad died and I left home, she took orders."

"That's amazing, sir."

"And I'm not even Catholic."

"When you go home, do you go to—"

"I don't go home," said Cooper. "I don't have a home to go to. I don't even have any relatives. I'm an only child."

"I'm a twin, sir," said Ben. Not that Cooper would give a hang.

"The heavenly twins," murmured Cooper. "What I miss on this island are the stars. The stars are different here. No Big Dipper. No Little Dipper. No Orion. No heavenly twins."

He resumed his knitting, and Ben supposed he had used up his ration of words for the day and was surprised when Cooper said, "Are you identical?"

"No, sir. My brother's short and I'm tall, he's right-handed and I'm a lefty. I bat both, though."

"A switch hitter," said Cooper. Then, in a softer voice: "Are you one of the great ones?"

"I don't think so, sir."

"If I could have my own team with my choice of players, dead or alive, I'd pick Christy Mathewson to pitch."

"Yeah, he'd be good, sir," said Ben.

A faint smile twitched on Cooper's lips.

"I thought you might say Lefty Grove. Some people favor him."

"I'd stick with Matty. He was really good."

"Grove is good. Walter Johnson was good. Grover Cleveland Alexander was good. But Matty was great. I don't care what people say. Matty was the greatest."

At lunch two days later, Cooper asked, "Who'd you put in the outfield?"

"Ty Cobb, Babe Ruth. Tris Speaker." Ben hesitated. "Or Joe DiMaggio. Maybe Joe DiMaggio."

At breakfast a week later: "I'd pick Mickey Cochrane for catcher, if I could have him the way he was before he got beaned. And Lou Gehrig at first, before he got sick. Second, now—who would you pick for second?"

"Gehringer, sir," said Ben.

"You lean toward the Tigers. Hornsby's the better man. But what good would it do to have Hornsby? A team that good, there'd be nobody in the whole world they could play."

21

Borrowed Clothes

Saturday morning, bagging groceries at Clackett's Fine Foods, Willie tried to keep his mind on his work. Mr. Clackett was out of sorts; his wife, who usually took the telephone orders, was sick, and he had to cover for her. And keeping track of the new ration stamps was enough to drive a man crazy; blue tokens for this, red tokens for that, stamps for sugar and butter and meat. And so many of his old customers expected him to put aside secret reserves of chocolate and cigarettes for them, in spite of the shortages.

At ten-thirty, after which no more telephone orders were accepted, Mr. Clackett put Willie to work packing the orders for delivery and told him he could deliver them when he came back from his lunch date with Marsha. Willie was careful not to mention that his lunch date was a fashion show at St. Joseph's. The fashion show was free.

In the chilly back room, lit only by a single bulb, Willie slipped around the damp floor prying apart the heavy delivery crates (lethal when dropped on a toe). No matter how often Willie swept the floor —and he swept it often; Mr. Clackett was very neat—there were always thin rivulets of milk and stray lettuce leaves crushed to a slippery pulp underfoot and a general dampness on everything. "It's condensation," said Mr. Clackett. "You should have seen this place before I got the electric icebox. You should have seen it at the end of the day with the blocks of ice melting all over the floor."

Willie separated the orders and was trying to read Mr. Clackett's handwriting on the first one when a square of light fell into the room. He glanced up to see a man standing in the loading door, which opened to the outside.

The man was large, but not fat, and he wore white shoes and a wool suit (expensive, but not in good taste, Willie decided; the checks were too large, too loud), and a gold watch gleamed across his stomach. The chain was not gold. It was leather, and Willie wondered why a man would wear leather if he could afford gold. The man laid his hand over the watch, as if it hurt him, and said in the friendliest voice imaginable, "Is Roger here?"

Willie was about to say that no one named Roger worked there, but suddenly he remembered seeing the name Roger George Clackett on his employer's ration book.

"You mean Mr. Clackett? I'll call him."

And he slipped into the store, where Mr. Clackett was ringing up purchases for an elderly woman in a green raincoat.

"There's a man at the loading door asking for Roger."

Mr. Clackett handed the register over to Willie, saying, "Everything's rung up, just bag it and carry it to the car," and strode to the packing room.

"How's the Packard running, Mrs. Reese?" asked Willie. He knew the style of chatter Mr. Clackett's customers appreciated, mostly well-to-do widows who expected good service. He loaded the two full bags into the trunk. A maid would unload them and carry them into her apartment.

"Every time I buy gasoline, the attendant makes me an offer on it," she said.

She cast a critical eye on the bags as he nestled them beside the spare tire.

"I suppose you'll be called up one of these days," she added.

He shook his head. "The army doesn't want me. I've got flat feet."

"Well, you're lucky, aren't you?" she chuckled. Willie did not know what to answer. He opened the door on the driver's side and handed her in. There were no shortages for these women, who still went shopping in silk stockings. Wanda had put hers away for the duration and bought a bottle of leg makeup which was guaranteed not to stain one's clothes and did.

An agitated Mr. Clackett met him at the door.

"What did the guy look like, Willie?"

"He was big and had brown hair, and he was wearing a checked suit and a gold watch on a leather chain. When he asked for Roger, I thought he was an old friend of yours."

"Never in my entire life have I been called Roger."

"He asked for Roger," persisted Willie.

"Not even in grade school did anyone call me Roger. If he comes around again, try to detain him till I get there."

"You mean he's gone?"

Mr. Clackett nodded. "There's a black market operating in the area, and a man has been coming around to grocery stores and gas stations, trying to get the help involved. The guy who came here sounds like the same guy who came to Peter's Deli last week and asked John's wife if Peter was there. He said they were old friends from high school."

Willie stared at him, perplexed.

"Peter was John's parrot," explained Mr. Clackett. "John named the deli for his parrot."

"I didn't know that," said Willie.

"Neither did this guy. It's the same business all over again, trying to sound like a close friend. I'd rather lose all my customers than go that way. My customers are patriotic."

But he did not sound completely certain.

"Trouble with the new rationing is, it encourages crime," he went on. "People are stealing gas, people are stealing tires off the cars, people are stealing ration stamps. And creeps like this guy come along and buy the stuff. I'm ashamed to write my boy about what goes on in this country."

The door opened and they both jumped. Helen Bishop came in, and Mr. Clackett said, "Go meet your girl. I'll take care of Mrs. Bishop."

Willie hurried home to dress. He opened his wardrobe and found nothing that suited him, nothing that made him look young and handsome, well educated and well bred. He tried on this, he tried on that. He opened Ben's wardrobe and was surprised to see so many shirts and ties identical to his own, though Willie had often found himself buying clothes like Ben's. If Ben bought a new blazer, Willie would buy one like it a few months later, a cheaper model. If Ben bought a new tie, Willie would ask for the same pattern. But he took care never to wear that blazer or that tie on the same day Ben wore his.

He selected one of Ben's ties: navy, flecked with gulls.

When he arrived at Marsha's house, he was astonished to find himself fifteen minutes early, and he sat in his parked car, looking at his watch, till a voice startled him.

"Since you're here, let's go. I'm all ready."

He had not expected her to be on time. She was usually late. She did not wait for him to open the door but slid herself into the seat beside him. A cloud of perfume stunned him. Perched on the edge of the faded upholstery, she glittered. The sheen on her hair and her stockings dazzled him. She had left off what Wanda called her war paint, and her face was as innocent and crafty as a stranger's. She might have passed for thirty; then she turned her head and was no older than twelve. And her dress, soft and plain and cut of some mothlight fabric that shimmered grey and brown and mauve—oh, he wanted to tell her how lovely she was, and he could not utter a word.

He realized she had also been appraising him.

"I love that tie," she said, and he wondered if she'd loved it on Ben and he said, "It's Ben's," hoping to catch her, but she said, "Oh, is it?" and he knew he'd wear it again the next time he saw her.

Still he could think of nothing to say. They drove three blocks in silence.

"What do you hear from Ben these days?" she asked at last, in an offhand way. She was searching for something at the bottom of her purse.

"Nothing."

"I'll never forget that evening I smashed all his stuff. That awful evening."

"Uh-huh," said Willie nervously. The memory chilled him.

"I'd like to know why he didn't go out with me. I'd really like to know." Her hand went on rummaging frantically through her purse, like a trapped insect.

"He went to visit a girl named Clare Bishop. I don't know too much about her. Her mother shops at Fine Foods."

He felt Marsha stiffen at his side.

"She's in a wheelchair," he added. "She got hit by a baseball."

"A baseball!" exclaimed Marsha. "Isn't that the weirdest thing you ever heard? To end up in a wheelchair because you got hit by a baseball. Who hit her?"

"Ben hit her," said Willie.

There it was. He kept his eyes trained on the road and went on. "He was fooling around with the old team down at Island Park and he batted one across the river and hit her. And ran."

"That's a terrible thing," said Marsha. "To hit her and run."

"He didn't tell her that he was the one who hit her. He didn't want to be paying her medical bills for the next ten years."

The steeple of St. Joseph's rose over the treetops ahead of them.

"Plenty of parking," said Marsha.

Willie passed all the spaces on the street and left the car in Father Legg's driveway, being careful to park the back half on the lawn so as not to block it. What else could you do? The new rationing encouraged all sorts of criminal activities. People stole gasoline, tires, even ration books.

The main door was locked, and he remembered it was always locked on weekdays. He was annoyed to find the side door locked also, but for this he had the key, and they stepped from the brilliance of the day into the cool darkness of the sanctuary. For a moment neither of them could see anything. Slowly the inhabitants of this place asserted themselves: the bronze angels holding up the pulpit across from the choir stalls, the golden eagle bearing the lectern on the Gospel side, the altar covered with a purple pall for Lent. The windows across the aisle brightened as the sun breathed life into St. Jerome and his lion, and St. Ambrose, haloed in amiable bees, and others whose faces and friendly beasts he knew but whose names he had forgotten, or forgotten to ask. And overhead shone the vaulted blue ceiling, painted with stars.

"What a beautiful room," exclaimed Marsha. "Ben never took me anywhere. He promised he'd take me to the Tiptop."

"You should have seen this place on Easter. Flowers everywhere."

"The Tiptop is the best restaurant in Detroit. My stepfather says so. He goes to St. Joseph's, " remarked Marsha, "but not often."

"I've never seen you here," said Willie.

"Mother and I don't go to church. I never did and I'm not going to start now."

Willie felt they were treading on dangerous ground. "Do you want to see the church?" he asked.

"I thought I was seeing it."

"Oh, there are lots of rooms you haven't seen."

They stepped into the parish house, which adjoined the sanctuary. Willie tried the door of Father Legg's office, but it was locked; the gargoyle door-knocker a parishioner had sent from Canterbury glared at them. The parish office was also locked; they peered through the window at the framed portraits of previous rectors, and he pointed out the row of buttons he used for summoning the children from Sunday School on special occasions.

The library was locked too; had he got the wrong day? It was nearly one o'clock. Fear settled in his stomach.

"Let me show you the downstairs."

Downstairs, in perfect darkness, Willie felt along the walls for the light switch.

"This is the boiler room," he heard himself announce, and thought, as the light snapped on, My God, why would she be interested in the boiler room? "We're collecting stuff for the rummage sale."

The furnace rumbled at them. They stepped carefully around mason jars, game boards, playing cards, magazines, outgrown clothes, torn piano music. Everything broken or cracked or worn out.

"I love bargains," said Marsha.

To his joy, a door slammed upstairs.

"People are arriving," he said and turned off the light.

In the corridor they nearly collided with Father Legg. "Willie, my lad, what are you doing here?" he exclaimed.

"We're here for the fashion show," said Willie.

Father Legg lifted his hands in mock horror. "Oh, my dear fellow, I'm terribly sorry, so terribly sorry. The fashion show was yesterday. Now, isn't that a shame, to have come here especially for it."

His face burning, Willie allowed Father Legg to escort them outside. "This is your car, is it?" said the priest. He bent over and studied the position of the back wheels, and Willie observed that his white hair was thinning on top. "You didn't happen to notice if my tulips were up yet, I suppose?"

"No," said Willie.

He waited till Father Legg disappeared into the rectory, then started the car.

"I promised Clackett I'd be back at work by two. Maybe we can find a place—"

But Marsha laid her hand on his knee and interrupted him. "Don't worry about it. This could happen to anyone. Just drop me off at Arnoldson's. I have some shopping to do."

"The Tiptop. On Saturday, I'll take you to the Tiptop."

"I'll be ready," she said and smiled at him.

When he reached Clackett's, the truck was loaded and ready to go. Clackett handed Willie the keys to the truck and asked, "Did you have a good time?"

The place where Marsha had touched his knee tingled, held itself apart from the rest of his flesh, superior to it. *Ben never took me anywhere.* They would go to the Tiptop. There would be other places she'd want to go, and he would take her, even if it cost him every penny he earned. He pushed open the door to Mrs. Hogarth's back porch and dropped the box of groceries on the blue wicker table, so she could see it through the French doors and tell her daughter to carry it in. She'd started locking the doors after her daughter came home from school to find an intruder in the living room.

Everybody else left their doors open. He carried their groceries into the kitchen, collected the ration stamps and tokens they left for him, and put away the perishables. He knew their kitchens as well as he knew his mother's. Mrs. Curtis kept seashells above the toaster. Mrs. LaMont called out, "Is that you, Willie?" and liked to order him around: put the Spam over here, the Dreft over there. Mrs. Johnson's kitchen was always spotless; her maid bleached the enamel on the icebox and the stove.

Today he was surprised to find her kitchen a mess: dirty dishes in the sink, a burnt pot on the stove, a dishcloth on the floor. No doubt the maid was sick, and Mrs. Johnson was fending for herself. He put away the milk and eggs and picked up the dishcloth and found a twenty dollar bill. Without a moment's hesitation, he slipped it into his shirt pocket, hoisted the empty delivery box to his shoulder, and closed the door behind him.

22

Hearts

The party was for him. That's what Aunt Helen had said when she called for him at school. But it was also for Clare, she explained, who needed some excitement to take her mind off Ben. No letters from Ben had arrived in a long time.

"Is it mostly my party or mostly Clare's?"

"It's a party for your birthday. Who would you like to invite?"

Davy hesitated.

"You and my mom."

"Don't you want any children at your party?"

There were lots of children in his kindergarten class, but he did not know any of them very well. He never saw them except in school. Probably they lived far away. And there were no children in this neighborhood except himself. Perhaps Aunt Helen hadn't noticed.

"No, just you and my mom."

"We should have someone besides the family, or it won't seem like a party. Now, what would you like to do?"

He looked puzzled.

"Games," Aunt Helen said. "At Clare's birthday parties we used to play Pin the Tail on the Donkey and Fish. Everybody loved Fish. You got a fishing pole and you put your pole over the top of the big screen and waited for a nibble. I was hiding on the other side of the screen. I put a present on the end of each line."

Davy did not like the thought of everyone getting presents. The presents might run out before his turn came.

"Will I get a present, too?"

"Oh, you'll get lots of presents. You'll get presents from everybody."

"Will I get springy shoes?"

"You mean those things in the magazine?"

He nodded. Every night he saw himself wearing those silver shoes with bedsprings on the bottoms, leaping over fences, fleeing Nazi spies, like the boy in the picture.

"Honey, things you send for from magazines never work right. But you'll get lots of presents."

"I want lots of presents," said Davy, thinking of the springy shoes.

"When I was little," said Aunt Helen (Aunt Helen little? he could not imagine it), "we played games outside. We played Red Rover, Red Rover. I wonder if children still play that one?"

"I want to play hearts," said Davy.

"What?"

"I want to play hearts. I want to play with Uncle Bill and Uncle Bill's wife."

He remembered with pleasure an afternoon when his mother and Bill and Bill's wife came to visit him. He was in bed with asthma, and Bill brought him a deck of cards and told Davy to call him Uncle Bill, and Davy did, but his wife didn't say to call her Aunt Heidi, so he just called her Uncle Bill's wife.

And Uncle Bill showed him how to play hearts. Uncle Bill and Aunt Helen and his mother sat around his bed and they all played hearts, while Uncle Bill's wife looked out of the window. The third-floor room was small and crowded, and he felt important and powerful, and he wished they would all be happy. Uncle Bill's wife was not happy. She paid no attention to the game but gazed with great interest at the snow falling on the garden next door.

That evening at dinner Aunt Helen said, "He wants to play hearts, and he wants to invite Bill and Heidi," and his mother said,

"That's all right. Heidi always comes along," and Davy wondered if he had asked for the wrong thing.

"I don't know why kids don't play Red Rover anymore," said Aunt Helen. She was using her special cheerful voice, but it did not cheer Clare, who ate in silence and looked on the verge of tears. Helen had warned him not to talk about Ben or the war. When he asked her why, she reminded him that Clare had not heard from Ben for a long time and was worried. And they must all be extra nice to Clare, even though it wasn't her birthday.

On the morning of the party, Aunt Helen vacuumed the dining room and opened the linen drawer in the sideboard and asked him, "Do you like this purple tablecloth? Or this ruffled blue one?" She had hardly any plain ones. She bought them white and dyed them when they got stained. Davy wanted a paper Mickey Mouse tablecloth, but she had none, and he did not want to hurt her feelings. So he said "Blue" and wished she could make up her own mind and didn't have to ask him about every little thing.

He wanted to run upstairs and see how his mother was getting on, but Aunt Helen said she was getting on just fine and she would be down very soon. When Aunt Helen went into the kitchen, Davy sneaked up to the third floor and saw the bathroom door closed and his mother's Madame Du Barry box open on her bed and a dress that looked like a nightgown hanging on the lamp—it was made of blue floating stuff, and you could see right through it, and it had no sleeves—and as he was thinking how nice it was of his mother to go to all this fuss for him, she put her head out of the bathroom door and hollered, "You wait downstairs with Clare."

But Clare was in her room, making a present for him, and she couldn't let him in till she'd finished it, and Aunt Helen was setting the table, so he sat on his little stool in the kitchen beside Grandma, who sat on her big stool and scrubbed the roasting pan, which was perfectly clean.

"It's my birthday," Davy told her.

She looked astonished. "How old are you?"

"Six."

"Already six!" She put down the pan. "Do you want to play 'Spin the Knife'?"

"Oh, yes."

He had never seen Grandma play anything. She took the carving knife from the wooden rack which Aunt Helen had hung well out of his reach, and she put it on the kitchen table between them.

"If it points to you, you can make a wish."

She gave the knife a flick and it turned, faster and faster, a knife no longer but a spoked wheel, and every spoke flashing at him, and they both held their breath and watched to see whom it would choose. And Aunt Helen came into the kitchen.

"Davy!" she shrieked. "You know you aren't to touch the knives. That knife could cut your finger *right off.*" She grabbed the knife and slipped it back into the rack. "I don't know *why* you can't mind. I just don't know *why* you *can't.* I do so much for you."

"Grandma said we could play Spin the Knife," whispered Davy.

"Go into the dining room and sit there till the guests arrive. I don't need another Eddie O'Toole."

He sat at the beautiful table, ready to weep. Such things should not happen to him on his birthday, and he was hurt that Aunt Helen would think him as bad as Eddie O'Toole, the little boy who had come long ago to one of Clare's parties and plunged his fist into the cake. Eddie O'Toole was now grown up, and in the army maybe, or dead. Davy would never forget Eddie.

"Someone's at the door," said Aunt Helen. "Go answer it."

There stood Uncle Bill and Uncle Bill's wife, all dressed up, and Uncle Bill's wife had on her blue dress made of floating stuff you could see through, just like his mother's, but she was fatter than his mother. And she wore nice perfume, the same as his mother's only stronger. And she curled her hair like his mother did, but frizzier. Davy was so pleased he couldn't think of a thing to say, not even when they handed him a present, and Aunt Helen had to nudge him and whisper, "Don't forget to say thank you."

"Thank you," said Davy.

He wanted to tear off the gold wrapping paper right away, but

Aunt Helen said no, not till his mother came, not till Clare came. And when he wanted to run upstairs and hurry her, Aunt Helen said that they must be patient with Clare and not upset her.

He waited till everyone had gathered in the living room, and then he sat on the sofa and opened his presents. And after every present they said "Oh" and "Ah" and told him it was just what he wanted. There was a teddy bear with an iron box in its stomach so you could feed it crackers ("to replace that knotted towel he takes to bed every night," Aunt Helen whispered to his mother) and a book called *Copy Cat* from his mother with very nice pictures of a kitten, a cow, a duck, and a dog, all of them orange, which was not the right color (if he colored a cow orange in his coloring book at school, the teacher always told him that was not the right color), but he liked it all the same. Clare gave him a box of stamps and envelopes and coupons cut from magazines which you could send away and get free samples of things in the mail, and a little book of pictures she'd drawn in which she'd hidden the faces of animals. Under each picture she'd written how many faces he could find: ten foxes, nine raccoons, five birds.

He was coming to the end of the presents, and he glanced around to see if anyone had given him the springy shoes, if they were hanging up somewhere, or if Aunt Helen had them in a box hidden behind her, but there was only one present left. On the white bow, something jingled. Davy picked it off.

"That's from me," said Uncle Bill. "It's a keyring."

"Isn't that nice," said Aunt Helen. "What's on it?"

"The Chevy insignia. I got it when I took my car for a tune-up."

"Isn't that nice," said Aunt Helen.

"I *bought* my present," said Uncle Bill's wife.

"What is it?" asked Uncle Bill.

"Open it, Davy," said Clare.

A wild idea overtook him—that now, in this last box, he would find the springy shoes, though he knew the box was much too small. He tore off the paper, which Uncle Bill's wife gathered and folded into a square and then a smaller square, and he lifted the lid and took out a tiny wooden toaster.

"Thank you." He was afraid he would cry.

"Isn't that nice," said Aunt Helen.

"Press down the lever," urged Uncle Bill's wife.

He did so, and a piece of cardboard toast popped up. It had writing on it.

"Read it so we can all hear," she said. She looked almost happy.

Shame flooded him. He did not know how to read so many words together. He searched for something friendly, a "the," an "and."

"Aren't you going to read it?" Uncle Bill's wife asked.

"No," said Davy.

Nobody spoke for a few minutes.

"I was taught to show my appreciation for a present," said Uncle Bill's wife, "when I *got* a present. And I didn't get many."

"He can't read yet," explained his mother. "He's only six."

"I could read when I was five," said Uncle Bill's wife. "I learned on the canned goods in my mother's cupboard."

"Clare, you read it," said Aunt Helen.

Clare read it. Her voice trembled. " ' "And now there abideth faith, hope, charity, these three; but the greatest of these is charity." —First Corinthians, Chapter 13, Verse 13.' "

"It's a sort of prayer," said Uncle Bill's wife.

"A prayer toaster!" exclaimed Aunt Helen. "Why, isn't that the darndest thing you ever saw!"

"I never saw one before," said Clare.

"Neither did I," said Uncle Bill.

"It has seven prayers and they're all different," said Uncle Bill's wife. "I got the Protestant version."

Davy wondered what else the toaster could produce besides prayers. As soon as everybody left, he would ask it for something better, like a stick of gum. The toaster was not such a disappointment after all.

"I believe I like this present best," said Davy.

Uncle Bill's wife smiled at him.

"Let's go into the dining room for the cake," said Clare and wheeled her chair toward the door. Grandma was sitting at the head of the table, still scrubbing the roasting pan. They had forgotten all about her.

"Grandma, you can put that pan away now," said Aunt Helen. "We're having cake."

Uncle Bill's wife gave Grandma a pitying look that said: You poor woman, used by your children, worse than a slave.

Grandma put the roasting pan under her chair and Davy sat at the opposite end of the table in Hal's chair and Aunt Helen turned out the lights in the dining room and vanished into the kitchen. Davy listened eagerly for her return.

"She's lighting the candles," said Clare.

A light gleamed in the doorway and the cake appeared, wearing its little crown of stars, six flames for him to blow out and wish on, and his mother started to sing "Happy Birthday," and Clare joined in, lower and louder, and Uncle Bill's wife trilled over them all in her piercing soprano, and Davy was overcome with the burden of their love.

"Make a wish!"

"Don't tell it!"

"Make a wish for Clare," said Aunt Helen.

"Davy, you wish for whatever you want," said Clare.

I wish I may get those springy shoes.

He blew. Five flames winked out forever and set up aimless trails of smoke. One flickered and came to life again. He blew once more, sure he had it this time, but again it burned brightly.

"Bill, did you sneak one of those trick candles on the cake?" demanded Bill's wife.

"That time didn't count, honey." His mother snatched the candle off. "Blow again and make your wish."

But he had already blown out all the candles except the trick one, and Aunt Helen was turning on the lights and telling Uncle Bill's wife how she served plum pudding with brandy sauce (you soak a sugar lump in alcohol and light it and it's simply spectacular), and Uncle Bill was handing Davy the carving knife.

I don't know why you can't mind. I just don't know why you can't.

He glanced at Grandma to see if she would help him, but she

was securing her hat with bobby pins, which she always did just before she announced she had to go.

"Cut the cake now, little man," urged Uncle Bill.

"Oh, he'll cut himself," exclaimed Aunt Helen.

"You baby him too much," said Uncle Bill. "Let him try it. He'll never learn if he doesn't try it."

"He's only six," cried his mother.

"When I was six, I could make a cake all by myself," said Uncle Bill's wife. "My sister and I got up one night and made a cake for Mother and told her the fairies did it."

"And she believed you?" asked Clare.

"No. Cissy forgot to wash up the dishes."

Clare, sitting beside Davy, guided his hand on the knife. Six pieces fell away from the blade, exposing chocolate, or maybe gingerbread, under the white frosting. He felt his happiness returning.

"There's plenty left for tomorrow," said Aunt Helen.

The sixth piece wore a fat yellow rose. His mother put the pieces on plates and handed them round the table. Of course she would give him the rose. He wouldn't have to tell her that.

"You can give me the rose," said Uncle Bill. "I'm allergic to chocolate. All I can eat is frosting."

"I'll never forget the roses Bob Larch sent Nell," said Aunt Helen. Uncle Bill was eating the rose; Davy pushed his own cake away. Grandma was wrapping and rewrapping her piece in the napkin and trying to fit it into her purse.

"Oh, let's not tell that story," said Nell.

But Aunt Helen could not resist. "Bob Larch had the most awful case on you." She turned to Uncle Bill and Uncle Bill's wife. "He was the mayor of Cleveland, I think. Or was it Bloomington? He sent flowers every day, in big wicker baskets, the kind actresses get."

"What happened to him?" asked Uncle Bill.

"He went to jail for embezzlement," answered Aunt Helen.

"What kind of cake is this?" asked Uncle Bill's wife. From her voice you could not tell if she liked it or not.

"Carob ginger, with custard filling," said Aunt Helen. It was the only kind Hal would eat. "Nell, do you remember the time you told Mother she never gave you enough custard for dessert, and she made you a whole dishpanful?"

"I don't know why you go on telling these stories," said Nell. "Let's start the game. I have the cards right here. Bill, you deal."

"I have to go," said Grandma. "I've had a lovely time."

"Grandma, I need you," said Clare. "I need you to hold my cards. Bring your chair close to mine."

Uncle Bill dealt and Aunt Helen sprang up and cleared the plates to the sideboard.

They all took their places.

"Remember, Davy," said Uncle Bill, "whoever gets the old lady tries to get rid of her." He looked significantly at his wife.

"What old lady?" asked Davy.

"The queen of spades."

"I don't think much of the old man, either," snapped Uncle Bill's wife.

"He's not so bad," said Nell.

"He has no power in the game," said Uncle Bill's wife.

"But he can take the queen," said Uncle Bill.

"Please, let's not fight," said Clare.

Uncle Bill's wife turned to Nell and asked, "What was *your* husband like?"

Nell closed her eyes. "He drank."

"Davy, do you remember your father?" coaxed Uncle Bill's wife.

Davy shook his head. Of his father he had a single memory, but he did not want to give it to Uncle Bill's wife, for fear that when she gave it back it would be changed. Once his father had come to visit Davy and wanted to take him for a drive, and his mother made Aunt Helen go along in the back seat. You have to go, his mother had insisted. What if he tries to kidnap Davy?

"A good Christian can get on with anybody," said Uncle Bill's wife.

"There were other things," said Nell.

"Hal and I never had a cross word," said Aunt Helen. "Never."

"Everybody pass three cards to the person on his left," said Uncle Bill.

Uncle Bill's wife glared at him. "Our church does not countenance divorce."

Uncle Bill rolled up his eyes. "Is snoring considered grounds for annulment?" he asked.

"I don't snore," she snapped.

"Yah, yah, I knew you'd say that!" shouted Uncle Bill, jumping up from the table so fast he knocked his own cards to the floor. "Well, I've got the proof. I've got the proof."

Clare buried her face in her hands.

"What proof?" inquired his wife in icy tones.

"Jack came over last night and he heard you. I've got a witness."

"Jack was in our bedroom?"

"That's the last time you'll ever tell me you don't snore."

"I was in my negligee and you brought Jack into our bedroom?"

"You were snoring so loud you never heard us."

"For God's sake, Bill, stop!" cried Nell.

"It's my birthday," quavered Davy.

"That's right, it's his birthday," said Uncle Bill. "Some people have to ruin it for everybody."

"Let's play," said Clare, lifting her head. "Please. *Please.*"

Davy looked at his hand. He had the queen of spades! He had the old lady.

"Pass three cards to your left," said Uncle Bill's wife.

To his left sat his mother, his good, kind mother. Perhaps he could pass to the right? On his right sat Aunt Helen, who had made the cake and invited the guests and gone to so much trouble for him. No, no—he could not pass her the queen. Pass to the left. Uncle Bill stood behind Davy and said, "Well, you'll want to pass this, of course, and this"—the king of spades—"and maybe the ten of clubs. You don't have many clubs. It's good to clean yourself out of one suit so you can discard."

If anybody could clean a person out of his suit, thought Davy, that person would be Uncle Bill's wife. She was so clean, always sweeping up crumbs, brushing lint off other people. He no longer wanted to play the game; he felt sleepy and wanted to take a nap. He thought of the moment when the cake was brought in, how happy they were then, how wretched they were now, and an earlier moment flashed across this one, a night long ago in Christmas week when he woke to hear children singing. Grandpa had called, "There are carolers at the door," and Davy rushed down and saw them through the glass—sixth graders, he supposed—and their tin lanterns dangled on long poles and the cutwork of the lanterns threw black diamonds over their faces and over the snow. He was the only listener at the door; Aunt Helen was running around the house, trying to find something for them to eat.

> Good King Wenceslaus looked out
> On the feast of Stephen.

By the time Aunt Helen returned with a box of Mary Lee chocolates, the carolers were gone, and she had let him put on his boots and his coat over his pajamas and run in the snow after them. But they had disappeared. Next year, Clare promised him, you and I will go caroling, even if there's just the two of us.

"Clare, can we still go caroling next year?"

Nobody heard him.

"Are we ready to start?" asked Aunt Helen.

Davy slipped the queen out of his hand and sat on her. Immediately he felt better, lighthearted. Danger was out of the world. He chose three low cards, three good cards, all diamonds, and passed them to his mother.

Hearts fell, Uncle Bill told him to play this and play that, and his mother said, "Well, somebody's got her," and Clare said, "She never shows up this late," and Uncle Bill whispered in his ear, "Play this" and "Play that," until the cards ran out.

The last trick. The end of the game.

"This deck has no queen," announced Uncle Bill's wife.

"She must be here," said Uncle Bill. "Davy had her and passed her on. I saw the queen in his hand."

"Cheating hurts nobody but yourself," said his wife, glaring at him.

"Who's cheating? Not with you around."

"Maybe she fell off the table," suggested Nell, and she crawled under it and Uncle Bill followed her.

"Shake out the tablecloth," said Aunt Helen. "She might have got caught in the ruffles."

Uncle Bill's wife bent down and peered under the table. She said not a word. She picked up the chunk of birthday cake when she saw Uncle Bill coming up and brought it down on his head.

Just like Eddie O'Toole, thought Davy. She's just like him.

And started to howl.

23

Charted Waters

It took Ben a long time to realize that Cooper was not cranky but shy, as unused to small talk as a hermit. When Ben admired the log he kept in the weather station, Cooper went so far as to show him the map he'd made of the island. A nervous line defined the coast, the five dead koa trees, and the patch of pigweed. A crude sketch of the government building defined the interior. He was also keeping a list of birds sighted:

The brown tern
The grey gull
The albatross
Rita Hayworth

"Is there really a bird called Rita Hayworth, sir?" asked Ben.
Cooper shrugged. "If I can't find it in the bird book, I name it myself."

One morning he invited Ben into the weather station and pointed to the ceiling. Ben followed his finger and gave a whistle of surprise. Over his head hung a dozen glass balls, pale amethyst and amber and luminous green like moss. On their shining surfaces Cooper had pasted the tiny silhouettes of cats, elephants, snakes, dogs, buffalo, otters, and voluptuous women. It was a galaxy of planets laced and fretted with shadows.

"Did you make it, sir? It's fantastic."
"Jap fishermen use these globes," he said, nodding ever so

slightly. "They probably drifted over from Tokyo. Or Manila."

"They're wonderful, sir."

"But I can't get any good glue here," Cooper went on. "Everything turns so brittle. The animals fall off."

As he spoke, his breath dislodged a lamb, which fluttered to Ben's feet.

"Everywhere I go—catastrophe," said Cooper. "Sometimes I think suicide's as good a way out as any."

"Suicide, sir? No, thanks."

"But if you had to kill yourself," persisted Cooper, "which way would you choose? Pills?"

"Not pills, sir," said Ben. "I'd probably botch it."

"I've always favored shooting. In the mouth. That's the quickest way."

"It's hard on the folks who find you, sir," said Ben. The subject was making him uncomfortable.

Cooper had clearly thought a lot about it. "Who would find us?" he asked.

"How about a firing squad, sir?" suggested Ben jokingly.

Cooper frowned. "Where would we find a firing squad on the island?"

The island felt as small to Ben as one of Cooper's gloves. He'd explored the grove of five dead koa trees, and he'd seen two of the three kinds of lizards Cooper told him lived here: the green lizard that sunned itself on the rocks in the morning and the brown lizard that came out to feed in the evening. All Cooper knew of the third kind was the message on a tube of sulfathiazole in the first-aid kit issued to him when he was assigned to Hewitt: "For the bite of the blue-horned lizard, apply twice a day. Also good for pigweed allergy."

There were no pigs and no other living plants on the island except pigweed. To Ben it hardly seemed worth God's time to make an island that had so little on it.

I gave unto Hewitt Island a host of microbes, seashells, sandalworms, terns, albatrosses, cormorants, the speckled shark, the striped marlin, all lovely and lively beyond description, said God. *Where were you when I made this island? Where were you when I broke the sea for its decreed place and said, "Hitherto shalt thou come but no farther, and here shall thy proud waves be stayed?"*

"Sometimes, on a good evening, I can pick up Harry Owens's band at the Royal Hawaiian," said Cooper.

Ben sat in the main room and fiddled with the dial on the radio, and Cooper watched him and went on knitting. Ben knew he would knit ten rows, and rise, and go to the weather station and check for fallen animals.

"Every day I lose a few," he explained. "They get torn or bent. I paste them back on. It's a losing battle. Are you going out?"

"Yes, sir."

"Far?"

"No, sir. Just to look at the stars."

"The Southern Cross is the best place to start. Once you find the Southern Cross, all the other stars fall into place."

The wind was up; the water was choppy. Ben tipped back his head to search the sky and was not prepared for what happened next, did not even know when there flashed over him a deep, familiar darkness, through which Tom Bacco was driving, because he alone knew how to keep the old green Packard from stalling. Charley and Henry and Tony and Stilts and Louis and Sol and George and Ben. They drove down to the river where night came early under the black willows and they could not see the families gathered at picnic tables across the water, though they could hear them talking and laughing and their dogs barking and their kids yelling.

Durkee's in Manila.

Look at that bird. Bet you can't hit it.

Bet I can.

A high fastball rushed toward him and Ben slammed it to the spot where the white bird would arrive in three seconds. In the darkness a girl cried out. Ben sank to his knees, sobbing, and the waves pitched their cold tents over him and rolled him to higher ground.

What woke him? The sun? The stiffness in his legs? The grit in his clothes? The smell of coffee?

When he walked into the kitchen, Cooper, his back to Ben, was marking the calendar. "The first of May," he said.

The date stirred a faint memory which came into sharp focus.

"That's my birthday, sir," said Ben.

Cooper did not hear him.

"The one thing you don't want to lose on this island is time," he said and crumpled April into a ball, which he threw with great dexterity into a basket on the other side of the room.

Time? To Ben they had more than enough time here—they had too much time. You could check the raft and the flashlight batteries and the ammunition—was it still dry?—and you could clean the floor and the dishes and your rifle—oh, you could clean your rifle for hours, burnishing each part lest salt and sand corrupt it—and you could hunt the rats, whose ancestors had come over on the ships of the first guano hunters when farmers started paying money for it, and you could fish for marlin and you could throw back to the sea the small yellowish-brown sharks that went for your bait if you used sardines or the green lizards that sunned themselves on the rocks in the morning, and you could clean the marlin and cook it (never would Ben forget the smell of cooking—kerosene and the dark dreams of smokestacks) and you could walk among the birds that nested in the rocks—there was no sand to speak of, just coral that cut your feet and raked your stomach when you swam, just a stinking network of small pools and the nests of birds; you could gather their eggs, still warm, feathers still clinging to the shells, smooth as if generations had touched them for luck, like alabaster trinkets from the tomb of a king; you could toss the garbage after lunch to the gulls and watch them dive for fish heads or a bit of gristle; you could shoot the plump terns and the skittery sandpipers which tasted like young ducks—but why bother? You could reach out your hand and take them. They were that tame and stupid.

You could watch the birds and maybe see an albatross. Cooper had seen only three since his arrival: large, distant, and unforgettable.

You could stand at the water's edge in the breeze that smelled of ammonia—or was it iodine? what was that smell?—and the birds would dart past, crossing and swooping and crying out to each other.

Those cries! Ben longed for wild geese winging south on nights chilled by the breath of the coming snow. All his life he had heard them and not known he was hearing them till Clare said, "Listen."

He waited for the mail plane. He wrote her long letters, not about the island, but about home, yet about nothing important, as if home were nothing, a rag-and-bone shop, all odds and endings. Remember the snow? Remember Precious Gems? His memory was caving in. The air was remembering for him, turning over, saving, throwing away. One day he could not recall his brother's face but could perfectly remember the timbre of his voice. Another day he remembered the smell of his father's glove but not the color of his hair. He remembered that Marsha was beautiful, but he did not remember how; was it her hair—the way it fell over her shoulders? What in the world had they said to each other? Whole scenes slipped away without telling him, without even saying good-bye.

It was early evening but already dark. The water was rough, the sky heavy with clouds. A westerly wind was collecting the stink of the guano; Ben could not imagine anyone paying money for it.

And on the fifth night of the fifth month a great wind arose, and the sun withdrew and the moon turned away, and darkness settled upon the parched face of Hewitt Island. And Ben Harkissian stood at the window and heard the roaring of the wind and the beating of the rain, and Captain Cooper hunched in the raft like a turkey buzzard wearing the yellow plumage of his life vest, waiting for the sea to take him.

And the wind carried away four cubits of the roof to the west and great was the noise thereof, and Ben Harkissian opened the front door, and the water rose up in a wall to meet him and advanced with an army of ten thousand waves joined into a single wave, which rushed into the house and loosed the tables and chairs upon the tide, and the papers and planets and the animals thereon—all were lost in the tide save Cooper, who had prepared the raft, and Ben, who climbed in with him when the water rose to his knees and to his waist and he saw that the koa trees were gone and the pigweed was gone, the three kinds of lizards who lived in the pigweed were gone, and the government building was splitting, board from board, and the sea was carrying it away, tree, weed, lizard, sand, house, the island itself.

And the heavens departed as a scroll when it is rolled together, and the waves pounded the raft and bruised the two men curled up on the floor of the raft, and the sea tossed cold water over her children, lest they sleep, she covered them with the cold salt spray of the storm.

When the rain stopped, Hewitt Island was gone.

Cooper raised himself and looked around. The gear was gone. The food, the water, the tarps, the matches, the staff and stuff of life: gone. Water sloshed around the bottom of the raft, chilling him. They would have to bail—with what? their shoes? Ben did not move. He lay on his side in the water, his face turned from the sky.

The sea had left them the clothes they wore, the two life vests, the rags they used for cleaning the equipment, and the things Cooper carried on himself: his knife and pistol, his fountain pen, his compass, his wallet. The wallet held a hundred dollars.

He uncapped the pen and scratched it on his life vest, and the ink appeared. Faithful friend! Over his heart Cooper drew a map. To his dismay the ink ran on the wet patches, but the sun was fast drying what the sea had washed. The salt winked and glistened on his clothes, his hands, his shoes.

He drew islands to the east and to the west, as if he were redesigning the Pacific. Above the islands to the east he wrote "friendly and inhabited." Above the islands to the west he wrote "Japs." If the raft drifted into enemy waters, they would be shot, of course. The Japs did not waste time taking prisoners. At the bottom of the map, he scrawled something large and vague and labeled it Australia.

Tonight, if the sky cleared, he could tell by the stars how accurate he was.

On the right side of his life vest he wrote "log" and made a mark for the first day so that they would not lose track of time, would not lose their bearings, and their intelligence would not turn against them, leaving them in a backwash of madness with no map, no sign, and no way home.

He picked up the bundle of rags and threw them over the raft, counted, and gathered them up again, and under the mark for the first day he noted the speed and direction of the wind and the drift of the water, wind out of the southwest, six knots, drift of one knot, while Ben fled through the long tunnel of fitful sleep, closing the hatches over the various shapes of terror as he passed them, and woke at last to find Cooper waiting for him.

"Where are we, sir?"

"Here," said Cooper, pointing on the map to the empty space over his heart.

We're not lost, thought Ben, and knew they were hopelessly lost. He sat up, and the sun nearly blinded him. The sea was the deep azure he'd loved when he first flew over it. Now its awful machine had wound down to a gentle lapping.

"Sir, I still have the flashlight."

"Does it work?"

Ben turned it on. There was nothing dark but the sea, and he pointed the beam straight down, over the side of the raft, and felt the flashlight glide from his grasp. It entered the water without a sound, its beam growing smaller and smaller, like someone walking down a road toward the horizon.

"Oh, Christ. Oh, I'm sorry, sir."

Cooper did not answer. Neither did he look angry. He seemed to have reached a state beyond anger, a benign indifference. He looked at his watch, a gesture so absurd that Ben wanted to laugh. The next moment he wanted to cry.

"It's one o'clock," said Cooper. "Take the watch at one o'clock."

One o'clock—what did that mean here? At one o'clock Ben fed garbage to the gulls and watched them dive for it. One o'clock on the island. That was when he wound the clock, just before he fed the birds. Yes. But it could not be one o'clock there now. At home it would be night. Lights turned on, fires lit.

By afternoon, thirst took hold of them, inhabited them; they could think of nothing else. The flashlight had attracted sharks. All day they hung like dark islands in the clear water below, and Cooper sat, still as a cat, mouth dry, pistol poised, licking his lips. He could not clear the taste of metal and salt, as if some secret corrosion were at work deep inside him. He could feel his body shutting down, a house closing up for the season.

Ben's shout jarred him alive.

"Look, sir—look! A boat!"

It hovered on the horizon like a friendly sliver, though they could identify neither the kind of ship nor the flag under which it flew. Cooper pulled off his life vest and his shirt and handed the shirt to Ben.

"Wave it."

Ben waved. He was certain he saw the boat slow down. When it glided out of sight, slipping over the curved face of the earth, he was not certain of anything.

"They didn't see us, sir," said Ben. He felt to blame for this. He should have waved harder. Longer. Higher.

Cooper shrugged.

"We're near Jap territory. Nobody is going to risk losing a ship for two men."

24

The News (in Six Reels)

MISSING IN ACTION

Everything in the house reminded Helen of Hal. As she went about her tasks, she reconstructed his day for Clare.

"If Hal were here, he'd be listening to the news now" (and they knew what he would be hearing at eight o'clock in the morning without even turning on the radio: the ad for Serutan, Natures spelled backwards).

When Helen brought up the breakfast trays—one for Clare, one for Grandpa—they thought of Hal driving to the chemistry building. He'd be there by this time.

At noon: he'd be coming home for lunch.

At one o'clock: he'd be going back to the lab.

At three o'clock, on another day a long time ago, school would be out and Clare would be walking to his office. She was just starting eighth grade. She would open the heavy door of the chemistry building and slip into the grey twilight. The stone stairs to the second floor had the soft dents of steps in old churches, worn down in the center by the feet of the faithful.

She hurried past the exhibit cases of molecules, past the closed doors of offices with names printed on the frosted glass. Her father had two rooms, his office and his lab. Today she did not find him in his office, but his desk lamp shone on unanswered letters and a shuffle of bluebooks.

In the lab she dropped her books on the black counter between the sink and the microscope, and she drew up a stool. The smell of the chemicals, the rows of fat beakers, the scales and balances weighing silence under glass, the shelves of brown bottles sealed with old corks or glass stoppers, and none of this subject to fear, heartbreak, or confusion—the mystery and patience of the nonhuman rolled over her.

She sat down and opened her social studies book and was startled by a soft whir from the high darkness over the bookcase in the office. From the lab she could see, through the connecting door, a great horned owl perched on the topmost case. Her father had told her not to be afraid; it lived in the forestry building across the way and belonged to a graduate student who had raised it from an egg.

If I had to be any other thing than what I am, thought Clare, I would be that owl.

After supper, Helen said, "He'd be taking his walk now." Hal would walk as far as the Blue Door magazine store (which he never entered) and turn around and walk back. Helen and Clare knew at what time he reached the store; he was so regular in his habits you could set your watch by him. At any hour of the day, they could look at each other and say, "Well, he's getting ready to leave the office," or "He's reached the magazine store, he'll be on his way back now," and sometimes it seemed that Hal had never left, only that they came and went at different times, and they kept missing him but would run into him very soon.

When loneliness washed over Helen like a huge wave, she straightened their closet and arranged on the top shelf the effects of their life together. Her hats, his cameras, her pocketbooks, his sock mender, which always made her smile. Hal knew she was only too glad to darn his socks, but he had been a bachelor for so long that he did not expect her to do the things he had always done for himself, and he loved gadgets that performed small services. In the time it took him to plug in the sock mender, wait for it to warm up (about fifteen minutes), put his sock on the mending platform with the hole exposed, arrange the patch (fifty cents for a package of five), and press it into place with the heating arm, Helen could have mended a dozen socks. And likely as not, the patch would fall off minutes after he'd pressed it on, and he'd sit on the edge of the bed with the sock mender in his lap and repeat the process, swearing quietly. He never said anything stronger than "Hell" or "Hell's bells."

At lunch and dinner, for which Clare and Grandpa came to the table, Helen read Hal's letters aloud. He wrote about sunsets, flowers, and fogs; you'd think he was living alone in nature. But of course the censor read everything first. The simplest statements were suspect. The censor had even paused over "I hope Clare is better" and had underlined it.

WAR EFFORT GOES UP IN SMOKE

"I can't believe it's finished," said Nell.

Nell had volunteered to sew everybody else's squares together if she didn't have to knit one herself. She wasn't unpatriotic, she explained, but counting stitches drove her crazy. Helen had finished Nell's square but then Clare had sewn them together because Nell found she broke into a rash whenever she got near wool.

But now she shook out the afghan with as much pride as if she'd knitted the whole thing.

"Debbie, you take the other corner," she said.

Mrs. Lieberman took the other corner.

The lady from the Red Cross said, "It's wonderful, just wonderful."

But Debbie said, "Girls, I can't understand why you all did the smoking cigarette. I thought you were doing a dog, Marie."

"I changed," said Mrs. Clackett.

Helen searched for her own square among the multitude, as one hunts for a familiar face in the newsreel. Mine has more smoke than any of them, she thought. Billows and billows. All the others showed a thin line of smoke straying from the glowing tip. She wondered if she'd made the smoke wrong.

KEEP AWAKE! THE ENEMY NEVER SLEEPS

When the air-raid whistle blew, Vicky had just finished putting Grandma to bed for the sixth time, and now she stumbled toward her own room, turning off lights as she went.

"Fred, are you going to bed in your shoes?"

"It's only eight o'clock," came Fred's voice from the dark space that was his half of the bed. "When I hear the all-clear, I'm going to get up."

"I'm so tired I could fall asleep right now," said Vicky and flopped down beside him. "Six more weeks to go. I just can't believe she cut up the ration books. I feel like I signed up for the duration."

They lay side by side, listening anxiously.

"She's still moving the furniture," whispered Fred. "What if she turns on the light?"

"I unscrewed the bulb," said Vicky.

Footsteps fleeing down the stairs unsettled them both.

"Fred, you go after her this time."

He found her playing with the dead bolt on the front door: an angry ghost looking for the way home. White nightgown, white braids springing from either side of her head like handles on a jug, mottled and milky by the light of the full moon which poured through the glass on both sides of the door.

"I just want to see if Vicky locked up."

"She locked the door," said Fred.

"It doesn't feel locked."

"Oh, it's locked all right." He rattled the knob.

"And the lights don't work."

"Grandma, it's a blackout. Because of the war."

"War?" she repeated, genuinely surprised. "Who are we fighting?"

"Germany, Italy, Japan."

"Oh, that's right. I forgot."

She followed him meekly up the stairs.

HEAVY LOSSES

Charley LaMont to Sol Lieberman
[censored]

Western Desert

Dear Sol,

Nothing new to write about, but I'll write anyway. Every day we bomb them. Every night they bomb us. Yesterday we bombed some German airfields. One of the ME 109's put holes in a couple of planes, including mine. For every enemy plane we knock out we get to paint a swastika on ours. I have six swastikas on mine. I also have the arming pin from the first bomb (500 lbs.) I dropped on the enemy.

I hear that Tony and Louis are on a sub somewhere in XXXXXXXXXXXXXX.

If you get a chance, send me the yearbook.

Your friend,
Charley

SIX HUNDRED DEAD

Tom Bacco to His Mother and Father
[censored]

Dear Mom and Dad,

At last I have the time to sit down and write you about what I've been up to. We just finished cleaning out a nest of Japs in XXXXXXXXXX. I'd rather fight the Germans any day. Japs are like those deadly snakes you never see till after they've bitten you or you happen to find one dead. They hide in the trees. It's a funny feeling to walk through the jungle waiting for the trees to open fire on you. The noise is deafening. There's sniper fire and machine guns (the Jap guns are higher pitched than ours) and strafing and mortars.

The mortars are the worst. They go high and you can't tell just where they'll land. I feel like an outfielder judging a high fly.

After the big push there were about six hundred Japs lying around. You can tell them from a distance because they wear wrapped leggings. I sure admire our medical boys. They go unarmed right into the fighting and find the wounded. If they can't carry them to the dressing station, they tag them: name, wound, what's been done to relieve the pain.

Say hello to all your faithful customers at the shop. We could use a little of your Fix-It oil out in the field.

Love,
Tom

TROOPS ON THE MOVE!

Lying in bed, Clare listened to the band practicing at the high school half a mile away. Twinkles of sound, she used to call what was not really a tune but the voice of a far-off brightness.

Then, the whistle of the train and Helen calling her for supper. That would be the Wolverine, coming from Chicago, headed for points east. When she was a little girl, Hal would take her to watch the train come in, her mittened hand safe in his gloved one. She loved the bustle of baggage carts, the shining blocks of ice hauled on the ice cart, the golden glow of the varnished benches in the station, the fireplace big enough for her to walk right into without lowering her head. And the fortune machine that gave you your weight and fortune on a little ticket—that was almost the best of all.

But not the best of all. No, not as wonderful as the train rushing toward them, setting everything into motion. Boys who put their pennies on the track for the wheels to flatten had left them by now, and the message man was standing on the platform with his mysterious rune, a fork pronged like a huge Y, on which he impaled telegrams, and the train roared toward him, and he held it high—O

brave message man!—and the engineer reached out of his high window and plucked it like a flower and was gone.

That was the best of all.

Sometimes the engineer waved at the people on the platform.
Hal and Clare waved back, always. And when the train pulled out
of the station, they went on waving at the faces behind the windows,
and sometimes a white hand waved back, or a black one.

25

Birdlight

At noon Cooper lay curled up in the bottom of the raft, and Ben, sitting on what Cooper insisted on calling the forward thwart (which was identical to the backward thwart) watched the tiny speck grow larger and larger. It did not appear to be a plane. It glided down and came to roost on the flat, dark sea.

Albatross.

Cooper had not told him about their wingspan, had not told him enough. This was no bird but a floating giant from heaven, majestic, though streaked with traces of its first mottled plumage. It did not stoop to the gull's tricks—coasting on the currents, spiraling and climbing, then the quick drop into the waves, all show and appetite. The albatross rested on the water, close to the raft, and watched Ben.

Ben! Ben!

He heard but did not stir. All day the calms had held him in a slow dream, and the bird was a dream as well, and the smell of leeks and clover and new-mown grass.

Ben, it's me. It's Clare.

He started; he was wide awake now.

Harvey's Bristol Cream, said the albatross.

"My God, you did it!" shouted Ben. "You found me! You're going to save us!"

I can't save you, said the bird. *I can only feed you.*

"I'd like a gallon of fresh water and a steak, medium rare," said

Ben. "Make that two steaks," he added, remembering Cooper asleep nearby.

The bird made a whirring sound deep in her throat. *You can't give the Ancestress orders. She has to do things in her own way. I told you about her.*

Of course. He should have known. Clare never traveled without her guardian spirit.

"Is she a bird or a woman?"

I don't know what she is. I don't think she's a woman except in the way I am a bird—

"But you're not a bird. You're Clare. Don't leave me."

I love you, said the bird. *Remember that.*

She was flying away from him very slowly.

"Wait! Come back!" called Ben. "I love you, Clare! I love you!"

He heard a dry cough and turned around. Cooper was staring at him.

"Get off the watch," said Cooper. "You're out of your head."

Close to the raft, the water broke and a fish leapt into the boat, and Cooper lunged forward and rolled over on it. The fish put up no struggle.

The Ancestress had sent them a small shark, about two feet long. Hell, thought Ben, she might have sent us something better. Immediately he felt ashamed. Cooper hacked at the skin and cursed till the knife slit the soft flesh of the underbelly, which opened as easily as a zipper, and his hand slid into that awful pocket and brought out the liver, slippery, dense, and bright with blood.

A second time he reached in and fetched out the heart.

A third time he reached in and found two small fish.

All these gifts he divided with great care and handed Ben his portion. Without a word they tore into the liver. Ben shuddered.

"Tastes just like chicken, sir." He fought back the urge to gag. "Chicken cooked in ammonia."

They ate the heart and each peered into the blood-smeared face of the other.

"I believe the blood is nutritious," said Cooper.

As if he had trained all his life for this office, he held up the head and the tail and drank the blood from the cup of the shark's body and passed the cup to Ben. The blood was thin, watery, and had a strong bitter taste.

Not the storms but the calms. That's what will kill us, Cooper told himself. He could hardly keep his eyes open, and what was there to see? Sea and sky, days and nights, all stretched into a flat, endless calm. His watch had long since rusted. You couldn't keep out the salt water forever. One day the pistol wouldn't work. He still kept the log. The stars would not rust. The moon would not rust. Not in his lifetime.

He put his hand into the water to feel the drift and felt his flesh ripped away; a shark dropped off, smacked the side of the raft, and plunged out of sight.

"Jesus!" said Ben. "Jesus! Right through the nail. Right to the bone, sir."

As Ben wrapped the hand in rags to stop the bleeding, neither said what each feared, that one quick thrust of a fin could put a hole in the raft.

"Good thing I did the log this morning," Cooper said. "I'm right-handed."

His voice sounded firm, but his face was bloated, and under the peeling sunburn his skin showed thin and waxen.

"A good thing, sir," said Ben.

The next evening Clare came again. Ben knew she was near by the scent of leeks and grass (tall grass, tall in the morning, cut down in the evening), and his thirst and weariness fell away as he scanned the horizon, fearing he might be wrong, that she was not coming, she had never come.

No, she was here! He gave a joyful shout. The albatross was resting in the trough of a wave.

She's sending rain, said Clare, *and a different kind of fish.*

"Turn me into a bird," pleaded Ben. "Turn me into a bird. I want to fly home."

And what would you do when you got there, with no body to keep you? The bird is what I travel in, my love, not where I live.

A shot exploded so close to him that the bullet grazed his ear and seemed to jar his hearing loose; waves, wind, the cry of the bird went on without him. Ben spun around, terrified. Cooper was lowering the pistol he'd fired with his left hand.

The violent break from the bird's body stunned Clare, left her scattered and confused, like water shaken from a bowl. She beat her spirit-arms, her spirit-legs, as the Ancestress had taught her. But she could scarcely move.

Stay in the shadow of my wing, said the Ancestress and raised her giant wings over her.

Why can't I fly? whispered Clare. She could not even hear herself speak, though she tried to put the broken pieces of her voice together.

The spirit set free by a death is not the same as the spirit set free by choice. It does not move as easily as we do.

I'm not dead, I'm Clare.

But the body you traveled in is dead, said the Ancestress. *After you have entered your own body, it will be a long time before you are strong enough to travel again.*

Behind them, below them, darkness had fallen, but the raft glowed with a silvery blue light which held the shadows of the two men and the body of the albatross, shining like a star.

There was phosphorus in its food, remarked the Ancestress.

By birdlight, Clare could see Ben crouching with his head on his knees so that he wouldn't have to watch Cooper tearing the bird with his teeth.

26

By Land and Sea

At first it looked like an island, and then he saw it moving toward
them.

"A boat, sir! A boat!" exclaimed Ben.

Cooper, huddled in the bottom of the raft, squinted toward the
horizon. For two days he had not been able to focus his eyes, but he
did not tell this to Ben.

"I can't see it," he said.

As if the boat itself heard him, it suddenly loomed much closer,
and now Ben clearly saw it was a lifeboat, manned by a single rower
whose back was turned to them.

"Shall I raise the flag, sir?"

"Save your strength. He's seen us."

The rower was a civilian, dressed—Am I dreaming? thought
Ben—in a three-piece suit and fedora, and though he made all the
motions of rowing, the boat appeared to be moving under some
silent power of its own, for when he lifted the oars it moved quietly
on at the same pace and drew up beside the raft.

"Wake up, sir. We're saved."

Cooper did not answer; he had fallen asleep just as the rower
turned and Ben's gaze met a familiar face.

"Good morning, children," the man said.

"Death," whispered Ben.

And time stopped on the high seas.

"You know my name, Ben," said Death. "I hope you don't mind if I call you by yours."

I'm going nuts, thought Ben. Where are the fires? The eternal torments?

"You've just passed through them," said Death. "You really are a glutton for punishment, Ben." He leaned into the raft and put his arm around Cooper's shoulder.

"Captain Cooper, I've come for you. There's plenty of room in my boat. You can leave your life jacket behind."

"Plenty of room," muttered Cooper and put his hand trustingly into Death's. And Death raised him to his feet.

"Don't go, sir!" shouted Ben.

But Cooper allowed himself to be led into Death's spacious dinghy, and the moment he set foot there, he seemed to revive, to become a new man.

"It's wonderful," he whispered. "I'm not thirsty."

"Plenty of room to stretch out, Captain," said Death, and Cooper stretched himself out to his full length.

"It's wonderful," he said, closing his eyes. "I'm not hungry."

"You forgot your map, sir," said Ben. He waved the life jacket in front of Cooper's closed eyes. "You forgot your log."

"I don't need them."

He lay perfectly still. Death drew a silver coin out of his pocket and laid it on Cooper's left eye.

"The other one, please," he said, holding out his hand. "Before I can do anything for you, Ben, I require my fee."

Slowly Ben slipped the coin on its elastic thread from around his neck and gave it to him, and Death broke the thread and laid the coin on Cooper's right eye. Then he looked up.

"You're next, Ben."

"You said you'd do something for me."

"Of course. A little reprieve. Will you come with me now or will you starve here and meet me later?"

"If I go with you now," said Ben, "can I ever come back?"

"Only one man ever came back in the flesh," replied Death, "and His was a rather special case."

The sea was as still as if someone had turned it off, and the silence as deep as if someone had turned it on.

"My dad told me if you make a bet with Death, he has to accept."

"You want to make a bet with me?"

Ben nodded. "If you win, you can take me on the spot. If I win, I want to live to be a hundred."

"The die is cast," said Death, with a smile at his own joke. "I suppose you brought your own dice?"

"No."

"A chess set? A deck of cards? I am the grand master of all games, but I don't furnish the pieces."

"I only know one game," said Ben. "Baseball."

"Baseball," repeated Death. "I know the game. Never played it myself."

"Could you get a team together?" asked Ben.

Death was still.

"Your team against mine. The South Avenue Rovers versus the Dead Knights."

"I'm interested," said Death.

"Of course I'll need time to get the guys together. I don't even know where they are."

"I do," said Death.

"George Clackett? You know where George Clackett is?"

"He's on a destroyer in the Coral Sea."

"And Louis and Tony?"

"Cruising off Honolulu," said Death. "In a submarine," he added.

"And Charley?"

"In the sky. Off the coast of Africa."

"And Stilts?"

"Australia."

"And Henry?"

"Thorney Island, England."

"And Tom?"

"The Solomon Islands."

"There's no way to get us together," said Ben, "unless you end the war."

"I can arrange furloughs," said Death. "Shall we set the game for June twenty-seventh?"

"We'll need three weeks to warm up," said Ben.

Death shook his head.

"Time is rationed. There are terrible shortages. I can only give you two."

"Okay, two. How are you going to let everybody know?"

"Through the time-honored channel of dreams," replied Death. "And a little finagling with current events."

"We'll need good weather," Ben reminded him.

"That can be arranged."

"And I'll want a few extra men on the bench."

"Agreed." Death nodded.

"And an umpire."

"Your choice," said Death. "Living or dead."

"Durkee," said Ben quickly. "I want Durkee."

"Durkee will do. He belongs to both of us now."

"And I'll need to get home right away."

Death nodded. "I'll send a boat to pick you up."

"The U.S. Navy, please," said Ben. "I don't want to end up in a boat with you."

"The contract, then," said Death.

And he wrote on the air with one pale finger, which trailed a thin line of smoke.

Agreed this day, that Death and his team, the Dead Knights, shall play the South Avenue Rovers on June the twenty-seventh, 1942. The game shall be played for three innings. If the Dead Knights win, Death shall take the South Avenue Rovers. If the South Avenue Rovers win, Death shall give the members of this team a new lease on life. They shall live through the war and beyond it. If any of the South Avenue Rovers shall be unable or unwilling to play, their places shall be taken by their next of kin.

At the bottom, Death tapped out two rows of dotted lines.

"What's this 'next of kin'?" asked Ben.

"Life is so uncertain," murmured Death. "One has to clarify the contingencies. Just sign on the dotted line."

"But who are the next of kin?"

"In case of unforeseen circumstances, the fathers would take their sons' positions."

"My father is dead. And Louis and Tony's father, too. You should know that."

Death blushed faintly. "If the fathers cannot play for their sons, the mothers will play for them. Naturally, I don't expect Teresa Bacco to play for both—"

"My *mother?* Holy God, Clare would pitch better than my mother!"

"That can be arranged," said Death.

And he wrote below the fading letters of the contract:

At the request of Ben Harkissian, Clare Bishop shall take his father's place. If Clare Bishop cannot play for Ben, his mother, Wanda Harkissian, shall take her son's position, in accordance with the above agreement.

"If I'd known you were going to do this, I'd have asked for Willie," said Ben.

Death's eyes lit up with pleasure. "Never let it be said that Death was unfair."

And he added yet another sentence:

Substitutes for the South Avenue Rovers shall include Mrs. Bishop, surrogate mother for Tony Bacco, and Willie Harkissian, who may play any position.

"Sign," said Death.

Ben wet his finger and signed and turned to bid Cooper farewell. The boat was empty.

"Where . . . ?"

"Buried at sea," said Death. "Quiet, dignified, cheap."

27

Love and Money

For the first time in his life, Willie was setting free his money. He bought gifts at Arnoldson's (for Marsha there was only one jewelry store in Ann Arbor, and she always checked the name of the store on the gift box), expensive showy trifles he knew she would like: sterling silver earrings, tragedy on one ear, comedy on the other. A silver Hershey bar for her charm bracelet. Nothing handmade, nothing useful or antique. Nothing that did not speak to her of a conspicuous cash flow.

For himself he also bought presents: a silver pen and gold cuff links, visible tokens of affluence which somehow seemed necessary for his evenings with Marsha. Sitting next to her, he felt as if he owned some valuable piece of lakefront property and was now obliged to keep up appearances. All those statues in her stepfather's house, all those books from the Limited Edition club, their pages uncut—he understood why people bought them, liked having them. He enjoyed the obsequious bows of waiters and the envious glances of other men. He had paid dearly for this property, and now he was ready to build on it, to move in. Marsha was beautiful. He knew it and she knew it, and he was determined to keep her. To keep her from Ben.

As they finished Sunday dinner at the Michigan Union, they turned to the newspaper and studied the movie listings.

"'*Moon over Miami*, with Betty Grable and Robert Cummings,'" read Willie solemnly. "'Yes, Boys and Girls, it's Betty in love. In Miami. In a bathing suit. In Technicolor. With Paramount News.' "

"Where's it playing?" asked Marsha.

"The Wuerth."

"I know a girl who got lice at the Wuerth. Let's see *Bahama Passage* at the Michigan."

After each dinner, after each large purchase, he suffered pangs of regret. He didn't need that pen; the salesman had gypped him—and what if he lost one of the gold cuff links? He was spending too much; he must pull in. He wrote down every purchase and the amount paid for it in a ledger bought especially for the purpose and realized that knowing where his money went did not keep him from spending it. He should be investing it, he told himself. He should not be taking money from Mr. Jackson at all. Tomorrow he would tell Mr. Jackson, "I'm through. Mr. Clackett is suspicious. I can't work for you anymore."

When had this work become so easy? When did he no longer feel as if he were committing a crime? At first he had simply pilfered bills, ration stamps, goods from the shelf: a bag of sugar . . . a bag of coffee . . . cigarettes from an open carton. Once, when Mr. Clackett was closing the register, he asked Willie if the crook had ever come back.

"Who?" asked Willie.

"That man who called me Roger. A bomb went off at the Salvage Collection Center last night and killed two people. The night watchman said a man had been coming around the last two or three nights asking for Harry. Sounded like your man, from the description of him."

"Who is Harry?" squeaked Willie.

"Somebody who worked on the day shift except when he did overtime. He was doing overtime when the bomb went off."

After that, for a while, Willie stole nothing. Then Mr. Jackson gave him the job of driving a vegetable truck to this building or that. On Mr. Jackson's orders, he parked his car behind the Stafford Arms, which Mr. Jackson gave as his address, and he waited at the bus stop till the vegetable truck pulled up in front of the hotel, loaded with crates of beans and tomatoes and a set of scales for weighing them. The man who handed him the keys to the truck asked no questions and gave no instructions. Willie knew that he sold vegetables on the west side of town, and he supposed that under the veneer of carrots and cauliflowers lay tires, cigarettes, sacks of sugar and coffee, and boxes of butter. When Willie returned with the truck, emptied of its contraband, Mr. Jackson would ask him, "Have you got enough spending money?" and press on him ten, maybe twenty—never a set amount but always more than enough. He never asked Mr. Jackson about his personal life, but after he spied the initials BBL on his wallet, he wondered if Jackson was his real name. Nor did Mr. Jackson ask Willie about himself; yet he seemed to know a great deal.

One afternoon when Willie was returning the truck, Mr. Jackson said, "Why don't you take Marsha to the Stafford Arms for dinner?"

Willie was surprised that he knew Marsha's name, and when he did not answer right away, Mr. Jackson added, "The evening's on me. Just tell the waiter. Or the man at the desk."

Ben and Willie had once gone to the Stafford Arms at the suggestion of two girls they'd met on a blind date. The girls had ordered lobster thermidor. At Willie's suggestion, he and Ben had retired to the men's room and climbed out the window, leaving the girls to pay the bill. Now Willie wondered what scene had taken place after their escape was discovered. Would the manager remember him?

He went home and changed into a suit. Before he picked up Marsha, he always got the runs, and now he allowed time for sitting on the john and reading the newspaper. *The Acquisition of Popularity* recommended reading the newspaper ("The well-informed man will never be at a loss for conversation"). He skipped the war news (Marsha did not like to talk about the war) in search of more entertaining fare. On the first page of the local news section he found an item that held his attention. A waiter in the Lotus Garden had been arrested for harassing a beautiful young nurse. The waiter was Chinese, and he had seen Miss Eileen Stark at the restaurant and fallen under her spell. He had hired private detectives to inform him of her whereabouts at every hour of the day and night. When she waited for her ride in the morning, she saw him staring at her, standing several yards away. In the foyer of her boardinghouse, he would be waiting for her when she came home from work. He never spoke; he never raised a hand against her. He followed her up the stairs, never taking his eyes from her, and watched her enter her room, and he was waiting for her on the front steps the next morning.

Willie turned the page and read Reverend Carpenter's "Thought for Today":

> A nation has as much religion as it can show in times of trouble. The men who were cast into the fiery furnace came out as they went in—except for their bonds. Their bodies were unhurt, their skin not even blistered, their hair unsinged, their garments not scorched, and even the smell of fire was not upon them. That is the way our nation will come out of the fiery furnace of trials—liberated from its bonds, but untouched by the flames.

He closed the paper.

As he drove to Marsha's house, the waiter's story spun various endings in his mind. What if Miss Stark went to the jail and gave herself to this man? What would he do? Nothing? Was he impotent? Crazy? Suppose he owned the restaurant instead of simply working there? Suppose he owned a chain of restaurants? Would she allow him to speak to her, would a friendship develop? Perhaps they would marry. How many women started out hating a man and ended up marrying him?

Marsha rustled into the seat next to his, and he climbed into the driver's seat (he always opened the door for her now, though he had never done this for any other woman, including his mother), and his old shyness overcame him. She was all blue silk and bare arms and throat and shining blond hair, and yet her loveliness intimidated him less than the suspicion that she was smarter than he was, that she saw through him, might even be using him.

They drove down Main Street.

They passed South Avenue Park, where boys gathered in the

early evening to play baseball. Darkness did not come on till nine.

They were the only customers in the dining room of the hotel; Willie remarked on this to the waiter, who replied that most of their customers dined later, around eight.

The menus were as tall as newspapers; Marsha read hers through very carefully and took out her pencil and corrected the French. Unlike Willie's date of that earlier adventure with Ben, she did not choose the most expensive item on the menu but asked for the watercress soup and a fruit salad, which allowed Willie to do the same. Waiters made him feel powerless, but he had his own way of getting back at them.

"I'd like my soup prepared without salt," said Willie.

"I'm sorry, sir, the soup is already prepared," said the waiter. "What kind of bread would you like?"

He pointed to the back of the menu:

DINING is DEFENSE when you dine on our health-and-morale-building victuals. Help to win by keeping fit! Strengthen nerves and resistance with the vital vitamins and minerals which you are assured in abundance in our finer selections of FRESH meats, vegetables, fruits, seafood, and dairy products, and our HOMEMADE breads:

Rye, French, Italian, pumpernickel, sourdough, white with raisins, whole wheat, whole wheat with raisins.

Willie studied the list and raised his head.

"Do you have Russian pumpernickel?"

"No, sir."

"Oh, let's have French bread," said Marsha.

"One order of French bread for her," said Willie. "Nothing for me," he added, in injured tones.

The waiter bowed and retired, leaving them alone in the cavernous dining room. Really, it's an ugly place, thought Willie. The hanging lamps threw a sallow light on the velvet drapes and the carpet, both a faded wine.

"What do you hear from him?" asked Marsha suddenly.

"Who?"

"Your brother."

"Ben's okay," said Willie, wondering if he really was. No letter had come from him for a long time. "He's stationed on an island in the middle of nowhere." Willie was systematically eating his fruit salad, finishing each fruit in alphabetical order: bananas, grapes, oranges.

"What kind of island?"

"I don't know. Some tropical thing."

"But what's the name of it?" Marsha persisted.

"He isn't allowed to say," answered Willie. "Why do you want to know?"

"It's nice to know things like that," she said.

He wanted to change the subject, so he told her about the Chinese man arrested for harassing the beautiful nurse. Marsha listened politely but without real interest.

"This hotel has seen better days," he said, in case she was thinking the same thing.

"Oh, I love this hotel," said Marsha. "When I was a kid I used to pretend I lived here. I was a princess and this was my palace. I used to ride the bus a lot and the bus was my coach. Everybody who got on worked for me, and I'd see who got on and decide who was my gardener, and who was my cook, and who were my ladies-in-waiting. When the bus stopped here, I'd pretend it was stopping just for me. The tower room was mine."

"Were you ever in the tower room?" asked Willie.

"No. I'd love to stay there. My mother told me the maids leave a chocolate on your pillow at bedtime. That was before the war."

The tower room, the desk clerk informed him, was the honeymoon suite. It had a fourposter bed and canopy and a private bath, and it cost nineteen dollars a night. *The evening is on me.*

"I'll take it for one night," said Willie. "Mr. Jackson will be picking up the bill."

At the mention of Mr. Jackson, the clerk's calm demeanor dissolved.

"One moment, sir."

He vanished, and Willie could hear him dialing and then talking in low tones. Presently he returned.

"Everything's arranged, sir. Here are your keys."

The soup had arrived. Marsha looked at him sternly.

"You were gone a long time."

"Sometimes it takes a long time to get what you want," said Willie.

"What did you want?" she asked.

"You wanted to spend the night in this hotel. You have the tower room for one night. Or for the evening, if you prefer."

Long afterward he wondered if Mr. Jackson had known this would all come to pass when he said "The evening's on me." Nothing Willie had thought or done had prepared him for Marsha— certainly not that girl from business school who asked him to carry her groceries to her apartment and then to stay the night, scared of losing him and too eager to please. For a month he stopped by her place a couple of evenings a week, but she had no finesse. At the slightest suggestion from him, she'd throw off her clothes as if they were on fire. The straps of her bra were dirty and dug into her shoulders, and her flesh bored him. She grew more and more afraid that she was losing him and found reasons to call him at work until he lied to her and said he was seeing someone else.

Now it seemed to Willie that he had mistaken the light of a small fire for the sun itself. When Marsha stepped out of her dress, he touched her breasts through the silky slip that did not look like a slip, and she said, "It's called a teddy," and he wanted to ask how you got out of it but didn't dare, and she said, "To take off a teddy, you have to take off everything," and pushed the thin straps from her shoulders and stepped free, naked before him in the twilight of the pulled blinds, pushing her hair back from her eyes. (It was that gesture of pushing her hair back from her eyes that he would never forget; long after he stopped seeing her, that gesture, made by a stranger, could stop his heart.)

"They have bubble bath in the john," she said and drew the tub full of water and waited for him to join her. "They do it this way in Japan," she called. "Everybody bathes together."

Afterward, whenever he heard or read of Japan's treachery, he thought of Marsha, her smooth back, her shoulder blades shifting under her rosy skin like budding wings, her face as young as a child's and as wise as an old woman's at the moment she pulled him down and was his for the taking.

28

Salvage for Victory

They had given up play reading for the duration and used their Thursday afternoons to pack boxes for soldiers and collect scrap. Mrs. Lieberman called the Salvage Committee and was delighted at the girl's suggestions.

"Scrap is vital," said the girl. "Fifty percent of the steel used in arms is scrap. One-third of the rubber our government needs can be reclaimed from scrap. Waste paper furnishes one-third of the material for new paper. You can have scrap parties. Ask everybody to bring something."

Mrs. Lieberman thanked her and called Mrs. Clackett.

It would be a costume party, they decided, and everyone would come dressed in scrap. There would be a scrap tease; of course you would be wearing your real clothes underneath. When Mrs. Clackett complained to Henrietta Bacco that all she had to cast away was her old girdle, Henrietta told her to come by the Fix-It shop and help herself; her husband had enough odds and ends to outfit a regiment, and her sister-in-law could practically spin straw into gold. Teresa worked for Bundles for America at the Salvage Sewing workroom, and she'd learned to make peek-a-boo blouses from torn curtains, bathing suits from tablecloths, bathrobes from auto upholstery, and leather jackets from pocketbooks. She'd won a prize for turning one torn bedsheet into seventeen pairs of children's underpants.

Henrietta was large, good-natured, and faintly moustached in spite of her best efforts. Teresa was small, sunken, washed-out, and widowed, and she consulted Henrietta about everything, never forgetting that she and her two sons lived on the charity of her brother-in-law, and the sewing she took in added very little to the family income.

The day after Marie Clackett stopped by Fix-It Land to appraise its bounty, she returned with Helen and Nell and Debbie Lieberman. Debbie brought along Kitty LaMont, whose husband owned the oldest funeral parlor in Ann Arbor and went to St. Joseph's Episcopal "for business reasons" instead of Sacred Heart with the rest of the family. Her friends had learned to tolerate the malty smell that clung to her red hair, which she washed in beer to keep the highlights.

They descended on Bacco's Fix-It Land full of plans and possibilities. They tried on water pipes, electric fans, and the finer parts of washing machines. They upset two bottles of Fix-All. They put plungers to their breasts and washtubs on their stomachs, causing Mr. Bacco to announce he'd rather fight the Japs than outfit these women, and only his responsibility to Henrietta and Teresa and the boys prevented him from enlisting. Henrietta almost remarked that the boys were overseas and didn't need much care but thought better of it.

Then Kitty LaMont decided to clean her attic and invited everyone over to choose parts for costumes. Her scrap, she assured them, was very classy stuff, things she hated to give away. She hated to give anything away when business was so bad. People were dying, God knows, but there was no more metal for coffins, and if the army started drafting men with one glass eye, she'd have to run the whole business herself. On the dark star in the front window, she had written her son's name: Charley. She wished on it every night.

When the women arrived, all her scrap was neatly arranged in the front yard. Helen was relieved to see that she had the usual things: fences, curtain rods, pots and pans, overshoes—nothing that might have been used to embalm people. Alberta Schoonmaker had donated a plow and an antique scythe. Kitty and Alberta had both graduated from Sacred Heart Academy, and Alberta had passed up a four-year scholarship at Beaver to marry a farmer. None of the other women knew Alberta, but they praised her generosity. The party broke up early when Nell cut herself on the plow and had to be driven to the hospital for a tetanus shot.

In the evening Helen and Clare pinned together half a dozen girdles to make a skirt, tassled with shaving-cream tubes.

Nell searched the attic for possibilities and found half a dozen rubber sheets that she'd put away after Davy quit wetting the bed and a bust developer she'd sent away for years ago. It had developed nothing, but the motor still worked, and if you took off the hose and the cups, it could surely be used for something.

The next day, two hours before the party, Nell called Debbie and said she couldn't go.

"I can't leave Davy," she said. "Suddenly he's getting all these strange fears. He takes my defense stamps to bed with him."

"They won't hurt him."

"And he says the Japs are coming through the walls with bayonets."

"So move his bed away from the wall."

Nell wept into the hard heart of the telephone and hung up. Ten minutes later Debbie called back, with joyful tidings.

"I'll send Ernestina over," she promised.

"But I don't need a cleaning lady," said Nell.

"She won't clean. I'll tell her to play with Davy."

She was, Debbie went on to say, a find. Honest, pious, and she always saw the silver lining. If you fell out of a tree, she'd tell you why things could be a lot worse. "Now if it was a fig tree, you'd never get well." If you broke your right arm, she'd say, "Praise the Lord, you'll get money. Now if it was your left arm, you'd get nothing but a heap of bad luck."

Furthermore, she had a son named Stilts who used to play baseball with Ben Harkissian.

The first time Davy saw Ernestina, she was boiling water for tea and talking to Aunt Helen's teakettle. She was polite and persuasive. She told it the advantages of boiling; she told it about the other pots waiting to take its place. She put her hands on her hips and said,

"Pot, what is your determination in this matter?" and the pot boiled.

Then she poured the water into Aunt Helen's flowered china teapot and added a tiny cheesecloth bag that did not smell like Lipton's and carried the tea out to the screened-in porch.

She sat down in the rocker and opened her purse, which was chock-full of khaki yarn. She was small, like his mother, but older, and her skin had the color of chestnuts fresh from the burr with the shine still on them, and her faded blue dress smelled clean and friendly as newly shelled peas. Davy drew his little stool near her chair and admired her. She did not appear to notice him, and he was much surprised when she said, "Loose tooth?"

He nodded—how did she know? He could wiggle that tooth without opening his mouth just by pushing his tongue against it.

"If you keep your tongue out of the hole, you'll get a gold tooth."

The blue jays screamed in the arborvitae; Cinnamon Monkey-shines lolled in the myrtle bed below, waiting for one false move. Davy breathed deeply the strong, sweet smell of the tea. Aunt Helen never let him sit near the teapot for fear he would knock it over and scald himself; and because she had forbidden him to touch it, he longed for nothing so much as a taste of tea from that pot. He gathered his courage and blurted out, "Can I have some tea?"

"Hoo! Not this tea," replied Ernestina. (Oh, would she let him try a different tea?) "This here is hog's hoof tea for my bad leg. You could bring me a cup. I don't know where your aunt keeps her cups."

Eager to please, he brought her a flowered cup from the cabinet that held Helen's best china. Ernestina thanked him gravely, as if he were a grown-up, and poured herself a cup and sipped it. Then she unlaced her shoes—black, with thick heels—and eased her feet out of them and wiggled her toes in their coarse black stockings. And what was that shining in her left shoe? A white stone?

"You have a stone in your shoe," said Davy, pointing it out to her, for she seemed not to notice.

Ernestina nodded. "The root doctor give me that when my leg got conjured. You can hold it if you want."

He picked up the stone and rubbed it between his fingers and thought he had never felt anything so old and gentle. And the rude doctor had put it into her shoe. That was a queer thing for a doctor to do.

"Can I keep it?"

"Nope. It come from the root doctor. My leg swole right up, and she dug under the doorstep and sure 'nough there was a conjure bag. Bones and hair and graveyard dirt."

Davy stole a glance at her afflicted leg, and she saw him; he could hide nothing from her.

"It do look fine, don't it?" she said. "The root doctor is a powerful healer."

Clackety clack, sang her needles, gathering the khaki yarn, arranging it to suit them. She held up for his inspection the front of a sweater for her oldest son. She had four sons in the army and one daughter away at college studying to be a teacher. Ernestina sent the money to keep her there, and it took a lot of money, she told him —it took practically all she earned. Her husband hadn't worked for a year; his liver was acting up. Before he got sick he wanted to join the Air Corps and be a pilot, but the Air Corps had no use for him, so he'd built a little plane of his own out of junk: broken radiators and old tires and rusty bedsprings, good scrap that the government wanted and would pay him for. He didn't tell anyone about the plane except a few kids in the neighborhood who came for rides. He had real pilot goggles for them to wear, just like his.

"Where do they go?" asked Davy.

"The Lord knows," said Ernestina. "The plane got no motor. But Henry keep a log book inside, with all the places."

Except for the lack of a motor, the plane was very well equipped, she assured him. She herself had never been inside to see where it went or how it got there because she was deathly afraid of flying. But she had seen the log and the names of the places. And she had seen the snapshots he took of the kids in those places. The backgrounds were always blurred, or common—a wall, a field— which convinced her that travel did nothing to improve your mind and folks might just as well stay home. Now *her* pictures were sharp;

you could always tell what you were looking at. Did he want to see some of her pictures?

Davy was delighted.

She showed him four pictures of her sons in uniform and then a picture of her husband, radiant and cocky in goggles and pilot's cap, leaning out of a cockpit, and a creased snapshot of a young man posing under a palm tree. The young man was her brother who had died in Bataan and come back a week later and asked his girl friend for a pack of Lucky Strikes he'd left in a bureau drawer.

"He came back when he was dead?" exclaimed Davy.

"His ghost come back."

"Did you ever see a ghost?"

"Nope. But I hear 'em when the trees murmur. They 'round all the time, crowds of 'em, the bad with the bad, the good with the good. They don't mix theirselves up like living folks. And the good ones is always flying. If you feel the air from their bodies, you get well. Anything that bothers you won't bother you no more."

But though she had not seen spirits herself, she knew lots of folks who had. The good spirits looked like children, or birds. But they could be any shape they wanted to. Why, she knew the brother of a man whose wife took a drink from the spring at night and drank up the springkeeper. It took the shape of a snake, and that snake used to pop its head out of her mouth and whistle.

She set down her cup, and Davy crawled into her lap. He could hardly wait to tell Clare about the ghosts and the springkeeper.

"Spirits is very fond of whistling," she remarked. "They do it to get your notice. If you ask 'em what in the Lord's name they want, they go away."

"If I ask one of the good spirits to bring me some springy shoes, will it bring them?"

And he showed her the picture in the magazine and told her about the birthday cake and the trick candle and the lost wish.

"Maybe," said Ernestina. "Maybe not."

A week later, when Aunt Helen and his mom were at the movies and Ernestina came over "to be in the house," as his mother put it, she woke him up and carried him to the window. The tops of the pear trees were blossoming hills of light.

"Full moon," said Ernestina. "You can wish on it. Show it what you want."

He opened the magazine to the page, and the moonlight fell on the springy shoes, a bargain at two dollars and ninety-nine cents. Directly below them he heard a familiar thud: Clare had let her book slide to the floor and fallen asleep with the lamp on.

"Is the moon watching us?" he asked. He loved the moon's dirty face.

Not the moon, Ernestina told him. The moon was just a lamp. But the Moon Regulator, who lit the moon every night—he would see the page. And he would send Davy those springy shoes. Not tomorrow, or the next day, perhaps. But he would send them. You never could tell which day he would choose.

She did not put Davy back to bed right away but let him stay up to see the stars. With the shortages, he was surprised to see so many.

"Hoo! They's just as many as they was 'fore the war," said Ernestina.

"Can they see us?"

"I 'spect they can. You never know who's watching."

From the solemnity of her voice, he knew these were grave matters, and he must not speak of them to anyone. Not even Grandpa. Not even Clare. And because no one had ever entrusted him with a secret before, he greatly looked forward to Ernestina's coming, and every morning he asked, "Is Ernestina coming today?" and mostly Aunt Helen would say no, but sometimes she would say yes, and then Ernestina would sip her tea (which she drank with ice in the hot weather) on the back porch, and he would sit in her lap, content to watch her hands twinkle the yarn off the needles. He had noticed that she never talked about herself to anyone but him. If Clare or Helen or Nell came into the room, the real Ernestina seemed to disappear, leaving behind a polite shell of herself. Only to him would she tell her troubles, and he listened politely, waiting for the squawk of blue jays, when he could turn the talk to his own liking.

"Tell about the jays taking sand to the devil."

"What's today?"

"Wednesday."

"They ain't doing it."

"Tell it anyway, please."

"Why you want to hear the same story over and over?"

"Tell about the jays."

"Well—they take a grain of sand a day till all the sand from the top of the earth is in Hell. They gonna ransom the folks down there."

The jays screeched.

"Tell about Hell," whispered Davy.

"Never been there."

"Tell about the coffins, then."

"Don't know why you want to hear the same story over and over."

"Tell."

"Well, there's Main Hell and there's West Hell. Bad folks' souls turn to rubber coffins and bounce through reg'lar Hell to West Hell. That's the hottest part."

She was fanning herself with a church program she'd found in her purse.

"I wish I were freezing, don't you, Ernestina?"

Ernestina shook her head no.

"I b'lieve I'd rather be too hot than too cold. I can't stand the cold."

And Davy, wanting to please her, said, "I can't stand it either," though just now he thought he would like it very much.

Mostly she talked about hot weather and cold weather, and how in the summer the iceman overcharged her, and how in the winter the furnace broke and once all her clothes froze solid in the washtub and Henry said, "I'll get 'em out," and he chopped them free with the ax.

"Chopped all my clothes to pieces," she said.

Davy never knew why, one night, after grieving over her ordinary disasters, she said, "The worst cold I ever heard of was Cold

Friday. A man got froze at the gate of his house with his jug of whiskey at his lips."

Davy shivered.

"There was a funeral, and the heat departed out of the church, and the preacher and all the families froze solid. And the preacher's dog froze on the doorstep. They stayed that way all Friday. The root doctor was a little bit of a girl, and she froze right along with the rest of 'em. But the Lord saw fit to thaw her out. And soon everybody callin' her Cold Friday, on account she's the only one made it through."

Except for the regular creak of the rocker, the air held perfectly still, as if it were listening.

"Lord, Lord, she be a powerful woman!" said Ernestina. "Five times she died, five times she come back. She froze and come back, she drowned and come back, her house burnt up and she fell in the fire and come back, she got the sleepy sickness and was buried alive and come back, she choked on a bone and come back."

"I hear an owl," whispered Davy.

"Too early for owls," said Ernestina.

"I hear one."

"The owl is old-time folks. She won't hurt you. Oh, she was born the year the stars fell."

And he did not know if "she" meant the owl or Cold Friday.

It was at night, when the stars looked huge, much closer than they looked at home, that Hal missed Helen and Clare the most. He wanted to show them the stars. They sparkled on the backs of the mountains that ringed the Lodge with the shapes of camels and laden beasts; he found himself lingering outside, though the Lodge had a very pleasant living room where he could sit around the fire with Stuart and Bob and listen to stories about what it was like on the mesa before the government came. Bob had camped around here as a boy. He'd lived in this very building when the lodge was a ranch school for boys; he'd seen the Indian ruins, which were still unexplored. You could find arrowheads and potsherds; they were so easy to find that the boys didn't set much store by them. There was an

Indian burial ground right by the lodge—would Hal like to see it? And Hal realized that he already had seen it and wondered why, on the manicured lawn of the lodge, this tiny square of land was fenced in and the grass allowed to grow rank and wild. No stones, no markers, nothing to tell you anybody was buried there.

Early in the morning he'd spied a horned toad sunning itself on the front steps like a little rococo dragon. And Bob told him the horned toads lived in the canyon. Bears lived there also and lumbered out at night to forage for garbage.

In the afternoon, he rode to Santa Fe with Stuart, who hired the station wagon that made the trip only on request; there was no other transportation if you didn't have your own car. The Indian boy who drove it never exchanged a word with the passengers, and in his presence the passengers did not talk much to each other. When he took the curves on the narrow mountain road at fifty miles an hour, they suffered in silence. Nobody asked him to slow down.

The driver of the station wagon gave you two hours to do your business, and Hal, who had no business in Santa Fe, strolled under the colonnade of the Governor's Palace and looked at the jewelry the Indians laid out on black cloths on the pavement. Necklaces, belts, rings, all turquoise and silver and so heavy—wouldn't it weigh you down?

He chose a small silver bracelet inlaid with turquoise for Helen and a silver ring for Clare which showed the rainbow god in garnet and turquoise and jet. He would send it home for her if he couldn't get there himself. But he would make every effort to go home, before the work here got under way. What a mysterious stranger I must be, he thought. I can't tell them where I live or what I do.

On the trip back to the lodge, the driver stopped only at the guardhouse on the road into town and stayed only long enough for the guard to check their passes. The guard glanced down at their photographs, glanced up at their faces, and waved them on.

29

Signs and Wonders

Ben didn't call first. He just walked through the door on Saturday afternoon and nearly startled Wanda out of her wits. She'd expected him on Friday and was sure his leave had been canceled. Now when she saw him in the hall—older, thinner, exhausted—she ran up to him and hugged him and burst into tears.

"Did you eat yet? I made some wonderful junket."

"What time is it?" he asked. He tried to hide his anxiety. Ever since he'd left the Pacific, he had heard, behind all other sounds, the ripple of seconds passing, like the clocks in Lieberman's jewelry store, which always reminded him of a swiftly flowing stream. Cooper, packing the raft, looking for lost animals, gluing them back into his glass galaxy—Cooper must have heard it passing for months. The sea rising, rushing over the island—why, it was only a matter of time.

"It's three o'clock. Are you hungry? We can eat early."

"No, thanks, I ate on the train," he lied. "Where's Willie?"

"He went out. He didn't say where. Tell me about the trip, tell me about everything!" she begged and realized that of course he couldn't tell her, not right away, that it would have to come out piece by piece, and she added, "Later. We can talk about the trip later. Let me *look* at you!"

He walked restlessly around the house, touching things, picking them up and putting them down. Ashtrays. The *Reader's Digest*.

THINGS INVISIBLE TO SEE

The framed photograph he'd sent her of himself in uniform. Queer to see it again here, like a gift coming back to the giver.

"You were in the *Free Press*," she said, "and the *News*. I saved the papers for you."

"Thanks, Ma. I'll read them later. I really am glad you saved them." He hoped this sounded convincing. But Wanda was not fooled.

"You don't have to talk to me right now if you've got things to do."

"Oh, Ma."

"I know you'll want to phone your friends. They've been trying to reach you."

Ben froze. "What friends?"

"The boys you used to play ball with. They're all home on furlough too."

She left him alone in the kitchen, and he knew he should call her back and tell her that none of his friends mattered, it was she that he had missed all along. Instead, he picked up the receiver and dialed Clare's number. Ten rings. Nobody answered. What right have I to expect her to be there always? he asked himself. He hung up and dialed the Liebermans. On the third ring, Sol picked it up.

"Hello?"

A hubbub of voices rose and fell in the background.

"It's me—Ben."

"My God! I can't believe it!"

"Speak up, I can't hear you," shouted Ben.

"My folks are having a party. Let's go to the park and talk. I'll take my dad's car and pick you up in ten minutes. All the guys are home."

His voice faded away; Ben pressed the receiver to his ear.

"Tom and Louis and Tony came in on Friday," Sol ran on, "and Henry and Charley and George got in last night. And Stilts phoned this morning."

"They all got furloughs? Why?"

"Death in the family. I'll be right over. I'll bring the contract."

"What contract?"

"The one you sent. It came in the mail last week. I'll bring it."

So it was true. That far-off conversation with Death had set these strange events in motion. Knowledge sank its invisible weight into his heart.

Outside the air was heavy with honeysuckle. Standing on the curb, Ben remembered how he and Willie used to suck honey out of the blossoms on the way home from school. That orange fragrance on their fingers afterward. Gone now, those secret rituals that made a truce between them. The well of contentment he'd carried around for years was poisoned now; Cooper rotted at the bottom, tainting everything.

When Sol drew up and honked, Ben, close to tears, could not utter a word. Sol babbled on to fill the silence.

"When they all got furloughs, I thought it was kind of strange. I know the army gives furloughs for a death in the family, but I didn't think you got one when your parakeet died."

"Henry got a furlough for that?" exclaimed Ben, astonished. Sol nodded.

"They all got one for a death in the family. The Baccos' cat died of old age. George's turtle got stuck behind the radiator. Stilts's dog got hit by a car. The only thing anybody could think of that died in Charley's family was the grass. Well, I thought that was pretty odd. But when they all started telling me the same dream, I got scared. Because I'd had the same one. We all had this dream about a telegram."

Ben found himself trembling.

"It was a singing telegram," Sol went on. And to the tune of "Row, Row, Row Your Boat," he sang, in an uncertain tenor:

> "Tom and Charley and Henry and Ben
> and Clackett and Stilts and Sol
> and Louis and Tony, together again,
> shall gather with glove and ball.
>
> "On the twenty-seventh of June
> at four o'clock they shall see

the contract, sink or swim, between
Harkissian and me.

"He sang it to each of us five times."

"Who sang it?" asked Ben.

"He looked familiar, but I couldn't place him. He wore a very
fancy three-piece suit and a winged cap. And he carried a caduceus."

"A what?"

"A staff twisted with snakes. You know—the symbol of doctors."

"Let me see the contract," said Ben.

"It's rolled up in the back seat. Real parchment, isn't it? You
won't mind if I stop to pick up a couple more people, will you?"

"Who?" Ben asked.

"Tony. He's practicing with a friend."

Bent over the contract, Ben had not noticed the route, and now
he lifted his head like a man digging a hole who stands up too fast
and for an instant knows nothing but the turning of the earth. Under
the gnarled trees, in tall grass, a girl in a white sun dress was sitting
in an armchair. She leaned forward and lobbed a ball to Tony, who
ran back under the branches, caught it, and lobbed it back. The girl's
hand, in its huge glove, shot out and plucked it from the air, and Ben
gave a shout.

"Clare!"

In Paradise, the Lord of the Universe tosses a gold ball which breaks
into a green ball which breaks into a black ball, and on the Burma
Road, a child carried on his mother's back quietly gives up the ghost
(his mother will not discover this till morning), and Ben pitches a
high fastball to Charley, who hits a line drive down center field and
lopes to second.

The players have not said much to each other since they stepped
into their old places, Tom at first and Henry at second, Sol on third
and Louis at shortstop, Tony shading his eyes in right field, George
chewing a licorice stick in left field, and Stilts behind the plate,
sweating in the awful armor of the catcher.

Charley takes center field, and Louis steps into the batter's box. He loses his sneaker halfway to first and flies out. What does it matter? They are not playing to win. Today they are playing to be healed, to let the eyes and mouths of the dead fall away from them, to step back into the eternal present of summer the way they lived as kids, playing till darkness came; to find the timeless space that turns ordinary men into heroes, where the only real world is the game itself, as old and reliable as the stars.

At home Ben wanted to get away, to be with Clare, but Wanda had set the kitchen table for three and spent all her blue ration tokens on a pot roast. She'd made brown gravy and biscuits and strawberry junket; how could he rush off? Had she not made all these delicacies for him? Willie, who cared for none of them, was eating stoically, the way he had eaten fried chicken in the Y camp when they were kids, moving systematically through each item in turn and stacking his dishes in a neat pile when he'd finished. Only when he was truing the edges of his dishes did Ben say, "We've got a game coming up, Willie. We might need you to sub."

"I haven't played baseball since ninth grade," said Willie.

"Come on, Willie, you're not that bad. We need you. It's an exhibition game."

"Against who?"

"An out-of-town team. The Dead Knights."

He could not go on, though both his mother and Willie were waiting for details. Death, you stingy bastard, you might have sent the subs a dream, too. Let Sol tell them. It'll have to be done just right. If they don't believe us, they'll blow the whole game.

After dinner Ben went to his room to put on a clean shirt and was aware of Willie hovering around the doorway.

"I don't know if Mother told you," he said. "Marsha and I are seeing a lot of each other."

"That's all right," said Ben.

"I didn't want any surprises or hard feelings."

"No, that's all right. I'm happy with Clare."

"I thought maybe you'd called Marsha about me."

"Why would I call Marsha? We're through."

What was it, then? Willie wondered. She had been so available to him, and now she was so evasive, so secretive. When he called her, her mother answered and said, "I'll give her the message, she'll call you back," which she never did, and when he finally reached her, Marsha herself found excuses for not seeing him, finally blurting out, "I don't need to give you reasons for the way I live my life."

He'd asked her right out, "Is it Ben?" There'd been a story about Ben in the newspapers, the hero coming home. But Marsha had said no. How did Ben find that easy happiness? How did he live his life that he could say so quickly, "I'm happy with Clare"? How could he set such store by this crippled girl?

"Are you using the car?" asked Ben.

"Yes," lied Willie. "I have a date with Marsha."

"Okay. I'll take the bike."

His bicycle felt like a stranger to him; Willie had lowered the seat for his own use. The headlight, too, was out. The air was hot and still, the streets nearly empty. He could be happy here again; Cooper would no longer nudge at the edges of his sleep. Danger was far away.

As he turned down Orchard Drive, the lights in Clare's house greeted him, and had he not been so eager to see her, he would have lingered under the trees and watched life passing in the windows, like a traveler, alone and in love with the familiar graces of strangers.

He walked his bike to the front door, threw it into the honeysuckle bush (the kickstand was gone), and knocked. After a long time the porch light flooded on, and Helen pushed open the screen door.

"Lord, it's Ben! And you're all out of breath!"

"Is Clare—?"

"She's on the back porch," said Helen. He heard her running through the house like a crier. "Ben's here! Ben's here!"

Clare was sitting with Davy on the glider, and she reached out her arms and Ben knelt and gathered them both into a hug.

"Da-*vy*," called Nell from indoors.

"No!" screamed Davy.

"Bedtime," said Helen, peeking out at them.

"Let him stay up a few minutes more," pleaded Clare, who remembered the loneliness of her own banishment as a child when the grown-ups wanted to talk.

"I want Ben to tuck me in," said Davy, sliding his hand into Ben's.

"Davy," said Helen, "Ben came to see Clare."

"It's no trouble," said Ben.

Davy skipped up the stairs ahead of him, past the wedding photos of Vicky and Nell and the smaller, faded photographs of ancestors, of whom no one remembered anything except that they were part of the family.

Overhead a cracked voice sang,

> "When we've been there ten thousand years,
> Bright shining as the sun,
> We've no less days to sing God's praise
> Than when we first begun."

"First we say good-night to Grandpa," said Davy.

The light on the third-floor landing laid a golden path to Grandpa's quarters in the attic. The floor lamp with the purple shade threw its glow over his bed, his books, and his chair, where he sat leafing through his hymnal. Like a moth he lived in a circle of light. The outer darkness bristled with the broken, the discarded, the out-of-season. Electric fans, cartons of outgrown clothes, boxes of puzzles marked "pieces missing."

"Good-night, Grandpa."

Grandpa looked up.

"Who's with you?"

"I'm Ben."

"Clare's Ben?" asked Grandpa.

"My Ben," shouted Davy. "He's *my* Ben!"

"On what evidence was Benjamin accused of theft by his brother Joseph?" asked Grandpa.

"Joseph hid a goblet in his sack and sent soldiers to search for it," said Davy.

"Very good," said Grandpa. "You may help yourself to a penny from my jar in the morning."

"Good-night, Grandpa," Davy said again and raced to his mother's room on the opposite side of the landing and climbed into bed.

"Aren't you going to put on your pajamas?" asked Ben.

"Uh-uh. I always sleep in my bathing suit."

Ben tucked the covers around him, averting his eyes from the bra and slip thrown over the back of Nell's chair. His hand met something hard.

"You don't want these in bed with you," he said, pulling a half-filled book of defense stamps from under the covers.

"I do so," said Davy. "Will you tuck me in tomorrow night too?"

"Sure," said Ben.

He snapped off the light and hurried downstairs, afraid that Davy might call after him. He did not call. Grandpa stopped singing. Helen and Nell had disappeared. The house felt deserted save for Clare and himself. He sat down next to her and put his arm around her shoulder.

"Where is everybody?" he asked.

"In the basement," said Clare. "They think we want to be alone."

"We do, but I don't want to keep your mother and your aunt shut up in the basement."

"They'll come up if we close the porch door."

He rose and shut the door that joined the porch to the dining room.

"Ben, thanks for taking Davy upstairs. He doesn't remember his father very well, and he's always looking for a new one."

"He had a book of defense stamps in bed with him," said Ben.

"He's scared of the dark. But he's a lot less scared than he used to be, now that Grandpa's back."

Ben sat down beside her and pulled her toward him, but her

body stiffened against his. Time. It would take time. He slid his arm around her waist, and she leaned her head against him. Close to them but outside the screen, a cricket chirped, regular as a heartbeat. Though it was still enough to hear time passing, now Ben did not notice the seconds ticking away like water. Cooper and his death were a thousand miles away. He can't touch us, thought Ben. He's powerless. He's dead.

"When you came as a bird," said Ben, "why didn't Cooper see you?"

"He did see me. He just didn't recognize me."

"The next time your Ancestress comes, ask her if she'll throw the dice my way," said Ben. "Make me lucky."

"She won't do it," said Clare. "She can't give you anything you don't already have."

"Would she turn me into a gorilla?"

"You don't turn into a gorilla. You go into the body of the gorilla."

"Could I go into the body of a gorilla?" asked Ben.

"Maybe. But it's better to start with something small. I started by going into the body of a cat."

"I don't want to go into the body of a cat," said Ben.

"A bird's, then."

"No."

"Whose?"

"Yours."

30

Death He Is a Little Man

If the Tigers had not defeated the Yankees the day before, if a twenty-three-year-old rookie right-hander named Virgil Trucks had not pitched eight innings of shut-out ball in Briggs Stadium, if the Dodgers and the Cardinals had not ended up in a free-for-all in the sixth inning after Ducky Medwick slid into second and spiked Marty Marion and if shortstop Creepy Crespi had not come between them, punching with both fists, more people might have noticed another story that appeared in the *Ann Arbor News:* the story of a local team, the South Avenue Rovers, whose members, through good luck and happy coincidence, had received furloughs and who had agreed to play an exhibition game with an unknown team from out of state, the Dead Knights. Proceeds to be given to the Red Cross.

Along with the story appeared a photograph of the contract. Many who read it found it disquieting. A new lease on life—what kind of trophy was that? And who was this challenger who called himself Death?

What one heart finds hard to believe, a hundred find easy.

It started with the sons, gathering every morning to work out, and it spread to the fathers, who had not played this hard since their boys were youngsters but who had never forgotten how. In slacks and undershirts they showed up on the field with their bats and gloves. Mr. Clackett was the first convert. He'd coached a church league when George was a kid, and he'd pitched softball for a couple of years till he fell on his knee and his body gave up running. But not hitting. And Mr. Clackett knew the game as well as if he'd invented it. When Ben asked him to coach the South Avenue Rovers, he accepted with pleasure. He made plans for a team picnic in Island Park on the eve of the game. He would hire a bus draped in bunting to carry them there.

"Make it the eve of the eve of the game," said Mr. Lieberman. "I want that we should enjoy ourselves."

When Mr. Clackett and Mr. Bacco and Mr. Lieberman closed their shops every afternoon to play ball, their customers took notice. By late afternoon there was a crowd, a gathering of the faithful. The bleachers filled up by four o'clock, and latecomers brought blankets and sat on the grass. The hot-dog truck, which usually appeared for evening games, opened at nine in the morning and stayed around till dark.

And word spread, from old to young, from husband to wife, from mother to daughter, from professor to car mechanic, from bank teller to tailor, that never had any team played for higher stakes.

This was the reason why Father Legg, who for five days straight never missed a practice and who had his own regular spot in the bleachers the way some of his parishioners had their own pews, took Ben aside one morning during warm-up and said, "Mr. Clackett is a fine coach but not, I think, the man for the job."

"Who else is there?" asked Ben.

Father Legg held up a warning finger, as if Ben had just said something dangerous.

"You believe that if you lose the game, you and your friends will die. Of course that's nonsense. But I have seen nonsense more powerful than sense. I have watched patients die because their doctors told them they would die. When I was a missionary in the Congo, I saw people die because an enemy had laid a curse on them—a promise that death would come to them on such and such a day. And if they believed that death would come to them on that day, they died, though they were in the best of health."

"What do you want me to do?"

"Let me be your coach. Clackett is a fine man for a game between the South Avenue Rovers and the Broadway Rangers. But

I do not believe he is the man for a game between life and death."

Ben was silent.

"I also know a lot about baseball," added Father Legg. "Your brother may have told you."

"No, he didn't tell me," said Ben. "I don't know what Mr. Clackett can do if he's not coaching. He's got a bad knee."

"Let me talk to him," said Father Legg.

The next day Father Legg bustled into the job. He scolded, he praised, he made rules. He allowed Tom to annoint his glove with Fix-All, which filled the air around him with a smell like rancid meat. He forgave an injured knee but not an injured dignity, and he knew the difference between Mr. Clackett's slow, painful gait and Mr. LaMont's slow, portly one. For Mr. LaMont he borrowed a nippy terrier and released her at the crack of the undertaker's bat. But with Mr. Schoonmaker, who was nearly as slow as Mr. Clackett, Father Legg was all patience, as if he knew without being told that Mr. Schoonmaker had never owned a new bat or ball in his life but always one handed down through four brothers. He could never lift the new bat he'd bought for Henry without pausing to admire it, to run his fingers over the satiny wood and to wonder: what kind of wood do they use that it hits so nice? And the glove—what kind of hide is this, and how is it tanned that it comes out so soft, fitting so good? And the ball—what do they stuff it with that makes it so strong that nothing breaks or loses its shape? Even in left field, he was shy at finding himself so near Mr. Lieberman, the jeweler, and Mr. LaMont, the undertaker with the pretty wife. Mr. Lieberman was so polite, so slim, so quick! Father Legg liked to kid him about being at home on any diamond.

The only player not at home in Father Legg's fold was Willie.

"Willie, don't try to kill the ball," Father Legg urged him as he took his stance at home plate. "Just meet it."

Willie stood straight as a pole, gripping the bat like a weapon, and Ben pitched a fast one right over home plate.

"Strike one," tolled Father Legg. "A bit late there, my boy."

Ben threw a curve and Willie lunged for it.

"Thou shalt not lunge," Father Legg cautioned him. "And choke up on the bat. Strike two."

Willie looked up for the next pitch and his glance caught a bright figure settling herself into the bleachers: purple shorts, pink halter, huge sunglasses. His heart raced. He longed to do something spectacular, something that would astonish them all. The ball sped from Ben's hand, and Willie lashed out with the bat. To his astonishment he heard a crack, as of a tree splitting, and Father Legg shouting at him, "Run! Run!"

He flew down to first, and at the burst of cheers he grinned up at Marsha. She was pawing through her huge purse. She had seen nothing.

"Ben, you bat now," said Father Legg. "George, you take the mound."

George went into his stretch. A high fastball.

"Let's see your *fast*ball, Clackett!" shouted Ben. "I could count the stitches on that one."

Willie turned to look once more at Marsha. She had taken off her sunglasses and was watching the game through binoculars. No, not the game. She was watching Ben, and Willie knew she had always been watching Ben, waiting for him, and in her sly way, faithful.

That night, eating supper with his mother, Willie rearranged the universe in his head.

"I don't ask for much," said Wanda, "but wouldn't you think he'd want to eat supper with his own mother?"

"Terrible, just terrible," said Willie. On the playing field of his mind, the South Avenue Rovers were losing to the Dead Knights.

"He could see Clare after supper," said Wanda. "There'd be plenty of time after supper. He doesn't listen to me."

"He doesn't listen to me, either." said Willie. The game was over. The Rovers were gone, erased, presumed dead. Father Legg and Willie alone were spared.

"Still, I wish you'd talk to him," said Wanda.

She noticed that Willie's attention was wandering, and she got up and turned on the radio that she kept in the kitchen for company while she scrubbed the floor. Its green eye flashed. They waited for it to warm up.

"Let's listen to the news," she said.

Lowell Thomas's urgent voice made them both sit up straighter.

"A smashing blow delivered yesterday by waves of German tanks, heavily supported from the air, crushed the defenses of Tobruk in Libya. The War Office tonight confirmed the loss of the town, already claimed by the enemy, who said twenty-five thousand prisoners, including several generals, had been captured."

"Pass the bread," said Willie.

"A bus carrying fifty-two children to a summer camp in Keene, New Hampshire, plunged into a ravine yesterday. All the passengers were injured, none critically. The driver of the bus claimed that the steering wheel broke off as he made a sharp turn. No charges have been filed against him."

"Fifty-two children!" exclaimed Wanda.

Willie saw in his mind another bus, draped in bunting, carrying the South Avenue Rovers to their team picnic at Island Park.

He saw the front left tire blow as it reached the bridge.

He saw the bus skid.

He saw the steering wheel break off in the driver's hands.

He saw all the passengers injured, unable to play.

He saw himself saved. He and Father Legg would have arrived earlier. And it would look like an accident—perhaps an oil slick? He could work out the details. He had time.

Although Ben came to visit every night, although he said he looked forward to seeing Davy and called him his special pal, Davy always remembered to ask him: "Will you tuck me in tonight?"

And Aunt Helen said, "Davy, he came to see Clare."

And Ben said, "Davy's my special pal. I always tuck him in, Mrs. Bishop."

Nevertheless, in the crumb of silence between question and consent, Davy feared that this one time Ben might say, "Not tonight,

Davy. I can't tuck you in tonight," so that when he heard the promise spoken, "I always tuck him in, Mrs. Bishop," he felt as happy as on the first night he'd taken Ben's hand and led him up to the third floor.

They said good-night to Grandpa, who expected it, and Davy climbed into bed and checked under his pillow for his defense stamps and thought of little ways to keep Ben sitting on the edge of his bed just a few minutes longer.

"Do you know any scary stories?" he asked.

"No," said Ben, smiling.

"Do you know any gory songs? Do you know 'The worms crawl in, the worms crawl out, the worms play pinochle on your snout'?"

"Everybody knows that song."

"Do you know 'Be kind to your web-footed friends'?"

"Oh, sure," said Ben. "I was kicking the slats out of my cradle at that one."

Those were funny songs, not scary songs. Only one song had the power to terrify Davy, and he did not sing it often, though he did not know if it was the tune, which was slow and wandering, or the words, which were simple and not gory or terrible, nothing that would make his mother say, "For God's sake, quit singing that terrible thing!" Sometimes he thought it was the way Ernestina sang it to him, crooning it, never looking at him when she sang but way out in the trees where the owl lived. But even when he sang the song to himself, he shivered, just as if she were singing it.

Ben stood up; in spite of all Davy's enticements, he was leaving.

"I know a really scary song," said Davy. "I can sing it for you."

"Tomorrow night," said Ben. "Save it for tomorrow night."

But Davy, who never took it as certain fact that there would be a tomorrow night, sang after him:

> "Death he is a little man
> And he go from door to door."

Ben, who was on the stairs, turned back.

"Where'd you learn that one?"

"Ernestina," answered Davy.

"Stilts's mother taught you that song?"

Davy nodded. He saw Ben turning to go again.

"She got it from the rude doctor on Catherine Street."

"What doctor?"

"Dr. Cold Friday."

It was his last secret, and he gave it up gladly to keep Ben there.

"*Who?*" Ben exclaimed. "Who did you say?"

"Cold Friday. Five times she died. Five times she come back—"

Ben did not wait to hear more; he was running down the stairs, whooping and shouting.

31

Where Your Treasure Is

When you cross Main Street into the west part of town, the streets that carry you over change their names: Liberty Street turns, after many adventures, into Goose Turd Lane. The roots of the elms run deeper than the roots of the people who live there and who will move on, looking for work in bigger cities. The houses are mostly duplexes, set close together, though here and there you see a small frame house with a hand pump in the yard. If you entered that house, you would find a wooden sink and a smaller pump in the kitchen, and you would admire how neatly some residents have tacked old sugar bags and newspapers on the bedroom walls for insulation.

If you walk along Catherine Street, just off Main, you will notice that on the left side live the black people and on the right side lives everybody else. On your left you will pass the barbershop, the Paradise Bar & Grill, and the harness shop; also the Oasis and the Promised Land. A sign in the harness shop says Furniture Cheap. The only suggestion of furniture for sale is a small table on which someone has arranged a family of old bottles. Those who know the owner of these bottles say that she has hidden something of herself in every building on this block—a bit of hair, a nest of nail parings —and this gives her power over the people who live there. It also gives them protection from devils, perturbed spirits, and the evil eye.

If you are a white man, it is unlikely you will ever meet this woman who lives over the harness shop and is known to everyone who cares to know such things as the root doctor, as if her name were too powerful to be pronounced. Her birthday and her given name, which she has never given out, were written in a family Bible and burnt up in a fire. So she says. She might be fifty or seventy, depending on the time of day, the light, and the weather. Sometimes she can be seen in the upper window over the harness shop, her conch shell applied to her ear; from this she receives messages, though in what language nobody knows. Probably Gullah, say the families who have come from one of the islands off South Carolina and speak that dialect. Trinidad, says the barber, whose father was born there and who hears his father's voice in her most casual greeting. Others claim she has a mynah bird's ear for picking up the accent of whomever she's healed, a chameleon's instinct for making a local color universal. She is a deep, brilliant black, as if newly arrived from the dark continent.

Several years ago she put her only competitor out of business. A conjure man from Georgia moved into the room over the barbershop and put his sign in the window there:

DOCTOR BUZZARD

MEDICINE—WATERS

INSPECTOR OF FISHING LICENSES FOR THE STATE OF MICHIGAN

He had skin the color of buckwheat honey and half a dozen testimonials from grateful patients which he hung on the barbershop walls. Shortly thereafter, the table of bottles vanished and a sign, of a size equal to his, appeared in the window of the harness shop:

COLD FRIDAY

MEDICINE—WATERS

INSPECTOR OF FISHING LICENSES FOR THE STATE OF ETERNITY

Below the printing was a little sketch of Elijah flying over the mountains of Detroit, an error to which Doctor Buzzard drew her attention.

"I never saw no mountains in Detroit," said Doctor Buzzard.

"You just ain't looked," snapped Cold Friday.

His medicine failed, his waters cured nothing, and Doctor Buzzard departed. What were his testimonials next to her power? She had stood in the very heart of healing. She had seen God sitting in his armchair, in full armor with a breastplate of feathers from all the birds that ever were and ever shall be, and He had handed her a pass, signed with her name, good for traveling between the lands of the living and the dead. She had a duster made of the feathers of the skypoke, which flies to the devil and back, and an ostrich egg laid on Good Friday over a hundred years ago, and the yoke of that egg was a pearl, which anyone could see when she candled it. The sight of that pearl had cured many a case of pinkeye on Catherine Street.

Further, she had a little whip made from the bristles of a hog named Bathsheba that ran five hundred miles from Virginia to Georgia with the devil in her. And she had personally met the Whooping Slave of North Carolina, who was buried with his master's treasure to guard it, and he had given her spells from beyond the grave and a speaking owl. Oh, there was no disease that a single feather from that owl could not heal. And she could beat off bad spirits with her cane which lay down and wiggled like a snake when she gave the command, but she never gave the command.

The illnesses of white people did not interest her, Ernestina explained, when Helen called to ask if Cold Friday was coming today. It was out of friendship for Ernestina that the root doctor had agreed to come at all. Possibly she might come today.

Helen asked about her fee.

"She do like treasure best," said Ernestina. "Something she can use in her business."

"What kind of treasure?"

"When she cured me of the rumatiz, I give her my little silver ring. Silver is 'specially bad for the devil."

She won't get mine, thought Helen, remembering the leftovers and hand-me-downs Debbie often gave Ernestina. And Ernestina was glad to have them. One person's trash was another person's treasure.

"Does she need bus fare?" asked Helen.

"No, ma'am. She got her own ways of gettin' around."

"How does she get around?" asked Helen nervously.

"In a car," answered Ernestina.

"I've got more treasure in this house than I know what to do with," said Helen. "If she wants treasure, she shall have it."

She asked Nell to help her carry out the treasure. First they sifted through the old clothes in the basement. There was a fur coat she'd meant to pass on to somebody, as it was worn and something had nibbled at the sleeve. And there was that awful fox stole Hal's sister wore before she died; Helen hated all those little heads and paws and tails hanging down and the grieving glass eyes and the dry noses painted black.

In the attic they found a glass orange tree that had most of its glass leaves and half of its glass oranges and some blue taffeta that Helen had bought for a dress she'd never made.

"We're redecorating, are we?" said Grandpa. "I shall scarcely know my own room anymore."

They arranged the treasure in a neat pile at the foot of the front lawn, and Helen remarked that you never knew how much treasure you had until you looked.

"I wonder if I should tip her," said Helen.

"Oh, you wouldn't want to tip her," said Nell. "Not with all the stuff you're giving her. You wouldn't want to tip her."

"Do you think she's honest?" asked Helen. "You hear so many stories about cleaning women who take whatever they can get their hands on. She doesn't have references."

"Ernestina wouldn't bring her if she were dishonest," said Nell.

"Ernestina has never asked to be paid in treasure," said Helen. "Have you ever heard of anyone else who asked to be paid in treasure?"

They agreed it might be prudent to hide what Helen called the really good stuff. Helen hid the really good stuff every time she and Hal went on vacation. She'd hidden her best silver coffee pot over a year ago and hadn't found it yet.

"It's in the house," she'd say when anyone asked about it, by which she meant that it was still hers, though she hadn't the use of it.

The tray and the sugar bowl and the creamer were safe, of course, under the four-legged bathtub on the third floor.

"Do you think the root doctor will be going to the attic?" asked Nell.

Helen shrugged.

When Grandpa heard the puffing and clattering in the bathroom, he called out, "Why not put all the good stuff together, in a pillowcase?"

"I don't want it all in a heap where she can just walk off with it," Helen called back. "I read in the newspaper about two gypsies that came to a woman's house, and one asked for a glass of water and the other stole her jewels. Would you believe it? She'd hidden her jewels in the wastebasket."

"Lay not up for yourselves treasure on earth, where moth and dust . . . " began Grandpa.

But the two women were already downstairs, turning their attention to the Dresden, though Helen agreed it would be hard to steal a dozen dessert plates without breaking them. "Of course, that won't keep some folks from trying," she added.

"Where should I put them?" asked Nell. All this secrecy had exhausted her.

"Under the love seat. Push them behind the fringe."

Deferring to Nell's bad back, Helen moved the larger pieces herself. She pushed the little jade pedestal under the piano and set the blue china clock under her bed as carefully as a hen on its nest.

Then she trudged downstairs. Nell had not moved from the love seat.

"One more thing," said Helen. "The vase."

"You'll break it, Helen. It would take two men to move that vase."

"She might have an accomplice," said Helen.

The vase was French porcelain and egg-shaped and showed a shepherd, draped in a magenta toga, offering his girlfriend an apple while two cupids ran interference. It perched on a gold stem which rose from an ornate base, agleam with gold leaf. The gold handles were badly glued and the lid was tied on with a black ribbon, which caused visitors to ask if the urn held the ashes of some dead relative.

"Oh, no," Helen would say. "It holds our important papers."

Mashed into the vase were birth certificates, old report cards, an AAA sticker, several public library cards, and a lock of auburn hair. Helen lugged it to the cellar, setting it down on every table she passed to rest her arms, and lifted it to the shelf of Bartlett's pears she'd canned three years ago and pushed it behind the mason jars. When she sat down in the living room with Nell, her arms ached, and she felt slightly ill.

"If I die in the next hour, don't forget where everything is," she said.

"It's well past noon," said Nell. "I believe she's not coming after all."

"I hope she doesn't expect lunch," said Helen.

The backfire of a car brought them to their feet.

"Is she here yet?" called Clare from her room.

Nell peered out the front door.

"Not a sign of her," she answered.

32

A Power That Never Fails

Sometimes Willie was a nuisance, Father Legg reflected. Hanging around the parish office with his good intentions, and now wanting the two of them to go ahead of the bus with the box lunches and the cake.

Wants to be helpful. Lord, give me patience.

"*I* shall ride the bus with my team," said Father Legg. "If you want to deliver the lunches and the cake earlier, you're perfectly free to do so."

"I thought we could set up the tables, Father."

"What tables? The picnic tables are already there."

"I thought white tablecloths would be nice."

Father Legg sighed. "If you wish to be responsible for returning them, laundered, you may use the church tablecloths. But we'll be needing them for the potluck next week."

"Oh, I will. I will."

"And, Willie—"

"Yes, Father?"

"The baker is putting all our names on the top."

He paused, rummaging his mind for further instructions, but found none.

"What if it rains?" asked Willie.

"We'll hold the picnic here, in the parish house. But it won't rain." He couldn't really predict the weather, now that weather reports on the radio were canceled for security reasons, but he could hope for the best. "And, Willie—"

"Yes?"

"I could use your help decorating the bus. Hutton's is donating the bunting. We'll give it to the Salvage Sewing Center afterwards."

The bus jouncing and creaking; Henry singing "Ninety-Nine Bottles of Beer on the Wall" and Charley and Stilts leaping over the backs of their seats to clap their hands over his mouth; the town jogging by them through dusty windows, hazy and strange, buried under dust and twilight like an early memory—oh, they might be riding to a game against Dexter High or Flat Rock last year, before Durkee got drafted, before death took him in the Philippines, when their whole lives lay before them, uncomplicated, empty.

Sol nudged Ben. "Did you say good-bye to everybody?"

"No."

"Me neither."

Behind the wheel, Mr. Clackett began to sing.

> "God bless America,
> Land that I love."

Mr. Bacco and Mr. Lieberman and Mr. LaMont joined in:

> "Stand beside her, and guide her,"

and now they were all singing with great feeling:

> "Through the night with a light from above.
> From the mountains to the prairies—"

"Praireeeees," howled Mr. Clackett, speeding up.

Lord, thought Father Legg. He's drunk.

He tapped the bellowing Clackett on the shoulder.

"Slow down, my good man. We're coming to the bridge."

The bridge was nowhere in sight, but Mr. Clackett slowed down. To their right, the river shifted from slow drift to frothing rapids.

"Over hill, over dale,
We will hit the dusty trail,"

sang Mr. Bacco.

"Look," said Sol. "Is that Willie?"

Ben followed his gaze out the window. On the other side of the river ahead of them he saw two picnic tables, their white cloths fluttering. Willie was sitting on one of them.

"He doesn't see us," said Ben.

"Yes he does. He's waving."

"Mr. Clackett, slow down," said Father Legg again. "You're taking the turn too fast."

The bus skidded around the curve, and Mr. Clackett started fighting with the wheel, and Father Legg reached past him and grabbed it as Mr. Clackett hit the brakes, and the bus, like a mad-dened animal, took off into freedom, leaving the bridge and lumbering into the air.

Early the next morning, Willie surveyed the eight women gathered at South Park.

"Mrs. Teresa Bacco, first base. Mrs. Schoonmaker, second base. Mrs. Lieberman, third. Mrs. Henrietta Bacco, you're our shortstop. Mrs. LaMont, you'll cover center field, and Mrs. Clackett, left field. I'll cover right field. Ernestina, you're our catcher."

They listened, sullenly, he thought. Their dislike was palpable; he could almost taste it. Not that he really cared what they thought of him.

"Who's pitching?" asked Ernestina.

"My mother. She's next of kin."

"Wanda's pitching?" asked Ernestina, raising her eyebrows.

Wanda, hearing her name, said, "How's Ben?"

"The contract says Clare's the pitcher," said Ernestina.

"Clare can't pitch from a wheelchair," said Willie. "She'll have to accept a substitute."

Ernestina frowned. "Why can't she pitch from a wheelchair?"

"It—isn't—done," Willie replied. "It's not the correct thing.

Clare will be on the bench with her mother. Besides, they're not here, anyway."

"They're waiting for Friday," said Ernestina. "They can't come till Friday gets there."

"Till Friday!" exclaimed Willie.

"How's Ben?" asked Wanda again, touching his sleeve.

"Mother, I told you. He's going to be fine. They're all going to be fine. Ladies, take your places. Mrs. Clackett, you're up first."

Not that he cared if they liked him. He knew they endured him because Father Legg had promised to come here directly from the hospital with news. What irked Willie the most was sitting in the waiting room and listening to Mrs. Lieberman and Mrs. LaMont babble to his mother about people who came out of comas suddenly and for no reason, after the doctors had given up all hope—not giving him the chance to tell her, taking the comforting words he'd prepared out of his mouth.

Over and over they had praised Father Legg's bravery. Although his head had required thirty-two stitches, he declined to spend even one night in the hospital; the shortage of beds was acute, and he would give his bed to someone who needed it more.

"Mother, it could have been worse," said Willie.

"How worse?" snuffled Wanda.

"Nobody was killed, Mother. Nobody's actually dead. Ben will wake up. Everybody will be out in a few days."

"Not everybody," Mrs. Lieberman reminded him.

Mr. Lieberman had cracked three vertebrae and had to be fitted with a cast and a brace, and Charley had broken his leg in two places and would be in traction for a month.

Mrs. Clackett struck out, but everyone cheered: at the far end of the park, Father Legg, his head turbaned in bandages, was striding across the field.

"How's Ben?" shouted Wanda.

"Sleeping," Father Legg called back, a little breathlessly. "Everyone else is wide awake." As he drew closer, the forced cheer dropped from his voice. "The brain is a mysterious instrument. You can't tell how long these things will last."

He didn't tell them he'd had to fight back tears as he walked through the ward with the doctor, asking about this one's arm, that one's back, to Intensive Care, where he asked nothing after the doctors told him they had no answers.

"What did I tell you?" said Willie. "Ben's going to be fine."

Not a trace of concern there, thought Father Legg. A cold fish, that one. The discovery unsettled him.

"Was it sabotage?" asked Mrs. Lieberman.

"There was an oil slick on the bridge," said Father Legg. "It's impossible to prove sabotage. But let's put all that behind us." He lowered his voice to get their attention. "Ladies," he said, "and Willie," he added, "I know the odds against us tomorrow are tremendous. But we have in our midst a power that no other team can boast. We have a power that never fails. We have love."

A few faces fell.

"A miracle wouldn't hurt," said Henrietta.

"A miracle would be nice," he agreed. He clapped his hands. "Play ball!"

Was it the sun beating down, Willie wondered, that made him feel so sick? There was not even a breeze. Wanda pitched, and the ball was weak and wild, and then Father Legg pitched. The more the women threw themselves into the game, the more Willie felt himself thrown out of it, a spectator removed to a distant peak. But not far enough. Though the names he heard were not his, every word Father Legg shouted seemed aimed at him.

"I want you to stand close to the plate, Mrs. Bacco."

"Don't worry about that one, Mrs. Bacco. Take your time."

"You got a piece of it, Mrs. LaMont. Now take one out and give it a ride."

"Come on, Mrs. Harkissian. You have to run full blast."

"Just meet it, Mrs. Schoonmaker. Just meet the ball. Step towards it."

"Take a lead there, Mrs. Clackett. Don't get glued to the bag. Keep your eye on the ball when you make that turn."

"Willie, you're up. Willie?"

He took his stance and turned to face Father Legg, and his legs felt like cotton.

"A little late, Willie my boy. A little late."

The ball rushed toward him and he swung.

"You got a bite on that, Willie. Next time you'll get it."

He swung again, and as his bat met the empty air, he heard behind Father Legg's encouragement the voices of his first tormentors following him off the field: Easy out. Easy out. Easy out.

By the end of the afternoon Father Legg felt his faith wavering. Never had he asked of God a thing that could not happen according to natural law. In cases where the outcome was uncertain, he always said, "Thy will be done." He was afraid to say it now. It would be like throwing the game, he thought, as he offered Willie a ride home. The women were all going to Mrs. Lieberman's house for supper.

"Thank you," said Willie, pleased that Father Legg had noticed he was not feeling well. But when the priest asked him a question, it had nothing to do with his health.

"Willie, do you believe Ben and his friends will die if the game tomorrow is lost?"

"They think so," said Willie cautiously.

"But do you think so?"

"You told Ben that if a person believes he is going to die on a certain day, believing can make it happen."

"Do you think we'll win tomorrow, Willie?"

Willie was silent.

"Or do you think we'll lose?"

"Miracles can happen," murmured Willie.

"Yes. Where there is love, miracles can happen."

33

Fire, Do You Know Her?

"Clare, I believe she's not coming," said Helen as they sat down to dinner, already postponed for an hour.

"Did she call?" asked Clare.

"No. I thought sure she'd come this morning. That's two days we've waited for her."

"Did you pray about it?" asked Grandpa.

"I pray for Clare every night," said Helen, "and now I'm praying for Ben. I didn't think I'd have to pray for *her*. I thought she could get here on her own."

When she comes, I'll ask her to heal Ben instead of me, thought Clare.

It was well after supper when Helen looked out of the kitchen window and spied a red Dodge pulling up in front of the house. A tall black woman in a long blue dress let herself out.

She stood over six feet tall, not counting the extra foot added by the white scarf wrapped around her head like the wimple of an eccentric nun. She had a long face with high cheekbones and skin so shiny that Helen longed to touch it. Her eyes met Helen's: one blue and one brown eye, and as she waited on the doorstep for Helen to let her in, she clattered and tinkled and glittered. The bodice of her dress was covered with medals closely set; they seemed a single fabric, a suit of armor designed to protect her against no ordinary enemy.

She wore three dog licenses, and a Little Orphan Annie button, and a medal citing the American Legion Bricklayers and Masons International Union, and a pierced Liberty-head quarter on a safety pin, and a Go Blue button with a tiny golden football attached to it, and a medal showing Andrew Carnegie saying, "My heart is in the work." She wore bells and buttons and bits of antlers and bones and a crucifix and God knows what else, thought Helen, who could hardly take her eyes from a necklace of dried lizards, brown and pinched as claws. And the leathern bag she wore on a rope around her waist—what horrors did that hold? Helen wondered, as she caught sight of the serpentine cane, which the woman did not lean on but held back, as one might restrain an ornery wand, chastising it: Stay put till you're needed.

"Clare, she's here!" shouted Davy, and he darted past Helen, almost knocking her down, and took Cold Friday by the hand and tugged her inside.

Her presence filled the entire hallway. The family photographs opened their eyes: a giantess was passing, jingling, rustling, smelling of juniper, like a ship bearing spices and bells.

Clare listened, her heart racing. She listened to the door of her room open; she listened for her mother's voice announcing that Cold Friday was here. Instead, Cold Friday herself walked straight into the room and the door closed behind her.

Under the bathtub on the third floor, the silver spoons quivered. And the Liberty-head quarter on Cold Friday's breast sent a message to the creamer and the forks and the knives: Remember me, sisters? I was with you before you were born, when our lode slept in the earth, a single vein.

Cold Friday unpinned the Liberty-head quarter, settled it in the palm of her hand, and turned to Clare.

"Open yo' mouth," she said, "but don't swaller."

Like a priest giving Communion, she put the quarter on Clare's tongue. It tasted cool, sweet, not like metal at all. Her mother always told her money was dirty. Wash your hands if you've touched money. You never know but what somebody used it to shut the eyes of the dead.

"Spit," said Cold Friday and held out her hand.

Clare spit out the quarter. But how changed! It was now as black as the hand that received it, a bright moon eclipsed. Cold Friday held it in front of Clare's eyes.

"You been conjured," she said. "That's the clear proof. Now we got to find the party that done it."

From the leathern bag she drew a folded paper which she spread out on the floor, a large colored poster of the human body, clothed in nothing but its veins and arteries and major organs, and standing on the words "Compliments of Henderson's Pharmacy."

Just like the pictures in Grandpa's books, thought Clare, and realized it wasn't. On the veins and arteries were the names of streets and the numbers of houses. Cold Friday took four glass bottles from the bag and weighed down the corners of the poster. In the first glowed amber water; in the second, amethyst; in the third, emerald; in the fourth, sapphire. A fifth bottle, which she placed in the middle, held—was that blood?

"Them bottles is for the spell to go into. It can pick the one it likes. I brought bottles and pretty stones and all what they likes. Open yo' hand."

Clare opened it, obedient as a child, and Cold Friday uncorked the fifth bottle and poured a stream of blood into her palm, and Clare thought again of Ben, of broken glass and crushed metal and a mind emptied of memory.

"Please," she whispered, "if you're going to heal anyone, could you heal—"

"Chicken blood," remarked Cold Friday.

She eyed the thick red pool, then reached out and slapped it, and Clare gave a cry as the blood spattered over the poster, gathered itself into a line, and rolled with great purpose along the arteries, past the heart, past the liver, and came to rest on the islets of Langerhans. Cold Friday read the inscription on it.

"Island Park," she said. "Do that signify?"

"That's where the ball hit me," said Clare. "That's where Ben hit it. And now he's the one that needs healing."

Cold Friday gave her a cold look. "It's you I be called for."

She tipped the fifth bottle on its side, and the blood rolled back into it as if summoned. Only after she had corked it and tucked it back into her bag did she speak.

"The one that hit it ain't the one that made the spell. You is conjured with one of the old spells the devil sent out when he took his third of the earth. Them is slow, traveling spells. They come from the darkness that moved on the face of the waters 'fore the earth *was*. And them no-words hid in the water and that no-voice talked it in the water, and it done traveled from water to water, and it done entered the body of Eve. And Cain said to his brother, 'You be firstborn and give me the brains. You kin have everything else. And that spell got itself handed down, hand over hand, 'cause that spell is so evil. The hand that worked the spell on you didn't make it. And now we's got to take that spell off."

Cold Friday opened the window, and the leathern bag at her waist began to throb. She reached a comforting hand into it and drew out a ring-necked dove and tossed it free, and then a red-winged blackbird and tossed it after the dove, and then another dove, smaller than the first, and this she threw away also, and then a chickadee, which she flicked outside, and then a sparrow, which did not wait to be sent but swooped to the window.

"O Lord," she called after them in a deep voice, "heal this girl. Don't send Your Son, Lord. Come on down and heal her Yourself."

She turned to Clare.

"Honey, when them birds cross the water, you gonna walk. But we got to help 'em. That old devil, he a powerful demon. He got his lyin' tongue a-clicking and a-clacking and he got his tail hooked around the good people, around you and me and President Roosevelt—amen!—and he want to pull the people's hearts from the truth."

Out of the bag she pulled a Maxwell House coffee can full of coals, which she set on the floor at Clare's feet. A sweet smell filled the room, as of leaves being burned in the fall. Cold Friday inhaled deeply and closed her eyes, and her whole body began to rock.

"Lord, take this demon from this child."

When she sang, her voice seemed to rise from the coals themselves:

"O graveyard,
O graveyard,
I'm walkin' through the graveyard,
Lay this body down.

"I know moonlight,
I know starlight,
I'm a-walkin' through the starlight,
Lay this body down.

"I'm a-layin' in the grave—"

She stretched out her arms and sat perfectly still, as if the very air were her grave, over which her white headscarf rose like a headstone.

"Lay this body down . . . "

Clare struggled to keep awake but felt her eyes closing; the last living creature she saw before she gave in to sleep was Cold Friday withering into a lizard, which warmed its thin claws over the fire and sang,

Fire, do y' know me?
Fire, do y' know me?

She awoke to the room full of smoke and Cinnamon Monkey-shines clawing at her skirt. The coffee can lay on its side, its coals scattered over the carpet, on which flames blossomed like a serpentine field of light.

"Fire!" shrieked Clare.

And because the bureau had now caught fire and the edge of the bedspread crackled into flames, and because the demon had met his match and the deep sleep of Clare's bones was ended, and because Clare herself wanted to live and wanted Ben to live also, she staggered out of bed and ran into the hall.

"Fire! My room's on fire!"

Smoke curled down the stairs in rolling gusts. Nell hustled Davy and Grandpa downstairs, and Clare pelted after them.

"Look!" screamed Davy. "Clare's *running!*"

Clare grabbed the phone in the front hall and dialed. Her mother rushed to and fro like a spirit, gathering the "good stuff"—silver teapot, knives, spoons, Dresden plates, jade pedestal, porcelain vase—hauling it out in a purple tablecloth.

"Operator," said a cheery voice.

"Fire!" cried Clare. "Send the fire department!"

"What address, ma'am?"

"Two-oh-one Orchard Drive. Hurry—there's smoke everywhere!"

Only when they were all gathered in the front yard waiting for the fire truck did Clare remember Cold Friday.

"Oh, Lord!" said Helen. "She's probably burnt up. Oh, it's a great day. Oh, Lord, what a tragedy!"

"I hear sirens," said Davy.

"Her car's gone," said Nell.

It was then they discovered that the good stuff was gone, along with the treasure; the lawn lay empty, as though neither treasure nor good stuff nor Cold Friday herself had ever been.

34

Than When We First Begun

What baffled the firemen was the damage. There simply wasn't any, though Clare swore she had seen flames dancing on the rug, and the bedspread had caught fire before her very eyes. The smoke was real enough, yet the odor did not cling to curtains and clothes, the way it generally did after a fire.

"God knows," said Helen, "my exhaustion is real."

She felt shorn of her past; she felt years lighter. I paid in treasure, she told herself. Paid for Clare to be made well again.

Nell announced they all needed a good night's sleep.

Only Clare would not go to bed; Helen called her and Nell called her, and at last Helen asked Grandpa to call her indoors.

"Ever since the firemen left she's been walking up and down, all through the house. First I found her in the fruit cellar, staring at my old wedding bouquet. Then I found her in the dining room, cradling the teapot. I asked her if she wanted me to make her some tea, and she said no, thank you, and put the teapot on her head."

"You should have let her visit Ben," said Grandpa.

"I thought it would upset her."

"Not seeing him upsets her more."

"But it's nearly midnight and she's walking around the garden!" exclaimed Helen. "Won't you go down and call her? She listens to you."

"Perhaps she's looking for something," said Grandpa.

"Nell asked her if she'd lost something, and she said no."

"Perhaps she's found something," said Grandpa.

"Grandpa, please call her. She needs her sleep."

"No she doesn't. She's been sleeping for months. Let her alone. Leave the door open, and she'll fly into the cage when she's ready."

The campus carillon began to chime. Ten, eleven, twelve—

Walking under the pear trees, Clare counted.

Thirteen.

Into the backyard crept the fragrance of fresh laundry and leeks and tall grass mowed early in the morning.

"Is it you, dear lady?" whispered Clare.

The forget-me-nots on her skirt nodded. *When we first met, you came to me on your spirit-legs. Now come to me on your flesh and bones.*

The Ancestress hovered over the lilac bushes, which had just passed their blooming, and Clare ran to meet her.

"Take me to visit Ben."

You don't need me to travel, my daughter. You know the way.

And her own breath carried Clare out once more. Out of her body. Weightless and fleshless, she followed the Ancestress into a cloud of unknowing that she knew would take her to Ben.

The crucifix on the wall: a broken sleeper.

Through the half-open window drifted sounds from the street: a car careening around the corner, its radio screaming "I got spurs that jingle jangle jingle."

This room is larger than the one I had when I was here, said Clare.

This room is the ward, said the Ancestress. *What do you see?*

I see two rows of houses with lamps burning in all the windows, answered Clare.

Those are the patients whose wounds are healing. Tomorrow they will gather around the radio to hear the game they wanted to play. Your game. Is that all you see, daughter?

They were entering a private room. Clare did not need to ask whose it was.

I see a dark house. Is Ben dying?

Everything alive looks dead and everything dead looks alive, said the Ancestress. *Daughter, his spirit is hiding.*

They floated toward Ben.

What does he love best in the world? asked the Ancestress.

Baseball, said Clare. *Summer.*

You've forgotten what he loves most.

What?

You. Go into his house, daughter, and breathe on all his lamps. But do not linger. The darkness of a house that is being abandoned is like no other darkness on earth.

Clare let herself in.

She never imagined that Ben's life would look like this: a dark corridor, off which opened dank rooms behind doors rotting on their hinges. The sconces in every room were black with soot. But the gas was still on. The lamps would light for her, if the gas didn't kill her first.

She breathed on the first lamp and it glowed softly. The tiniest pilot light awoke at the bottom. She hurried on to the second, and it too awoke at her breath and encouraged the third, which flamed quicker and brighter than the others. She began to feel ill, as if she were trapped in a mine. The air was poisonous. She breathed the fourth lamp to life and the fifth and heard the Ancestress calling her.

Come back now, daughter, or you will never come back.

Once outside, she turned to look at him. Every room was sending out a warm, clear light.

When Hal arrived at the airstrip early in the morning, his heart sank a little. He would have preferred a train, with its ponderous courtesies, not this six-seater, this toy. The pilot, a young man with sandy hair and a sleepy expression, took his valise.

"You're traveling light," he remarked.

"Presents for my family," said Hal. "I can't stay long."

"Oh, that's nice. I got some jewelry in Santa Fe for my mother."

Hal thought of the stuffed horned toad mounted on a piece of petrified wood he was bringing for Davy. The little box of minerals for Clare and Helen. Clare would love the names: desert rose, Apache tears.

"We'll stow this in back," said the pilot. "There's not much room under the seats."

"But I'm the only passenger," said Hal.

The pilot nodded. "It's you and me and my copilot and the cargo."

Hal wondered where they were taking the cargo—it was packed in three steel boxes, padlocked and unmarked. To Willow Run? He wanted to ask how many stops they'd be making between here and Willow Run, but these last months had taught him to mind his own business.

He climbed in behind the copilot, a thin, blond man with protruding teeth who reminded Hal of a white rabbit.

"Nice day for flying," the rabbit said to Hal. "You'll get a nice view of the sun rising over the Sangre de Cristo mountains. I saw a mountain goat once. You hardly ever see them so well on the ground."

The plane taxied for takeoff, and Hal peered out of the window, not wanting to miss the goat if it was there. He would tell Clare and Helen about the goat and about the aspens shaking their leaves like coins and about these two men and their mysterious cargo. He would walk into the house around supper time, just walk in. No calling beforehand, no letter announcing his arrival. Just walk in, calling, "Hi. I'm home."

Father Legg ran up to Clare.

"You're the second miracle," he said and hugged her.

The first miracle, he told her, was Ben. He was wide awake. Too weak to play, the doctor said, but wide awake. And though it was still too early to say for sure, he appeared to have lost neither speech nor memory nor movement.

"What did he talk about?" asked Clare.

"The game. He can't think of anything else."

"Of course," said Clare.

"The other team hasn't arrived yet," said Father Legg. He

avoided uttering the name Dead Knights. "We're warming up. I hope the crowd doesn't make you nervous."

No, she wasn't nervous. No. Because there was only the game and the no-game, the players and the watchers, the inside and the outside. Right now only the inside mattered. The people in the bleachers rustled like so many blades of grass, faceless, innumerable.

The very hairs of your head are numbered, said God.

"Here are your positions," said Father Legg, addressing the little group on the bench. He could not accustom himself to seeing the women in slacks and shirts. Look like they all work in a defense plant, he thought. "And we would especially like to welcome Sol Lieberman and Mr. Clackett."

The two grinned, their right arms in nearly identical casts.

"Sol will coach first base and Mr. Clackett will coach third. Please—give me your attention. Mrs. Teresa Bacco, first base. Mrs. Schoonmaker, second base. Mrs. Lieberman, third. Mrs. Henrietta Bacco, shortstop. Ernestina, you're our catcher."

He wanted a tight outfield, he told them. He was counting on Mrs. LaMont in center and Mrs. Clackett in left. Willie would play right field. Wanda and Helen would wait on the bench in case they were needed.

"And Clare Bishop will pitch," he added with a grin. A current of warm feeling ran through the women. "And you all know the good news about Ben."

He lowered his voice.

"Dear Lord, Who knowest our needs before we ask them, be with us all, now and in the world to come. Ladies—and Willie—take your positions."

Kitty helped Ernestina into her chest protector, and Ernestina laughed nervously and said she felt like an old crawdaddy rigged up like that, and then they all fanned out and trotted to their places. Helen and Wanda made themselves comfortable on the bench.

Poor Wanda, thought Father Legg. She feels useless.

"Wanda, let's see you take a few cuts at the ball," he said gently.

Wanda took her stance, knees flexed, at home plate. Clare did not move. The two women stared at each other.

"What's wrong?" asked Father Legg.

"I was just thinking, this is a funny place for us to meet," said Clare.

"Good heavens!" exclaimed Father Legg. "I thought you knew each other."

Out in left field, Willie shaded his eyes. Were they talking about him? Or was Father Legg giving his pitch on love?

Suddenly the murmurs of the crowd ceased. Wanda let the bat drop. The air grew faintly chill, as if rain were not far off—yet not rain, either, but the dank moisture on the undersides of stones.

"They're here," said Father Legg.

They did not run onto the field. They simply appeared, as if they had broken through a wall of air, or an invisible ray into visibility. First, Durkee, tugging on his visored cap, in his old maroon jacket with "AA Pioneers" in white script on the back. Then the players: big, slow-moving men in the uniforms of the teams they had served. They lumbered onto the field and their feet touched the earth, yet the earth did not take note of them; they raised no dust, disturbed no blade of grass.

Lord have mercy on us, thought Father Legg. They've got Lou Gehrig on first.

And yet he was not as Father Legg remembered him. This man was a shell, its passenger gone; tossed through hurricanes, through deep silences, it had washed ashore intact, luminous, dead.

Their coach strolled over to Father Legg and offered his hand; Father Legg shook it gingerly.

"My name's Death," he said.

"I know," said Father Legg.

"Both of us in black today," Death observed with a smile.

Father Legg said nothing.

"I see you're expecting an easy three innings. You're giving the women a chance."

"A bus accident," said Father Legg. His mouth felt dry. "Everyone was hurt. Nobody killed, fortunately."

"Fortunately," said Death. "I believe most of my players are familiar to you," he added.

Father Legg nodded.

"I never thought I'd live to see Christy Mathewson pitch again. What did he die of?"

"TB," said Death. "Naturally, it doesn't bother him now."

"Naturally," said Father Legg.

"Those who play for me never tire. They never get hurt."

"Very convenient," said Father Legg.

"So many wanted to come. You can imagine. They haven't picked up a bat and ball since the day they died. Durkee was ecstatic. Not all of you can keep your positions, I told them. And they still begged to come. The pitchers even offered to play in the outfield. Baseball was their whole life."

"Do they need to warm up?"

"Some things you never forget," said Death. "Baseball is one of them."

What were the others? Father Legg wondered. Once he would have said "love." Now it did not seem that simple.

The nurse wheeled the radio toward Ben's bed and stopped in the middle of the room.

"I'm sorry. The plug won't reach. We'll push all the beds down to this end."

By the time she found the station, the announcer was halfway through the lineup.

"Mrs. LaMont, center field."

"Give it to 'em, Kitty!" shouted Mr. LaMont.

"And Willie Harkissian in right field. And now the lineup for the Dead Knights."

A hush fell over the room.

"Starting pitcher is Christy Mathewson of the New York Giants. At first base, Lou Gehrig, New York Yankees. At second base, Joe McGinnity, New York Giants."

"Lord," said Mr. Lieberman. "Not Iron Man McGinnity."

"At third base, Eddie Plank of the Philadelphia A's."

"They're playing the wrong positions," said Ben.

"There's a reason for it," said Mr. LaMont. "There's a reason for everything."

"At shortstop," the announcer went on, "Hughie Jennings of the Baltimore Orioles."

"The ee-yah man," said Mr. Schoonmaker. "I used to think the world of him."

"In center field, Rube Waddell of the Philadelphia A's. In left field, Big Dan Brouthers—"

"Rube Waddell!" exclaimed Mr. Bacco. "He's the guy who used to run off the field to chase fire engines."

"In right field, Ross Youngs of the New York Giants. And the catcher: Moses Fleetwood Walker."

"Who's he?" asked Mr. Bacco.

"He played with the Chicago Lincolns," said Stilts.

"There's a Negro on this team?"

"He's dead, isn't he?" said Stilts. "This ain't the majors."

They were flying over Lake Erie when Hal realized he was listening to the engine of the plane. The steady hum had shifted into a lower pitch, then a quick, polite cough. Another, and another. And then it hummed as before, but Hal kept listening, noting the smallest changes in its voice. The two pilots had stopped talking and were listening, too. As the hum steadied itself, Hal felt his muscles unclench.

Whef-a-whef-a-whef.

The pilot checked the fuel gauge.

Whef-a-whef.

"Engine trouble?" inquired Hal.

"Not really," said the pilot.

They were all listening intently now, and each knew the others were listening too, and waiting for the cough in the motor, the rattle in the chest, blood in the urine, numbness in the leg, a dizzy spell, a lump: Doctor, will I die?

. . .

Christy Mathewson, five years dead, translucent as a leaf through which the sun scatters shadows, had not lost his pinpoint control. He hurled a fastball at Mrs. LaMont, who swung under it and missed.

"Makes 'em hit on the ground," observed Mr. Clackett to Sol. "It's a damned hard pitch to hit in the air."

"God help us if he throws his knuckleball," said Father Legg.

Dear Lord, he whispered, Dear Lord Who stopped the sun for Joshua, Thou knowest the score is three to nothing in the bottom of the first. Thou knowest the Dead Knights are winning. Stop the ball, Lord, so that Mrs. LaMont may hit it.

But the Lord did not stop the ball, and Mrs. LaMont struck out.

"It's a bad time to need the bedpan," said Charley. "There must be fifty people in here."

"Do you have to—?" asked the nurse.

"No," he answered quickly.

The nurses from the floor and the ambulatory patients from the private rooms had gathered in the ward. That nurse's aide by the door—Ben was sure he'd met her before, in an earlier life.

"I'm Ginny," she said. "Remember?"

Of course. How could he have forgotten?

"The kid with the St. Anthony medal—remember?" said Ginny. "He finally went home. He asked if I'd take him for a ride in my old Studebaker next time he's in the hospital."

"He's probably listening to the game right now," said Ben.

"There's one out in the bottom of the first," said the announcer, "and three–zip is the score. This is a big game for the Rovers. 'Course, it's a big game for the Dead Knights, too . . . Mrs. Schoon-maker's at the plate. There's the windup—the pitch—it's an easy grounder toward first base. Gehrig fields it, steps on the bag. That's two out, nobody on."

It was terribly quiet in the ward. Everyone seemed to stop breathing at once.

"Mathewson winds up. The pitch—it's a slider. Mrs. Lieberman swings and misses. Strike one."

Ben climbed off his bed and threaded his way to the door and nudged Ginny.

"Where are your car keys?"

"In my coat pocket. Why?"

"Don't ask. Where are you parked?"

"In the first row behind the hospital, but—"

Clare stood up and walked behind the dugout. If she was going to cry, she wanted to get it over and done with, out of sight. A fly buzzed at her ear; she swatted it fiercely.

Don't, daughter. You know me.

"Dear lady," whispered Clare, "can't you go into the ball and make us hit it? Or make them not hit it?"

I can't give you anything you don't already have, murmured the Ancestress.

"You got into the knife."

Ben has a way with a knife. He just hadn't discovered it.

She could still taste the dust from the field, chalky, all the way down her throat. "I don't have a way with the ball," said Clare.

True, said the Ancestress. *Therefore, do as Ben does. Put some stuff on it. The Dead Knights can never hit a ball with some stuff on it.*

"What kind of stuff?" asked Clare.

The stuff of being alive. Morning, evening, the first snow and the last snow, bells, daisies, hubcaps, silver dollars, ice cream, hummingbirds, love.

Clare drew a deep breath. "How do you put that kind of stuff on a ball?"

You say it very softly over the ball before you throw it.

She heard Father Legg calling her.

And when you pitch to Mr. Gehrig, say "Mother." There's nothing he wouldn't do for his mother.

. . .

His clothes—where were his clothes? The nurse's lounge was empty. Ben darted in and opened the closet. Nothing but a blue raincoat and a pink silk scarf. He pulled them on over his hospital gown.

He had almost reached the stairs when Ginny grabbed his arm.

"My raincoat! My scarf! Where are you going in my clothes?"

"I'm going to tie up the ball game."

"You can't go! You haven't been discharged."

"That's why I took your clothes. Ginny, please!"

"You can't go—"

"I can't wait to be discharged. I'm needed *now,*" he cried and yanked himself free of her grasp. She let him go, down the stairs and through the lobby past the receptionist and out the front door, past the patients in wheelchairs who were brought out every afternoon for fresh air and a change of scene. He did not stop running till he reached the parking lot. Ginny's car. Ginny's car—which was Ginny's car?

A window opened on the sixth floor, and her voice called out, "It's over there, to your right, the blue one."

Thank you, Ginny. Thank you, car. Thank you, God. Ben drove out of the lot and headed toward the ballpark.

By the time Youngs and Jennings had struck out, everybody in the ward was cheering, and everybody in the bleachers who knew anything about baseball realized one thing:

They'd never seen a ball behave like this one.

"Will you look at Bishop's unorthodox delivery!" exclaimed the announcer. "A high kick, then she bends down as if she's talking to the ball. Good breaking pitch by Bishop. Strike two. Two quick strikes on McGinnity, two out in the top of the second. . . . Watch that pitch. McGinnity is swinging at her motion, not at the ball. Halfway into the swing he decides not to swing. Ball one. It's one and two."

Over the ball, Clare whispered: "A cold beer. Your first home run."

The ball sped away and McGinnity started to swing, then stepped back as if he'd gotten a whiff of something it was carrying, something that took his eye off the ball, off the game, everything.

Strike three.

Clare glanced up and saw, over the bleachers, a vast, silent throng that receded as if on invisible waves, the women in white, the men in black, the lovely fabric of their presence growing faint among the far-off dead, turning in those farthest from her to feathers, wings, the faces of birds.

Willie was bending over the drinking fountain behind the bleachers when someone tapped him lightly on the shoulder.

"Willie," said Death, "nobody appreciates you."

"I know," said Willie. Immediately he felt embarrassed. He hadn't meant to say it right out.

"You're a good, steady worker. You're smart. What's a girl like Marsha in the eyes of the great world? She'll marry a doctor and live unhappily ever after. There are thousands of girls more beautiful where I come from. Don't look so surprised. I know both the living and the dead; they all come to me eventually."

Willie rolled the water around in his mouth thoughtfully, as if he were judging a fine wine. A cheer from the bleachers startled him.

"Matty just walked Mrs. Henrietta Bacco," remarked Death.

"I'm up now," said Willie.

"I give good benefits, Willie," said Death. "Wonderful vacations. Willie, I want *you*. Join my club and see the world. I've got a job for you."

"What kind of job?"

"I want you to keep my records, plead my cause. Snuff out hope wherever you find it. It's what you've always done, Willie. And you can start right this minute."

"No, thanks," said Willie.

"Willie, last night Mr. Jackson was arrested. He named you."

"He named me?"

"There will be a trial, of course. These are patriotic times. You won't get off easily."

The pilot broke the silence.

"The fuel gauge has been reading empty for the last hour," he observed. "According to my instruments, we should all be dead."

None of them was ever to know for certain exactly what happened next. The pilot said it was the clouds; they played tricks on you. Made you think you were seeing whole cities, armies. The copilot blamed it on magnetic currents: there were currents you could hit up there that made all your instruments malfunction.

Only Hal believed his eyes. The engines were silent. But under the wing he saw the ghostly shapes of children, animals, birds, bearing them up.

Willie struck out, and the crowd roared its grief: "*Awwwwww.*"

"You see, Willie," murmured Death as Willie walked toward the dugout. "You have a calling."

"What's the pay?" asked Willie.

"Every living thing in the world shall be yours."

"Then I'm your man," said Willie. "But I'm not packed."

"No need to pack," said Death. "Everything you'll ever need is furnished."

From his pocket he drew a coin—a skull on one side, a man in a winged cap on the other—and slipped it into Willie's hand.

"Come."

"The game's not over," said Willie. "And you're winning."

"We're losing," said Death. "Can't you see? Do you think Gehrig and Waddell and McGinnity and Jennings couldn't hit if they wanted to? Do you think Matty had to walk Mrs. Bacco? They want the living to win. Even the umpire wants the living to win. They remember how it was. All the pain, all the trouble—they'd choose it again—they'd go extra innings into infinity for the chance to be alive again."

· · ·

It seemed to Helen that she heard Hal singing, heard him so clearly behind the murmur of the crowd that she could even make out the words:

"When we've been there ten thousand years
Bright shining as the sun—"

She looked around for Grandpa, knowing full well he was in the bleachers. It was Hal's voice, she was sure of it now, and her heart fluttered a little. She had not heard any sound that far off since the last snowfall. All spring she'd heard the usual sounds, the chirp of crickets but not the silence of crickets; the drumming of rain on the roof but not the plotting of rain in the clouds. And now she heard Hal's voice drawing nearer and nearer like an approaching parade.

"What does it mean?" she wondered, and Father Legg next to her said, "It's a miracle," as Clare swung and connected.

The next moment Helen was shouting at him. "Who is that coming out on the field?"

It was a figure to make the dead sit up and take notice: a tall woman in a blue raincoat, a pink babushka and slippers, and as she ran she threw off her clothes, one garment at a time. First the raincoat; the hospital gown she wore underneath did not even reach to her knees. When the babushka was tossed away, the players gaped in astonishment, and Clare, digging her toe into first base, gave a shout.

"It's Ben!"

In the ward, the announcer's voice crackled with excitement.

"Folks, that's two on for the Rovers, only one away. A home run now would tie it up, and ladies and gentlemen, coming to bat" —his voice broke—"is Ben Harkissian!"

"*Who?*" exclaimed Charley.

"Listen!" hissed Ginny.

The room grew still, as still as the day before creation.

"Here's the windup," said the announcer, "and the pitch."